THE QUEEN IN THE MOUND

JOHANNA WITTENBERG

BOOKS BY JOHANNA WITTENBERG

The Norsewomen Series
The Norse Queen
The Falcon Queen
The Raider Bride
The Queen In The Mound

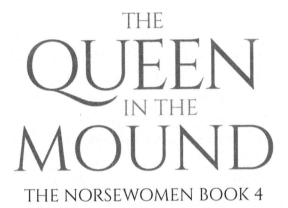

THE
QUEEN
IN THE
MOUND

THE NORSEWOMEN BOOK 4

JOHANNA WITTENBERG

For my readers.

CONTENTS

MAPS

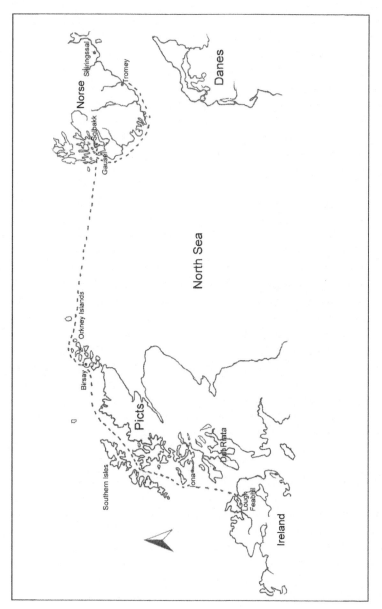

Sailing Route from Ireland to Norway 1

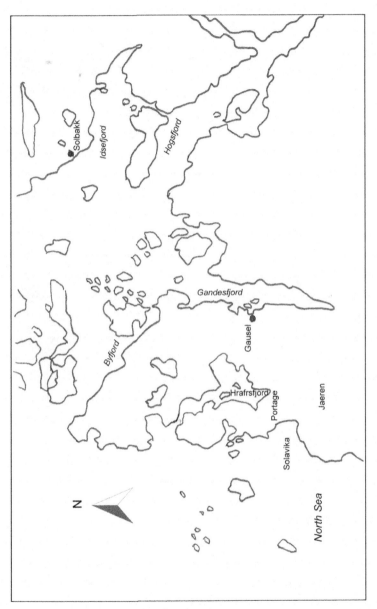

Gausel area 1

CHAPTER 1

The Orkney Islands
September, AD 822

Ragnhild eyed *Raider Bride*'s blue-and-white striped sail, its belly full of the westerly wind and straining at the sheets as the ship galloped over the indigo waves. Beside her, Murchad steered, hand on the tiller, gaze fixed on the sail. Ragnhild was proud of how quickly her husband mastered handling the karvi. The Irishman was no stranger to boats and the sea, but the rounded, hide-covered currachs of Ireland were as different from the sleek Norse longship as a farm cart was from a sleigh.

Voyaging north from Ireland over the past week, Murchad had grasped those differences. Though he was in his mid-thirties, his wiry, compact body had the energy to match the youngest of the crew, and he'd gained their respect. Even Ragnhild's three húskarlar, Einar, Thorgeir, and Svein, found him a tolerable companion. The Norse had no love for the Irish after their treatment at Irish hands, but Murchad's cheerful disposition and willingness to work, whether bailing, rowing, or cooking, had won them over.

Though he'd lost his kingship, Murchad's royal blood and family connections had ensured their welcome in the Irish-held island kingdom of the Dal Riata, but once they'd passed the island of Iona, they entered Norse waters. The Norsemen here were no friends.

Raider Bride had emerged from the shelter of the Southern Isles early that morning. A brisk wind filled her sails as she skirted the west side of the Orkney archipelago. Ragnhild set their course well offshore, hoping to make it past the island of Birsay without the notice of Jarl Ivar, her brother's ally—her enemy.

"If this westerly holds, we'll raise Tromøy in less than a week," she said to Murchad. "I can't wait for you to meet Åsa. She'll help us recruit our army and train them over the winter. Then in the spring, we'll sail to Gausel and claim what's mine." She grinned in anticipation of taking charge of Gausel. It would be like commanding *Raider Bride*, where she made the decisions and no one could tell her what to do. With her own kingdom, she would never be anyone's pawn again.

Murchad smiled as he watched the sail. "You seem very sure that Åsa will support you."

"She knows that Harald has no right to withhold my inheritance. She'll help us set things right."

"I hope so, *a chroi.*"

Ragnhild wrapped her salt-stiff brown braid around her hand. "What do you mean? You don't know Åsa. She'll come to our aid."

"If it's to her advantage, she will."

"Åsa's not like an Irish king. She's loyal to her friends."

Murchad shrugged. "You know her better than I do."

Ragnhild twisted the braid tighter and looked up at the sail.

The ship rolled in the ocean swell, lifting the foot of the sail. Beneath it, Ragnhild glimpsed a flash of white against the low, dark hulk of the distant island to the east. The sail dipped and hid the flash. As it lifted again, she squinted across the water. There— a white shape too square to be a wave.

"Sail ho!" cried the lookout.

As the shape resolved into a longship, Ragnhild could see that it was on course to intercept *Raider Bride*. So much for luck and the blessings of the gods.

"To arms," she ordered. The crew were already rooting in their sea chests, bringing out bows and quivers of arrows, tucking battle-axes in their belts, donning steel helmets and padded linen battle-jackets hardened with many coats of varnish. Though a few owned chain mail brynjas stowed in their sea chests, nobody wore them in a fight at sea, for the weight hampered balance and if you went overboard, dragged you down to Ran's feasting hall at the bottom of the sea before you could swim a stroke.

Ragnhild drew her own battle-jacket from her chest and pulled it on, then settled her helmet on her head, stuffing her braid up under it. She strapped on her sword, Lady's Servant, then took the tiller so Murchad could arm himself.

"They're coming out of the Brough of Birsay," said Einar.

Ragnhild nodded grimly. "Ivar's stronghold," she said to Murchad.

"Do you think they recognized us?"

"Probably not at this distance, but they're pirates. They'll attack any passing ship."

Murchad nodded, belting on his sword.

"We've got the advantage of the windward position," Ragnhild said. "But the wind is setting us toward shore—and our enemy." She pointed her arm into the wind. "We need to maintain a position due west of them. They can't sail directly into the wind to intercept us. The best they'll be able to do is to stay on a converging course and wait for the wind to set us down on them. We need to keep our windward advantage. I'll stay on the helm."

Murchad nodded. Right now they needed Ragnhild's expertise to steer *Raider Bride*. He kicked off his shoes and shouldered a bow and a quiver of arrows. "I think I can do them some damage with this."

Ragnhild altered course a little closer into the wind, away from land and more parallel to the oncoming ship. The crew tightened the sail in response to the course change and *Raider Bride* heeled over more, throwing up spray.

It became a race between the two ships. Ragnhild fought the helm, striving to coax more speed out of *Raider Bride* while still heading as close to the wind as possible. The two ships would converge eventually, but Ragnhild intended to put that off as long as she could.

Their pursuer was faster, and the wind was setting *Raider Bride* down on them inexorably. The other ship was close enough now that Ragnhild recognized the red-checked sail. "*Sea Steed*— Kol's ship." Her brother's spy.

"We're not going to get past him," said Einar.

Ragnhild nodded sharply. "He's bigger and faster than we are. We can't outrun him."

"Then we'll fight him," said Murchad with a grin.

"I'd rather avoid that," said Ragnhild. "I'm sure he's got us outnumbered." Coming from his home port, Kol would have a fresh crew of forty or more bloodthirsty warriors, while *Raider Bride*'s battles in Ireland had reduced her original crew of forty to thirty-four—six dead, and four of those who survived still nursing injuries that hindered their fighting ability.

"Archers," she said. Half the crew readied their bows while the others took up shields from the racks.

"Sail ho!" cried the lookout. Sure enough, another ship had materialized behind *Sea Steed*.

"I have to maintain our distance from Kol," said Ragnhild. "If he forces us to engage, the second ship will have time to catch up. If the two ships flank us, we don't have a chance." That could be as many as eighty warriors against her thirty-four. She had to elude them.

The wind strengthened and *Raider Bride* heeled more, dipping her rail in the seas. The crew crowded the windward rail, adding their weight to help level the ship. They couldn't afford to shorten sail. Ragnhild prayed to the sea goddess that they could keep this speed without broaching. If they heeled over too far, the open decks could take on enough water to swamp them.

Kol and his companion ran the same risk, but they were bigger, faster, and higher-sided.

Sea Steed's archers sent up a hail of arrows. Murchad balanced against the leeward side, sheltering Ragnhild beneath his shield while she concentrated on keeping the ship on the edge of the wind.

All along *Raider Bride's* side, shield men gripped the rail with one hand while they covered themselves and the bowmen from the missiles. Kol's archers were shooting into the wind and it stole the force of their arrows. They bounced off *Raider Bride's* shields into the water.

Murchad racked his shield, unshouldered his bow, plucked an arrow from his quiver, and nocked. He steadied himself against the gunnel as he drew, firing toward the enemy as a dozen of his shipmates loosed their arrows.

The favorable wind carried *Raider Bride's* volley farther and gave it more force. Screams rose from *Sea Steed* as arrows found their marks.

While their enemy recovered, *Raider Bride* surged ahead, gaining ground to the north. Would it be enough?

The other ship had nearly caught up with Kol and now the two pursued *Raider Bride*. All three were on the same point of sail, but the bigger vessels rapidly ate up the distance between them as Ragnhild fought to keep her slim lead.

Murchad fired from the stern quarter, joined by Einar, Thorgeir, and Svein. They had to compensate for the westerly wind that blew the missiles sideways, and the narrow stems of the pursuing ships made slim targets. Fortunately, their enemy had no viable shot from their bows either, fouled by the wind. They didn't even try.

"I wonder if Kol recognizes us yet?" Ragnhild asked, eyeing her distinctive blue-and-white striped sail.

"We recognized him," Murchad pointed out.

"True, but he's not expecting to see us."

Murchad shrugged. "There's not much we can do about it either way, *a chroi*."

"No, but he'll report to Harald that we're on our way home. Our element of surprise will be lost."

"It'll be a moot point if we don't survive this encounter." Murchad frowned and put a protective hand on the small of Ragnhild's back. The gesture eased the stress that had been building inside her.

Sea Steed was closing fast, the carved horse head mounted on her prow clearly defined. The companion ship, probably the chieftain Ivar's, was right on Kol's stern. Soon they would overhaul *Raider Bride*.

Ragnhild kept the prow pointed as close to the wind as she dared to maintain her windward advantage. She hoped *Raider Bride* was more weatherly than the two bigger ships. If one of them got upwind of her, the race was over.

The rail dipped into the seas and scooped a wave on board. A few sailors set aside their weapons and sloshed to leeward to bail with their helmets. But their added weight deepened *Raider Bride*'s heel dangerously and Ragnhild ordered them back to the windward side.

She glanced over her shoulder and caught her breath. *Sea Steed* was nearly on them.

Murchad followed her gaze and his eyes narrowed. "Here they come."

The enemy ship pointed her prow impossibly close to the

wind and slid to windward of *Raider Bride*, her giant sail shivering on the verge of a luff. Her rail was deep in the water, her crew massed on the windward side, clutching the shrouds. As they passed, Ragnhild could make out every detail of their bearded faces, the murder in their steely eyes.

As *Sea Steed* pulled alongside, Ragnhild recognized Kol at the helm. She met his vicious glare, fury and hatred coursing between them. Ragnhild took a deep breath and forced her eyes back to the sail, keeping *Raider Bride* moving.

Ragnhild glimpsed the other ship gaining to leeward and tensed. In a few moments the two bigger vessels would trap *Raider Bride* between them, and all that would be left for her crew would be to fight and die.

Murchad steadied himself against the windward rail, his bare feet gripping the deck. He plucked an arrow from his quiver and nocked, training his aim on *Sea Steed*'s helmsman. Ragnhild heard Murchad's arrow whisper past and her gaze darted sideways to see the point drive into the shield one of Kol's men flung up. Murchad nocked again and Ragnhild focused on the sail.

As Murchad took aim, they entered *Sea Steed*'s windshadow. *Raider Bride* jerked upright and slowed as the bigger ship blanketed her sail. Ragnhild brought the ship off the wind until the sail filled, and risked a glance at her husband.

Somehow, Murchad had maintained his position and he held his fire until *Sea Steed*'s rail dipped, leaving Kol open for an instant. The Irishman loosed. His arrow flashed by, drawing Ragnhild's gaze. Kol reflexively turned his head toward the movement and took the arrow full in his eye.

Kol's corpse thudded to the deck and his shield man grabbed for the tiller, but Murchad had already loosed another arrow that struck the man in the shoulder. He fell against the tiller and *Sea Steed* spun up into the wind, dead in the water. Its huge sail flogged across the deck, sweeping crewmembers overboard.

Raider Bride's crew cheered as they slipped past *Sea Steed*.

Ragnhild hoped the other ship would stop for survivors, but they came on relentlessly. Murchad turned his attention to their new pursuer as it charged down on them.

A gust hit *Raider Bride,* heeling her over until the foot of the sail kissed the sea. Off to leeward the pursuing ship luffed up and spilled their wind to avoid a knockdown. Ragnhild gritted her teeth and kept her sail full while the crew put all their weight on the windward rail.

The gamble paid off and *Raider Bride* shot ahead, gaining a boat length on her pursuer.

They rounded the island to the north and Ragnhild shifted her course easterly into the broadening sea between islands. With the wind on the stern quarter, the ship heeled less while picking up speed.

"Bail!" shouted Einar. The crew put down their weapons and began to rid the ship of water, using helmets, buckets, any container that came to hand.

The bailing lightened the ship and helped their speed. Ragnhild set a course for the distant headland. The enemy came up behind them, the vast sail blanketing *Raider Bride's* smaller spread.

"The bastard's stealing our wind!" shouted Einar. *Raider Bride* lost momentum and the bigger vessel overhauled her quickly, its crew sending a volley of arrows. Favored by the following wind, the enemy arrows struck hard on hastily raised shields. Murchad sheltered Ragnhild from the hail of missiles. She cried out a warning as an arrow sliced into a shield-maiden's cheek. The girl crashed to the deck.

There was no time for anyone to look to her as they dodged incoming missiles.

"Hold your fire," Ragnhild shouted. "Don't waste your arrows." She watched the pursuing ship sail down on them. "Get ready to repel boarders."

Ragnhild let go of the slack tiller as the enemy threw grapnels and hooked onto *Raider Bride*'s side. She drew her knife and slashed the grappling line, but more grapnels latched all along the side.

Murchad grabbed a javelin from the midship rack, pivoted and hurled it at an enemy who was hauling on a grappling line, pulling the two ships together. The impact sent the man stumbling backward, his beard pinned to his throat.

Raider Bride's crew hurled spears and slashed lines but the enemy crew succeeded in pulling the two ships together and made fast. Now they were rafted side by side, hove to with sails backed. The ships pitched in the seas while the crews fought hand-to-hand. Ragnhild drew her sword and hacked off a hand that gripped the rail beside her. Blood spouted from the stump, spraying Ragnhild in the face as the man fell back, screaming.

"Catch!" cried Murchad.

She caught the shield he tossed her and blocked a swordblow, bashing the owner in the face while Murchad drove his spear into her attacker's side, piercing the man's padded battle-jacket.

Screams filled the air from both sides as blades found their marks and warriors fell. For the moment *Raider Bride*'s crew only had to battle one ship and managed to hold their own, but *Sea Steed* would soon recover. *Raider Bride* had to fight her way free and escape before they caught up.

Murchad whirled and hacked with his sword. He leaped onto the gunnels, balancing with a foot on each ship, and slashed down on the enemy, setting helmets ringing and enemies stumbling.

From the enemy crowd, a huge man lunged at Murchad. He wielded a double-handed ax, flailing it like a wind vane straight at the Irishman's head. Ragnhild shouted a warning and Murchad ducked just as the blade whizzed by, knocking his helmet off and sending him stumbling onto the enemy ship.

Ragnhild's heart lurched as another warrior raised his axe to deliver a blow that would crush the slender Irishman.

"Look out!" she screamed as the axe hurtled down on Murchad. She shoved her way toward them, roaring, but there were too many bodies in the way.

The Irishman leaped nimbly aside and slashed his sword across the big man's hamstrings. The brute roared in pain as he dropped to his knees. Murchad hacked his sword into the Norseman's neck, taking the head half off.

The lifeless body collapsed on the deck. Murchad slashed the rope that held the clew of the sail. He dodged as the huge expanse of fabric whipped out of control.

Murchad jumped back onto the gunnels and swept his blade along the walrus-hide ropes that bound the ships together, then landed lightly back on *Raider Bride*'s deck as the gunnels separated.

The ships parted and *Raider Bride*'s sail caught the wind. Ragnhild grabbed the tiller and brought the ship back on course. The enemy ship lay dead in the water while its crew tried frantically to get the sail under control. As *Raider Bride* slipped out of the enemy's grasp, Ragnhild recognized Ivar, Lord of Birsay, screaming orders. Their eyes locked. She grinned in triumph as she watched surprise change to recognition on his face.

The sun grazed the western horizon. "It's a risk to skirt the northern islands after dark," said Ragnhild. "None of us are that familiar with the islands, but we have to maintain our lead before the enemy recovers. Who's got lookout?"

"I'll go," said Svein. White flag in hand, he went up to the bow to signal telltale surf breaking on rocks and reefs.

Murchad stared aft, watching their pursuer.

Groans rose from amidships as Einar and Unn tended the wounded. Ragnhild braced for the splash of a corpse heaved over the side, but none came. So far, it seemed everyone had survived the battle.

She glanced back to see Ivar's crew recapture their flogging sail. "No sign of *Sea Steed*."

Yet. Ragnhild took slow, deep breaths. They had a long way to go.

"They're turning back," said Murchad.

Ragnhild squinted at their pursuer. Against the brilliant sunset, the enemy sail was indeed changing shape. It narrowed and then billowed out on the opposite tack as the ship turned for home. Apparently Ivar didn't think they were worth the risk of the treacherous waters after dark.

"They can probably just make it home before full dark," said Ragnhild. Her hands on the tiller trembled with relief.

"I'll take the helm," Thorgeir offered.

"Thanks." She peeled her fingers from the tiller. Murchad put a steadying arm around her.

They made their way forward where Unn tended the wounded in the shelter of the high prow. Groans and the stink of blood filled the air. Unn had trained as a shield-maiden but also proved adept at healing. Einar was helping her bathe wounds in seawater and wrapping them with strips of linen.

Four of *Raider Bride's* crew lay on the deck: three lads and a young woman. The shield-maiden had a gaping wound on her cheek. It was she who had taken the arrow to the face. The girl was conscious, but she made no sound. Ragnhild's heart twisted as she recognized Ursa, one of Unn's younger sisters. The sisters had once numbered five, but the eldest had been killed in battle the year before. If they lost Ursa, too…

"How are they?" asked Ragnhild.

Unn shook her head. "The three lads will heal well enough. They're sleeping. As for Ursa, I got the arrowhead out of her cheek, but I don't know how she will heal." She didn't say, *If she will heal.*

"I pray the gods she will recover well," said Ragnhild.

Unn nodded and cast an appraising eye over her. "There's nothing you can do here, Lady. You need some rest."

Ragnhild nodded, suddenly aware of how weary she was.

Murchad had stayed at her side, and he helped her to the shelter of the bow before she sank to the deck. She eased her back against the hull, rubbing the tingles out of her stiff hands.

Murchad settled in beside her and his arm went around her. She let her head rest on his shoulder and whispered thanks to the sea goddess Ran that he was here, hale and whole.

"Ivar recognized me. He'll get word to Harald and he'll be ready for us," she said.

"We'll take care of that when the time comes," said Murchad. "Spring is a long time off."

The first stars appeared and Einar measured their distance above the horizon with his fist. He directed Thorgeir to come around due east.

To home.

Ragnhild closed her eyes and nestled into her husband's arms, lulled by the shushing trickle of the sea running along the hull.

CHAPTER 2

Southern Coast of Norway
September, AD 822

Murchad watched Ragnhild deftly steer *Raider Bride* between the high-sided rocks that protected a flat, sandy beach in a deserted cove. After the two-day passage from the Orkney Islands, he was glad to make landfall. They were on the southern tip of land, south of Tromøy and far from Ragnhild's treacherous brother. The westerly wind that had carried them so far had petered out and now they were becalmed under a light drizzle.

The fury of battle had long since ebbed, leaving him tired and homesick. He shrugged off the feeling, knowing that a full belly and a warm fire was the cure.

Einar picked up the anchor and at Ragnhild's nod heaved it over the side.

"Stroke!" she cried. The rowers dug their oars in for one final push and the anchor line paid out. The surge lifted the longship's keel and with a jerk, the anchor grabbed and held.

"Ship oars." The rowers pulled their oars in through the notched holes as the surge carried the ship onto the beach. The keel ground into the sand and held fast while the stern swayed in the waves, tethered by the anchor. The oarsmen stood and laid their long sweeps in the midships rack. Murchad joined those crowding the bow. Taking a firm grip on the gunnel, he vaulted over the side into the knee-high water.

"Heave!" At Ragnhild's command, they hauled *Raider Bride* onto the sand. She shipped the steering oar and sprang onto the beach beside Murchad, then stood by to help the wounded crewmembers disembark. The three injured lads were able to climb down with assistance. Ursa was gently handed down, wrapped in furs. The shield-maiden moaned as Murchad and three others carried her up the beach and lowered her onto the sand.

Murchad knelt beside Ragnhild and Unn as the healer removed the bandages on her sister's cheek and sniffed. He braced for the stink of rot, but the wound was still sweet. Unn nodded, though worry creased her brow. They all knew wounds could sour quickly.

"Tova, Ylva," Unn called to her younger sisters. "Go find me some cobwebs."

Unn dipped a clean linen cloth in saltwater. She bathed the injury gently, but Ursa moaned and writhed weakly under her sister's touch. Ragnhild restrained the injured girl while Unn soaked away the dried blood. Tova and Ylva returned with handfuls of clean cobwebs which Unn laid over the injury, sealing it with a salve of herb-laced honey from a little pot. Then she bound the girl's face with a clean strip of linen. Ursa groaned and sank into that limbo of half-consciousness, the pain rousing her each time she dozed.

Ragnhild rose, brushing the sand off her breeks, and Murchad followed her to join several crewmembers gathering driftwood while Thorgeir sparked a pile of shavings with his firesteel, hulking over his work to shelter it from the light drizzle. The fire caught and Svein fed the tiny flame with twigs. Soon the blaze crackled, scenting the air with woodsmoke.

The day's trolling had been successful and they cooked fresh haddock on a stone at the fire's edge while Einar broached their last cask of Irish ale. Murchad sipped his with regret. He'd have to get used to Norse ale from now on. He turned to his food with relish. The Norse did know how to cook fish.

When they had eaten, everyone sat back expectantly, picking their teeth. It was time for stories. Svein turned to him and said, "Lord Murchad, it's high time I told you the tale of Hervör, the greatest shield-maiden of her day. Your wife is much like her."

The story was obviously well-loved, for everyone cheered. Murchad stifled the regret at being addressed as "Lord" instead of "King" and smiled at the big Norseman.

Svein took a great drink of his ale and launched into the tale. "Hervör was the daughter of Angantýr, a famous berserker who was killed in battle, along with his eleven brothers, before she was born. Even as an infant, the berserker's daughter was feared as cursed, and many thought she should be set out in the forest for the wolves. But her mother's father was a mighty jarl, and he decided she would live. He forbade anyone to mention her father's identity, and eventually it was forgotten.

"Hervör grew up strong and tall, mastering the arts of war. There was not a boy who could stand up to her." The shield-maidens around the fire raised their cups to this. "When she came of age, she discovered the truth about her father, and that he was buried on a haunted island with the family's sword, Tyrfing. Now Tyrfing was cursed, but it brought victory to everyone who wielded it, and Hervör lusted after the sword.

"She disguised herself as a man and joined a fleet of raiders. Hervör fought and bested every man in the crew until they elected her leader. She sailed with her ships to the island where her father was buried along with his brothers. An eerie light shone from the grave mounds, a sign of magic. Lightning flashed and thunder boomed in the sky over the island. Her crew refused to go ashore, so brave Hervör set off alone.

"She strode boldly up to the biggest mound and cried out, 'Angantýr, I am your daughter, Hervör. I command you to come out and surrender my birthright, the sword Tyrfing.'

"The only answer was shooting flames and roaring thunder." Svein threw a stick on the fire and it snapped and flared. "Hervör cursed her father and his brothers. 'Ants will shred you, dogs will rend you, you will rot away if you do not give me what is mine.'

"Angantýr appeared in the flames and said, 'No, daughter, you do not want my sword. Tyrfing is better here with the dead. The dwarves who made it cursed the blade. If you wield it, our bloodline will be annihilated.'

"Hervör answered, 'Nevertheless, Father, it is a mighty sword and rightfully mine. I would wield it. Give it to me.'

"'No, little maid,' said Angantýr, 'I will not lay this curse on my only child.'

"You can imagine how Hervör reacted to being called a little maid," said Svein. Murchad groaned, thinking of Ragnhild. "She said, 'Then I will come and take it, Father.' And she stepped into the flames.

"Angantýr shouted, 'No, daughter, don't come any farther into the flames of Hel. Here, take the sword.' And Tyrfing came flying out of the fire and straight into Hervör's hand. But her father gave her one last warning. 'Beware, daughter. Though the sword will always bring victory, Tyrfing must kill a man every time it leaves the sheath.'

"Thank you, Father, may you sleep in peace,' Hervör said. She took up the sword and strode to the beach to discover that her cowardly crew had sailed away without her.

"Hervör jumped into the water and swam across the sea until

she arrived at a king's court. Still disguised as a man, she became a confidant of the king. She won his favor with her advice on hnefatafl strategy."

"That's one big difference between Ragnhild and Hervör," said Unn. "Ragnhild is no strategist."

Ragnhild blushed. "It's true, I lose more often than win at hnefatafl."

Grinning, Svein resumed the tale. "Hervör stayed at the king's hall and became one of his most favored warriors, but she took care to keep Tyrfing in its sheath. The other húskarlar, jealous of her high favor with the king, conspired against her. One day while Hervör was advising the king at tafl, one of the húskarlar sneaked up and pulled Tyrfing from its sheath. The curse left the shield-maiden no choice but to take the sword away from him and run him through.

"She sheathed Tyrfing and fled to the harbor, where she joined a crew of raiders. With them she marauded far and wide, gaining fame and wealth."

"And died a noble death in battle, no doubt," said Murchad. He knew enough of their culture to predict the ending.

Svein laughed. "No, no, eventually she fell in love and married. She took up embroidery."

"She did not!" cried Ragnhild, throwing her cup at him.

Svein dodged and plucked the cup out of the air. He swigged the remaining ale and said, "That's how the story goes. Hervör raised two sons, naming one Angantýr, and the other Heidrik. Angantýr was brave and good, like his grandfather, but Heidrik was evil. Hervör gave Tyrfing to Heidrik. But that's another story." Svein filled his cup with ale and sipped.

The fire burned down and the crew crawled into their sheepskin hudfat. The skies had cleared and the September weather was warm enough for them to sleep under the stars.

Unn and her younger sisters bedded down beside Ursa. Murchad sent a silent prayer to let the young shield-maiden survive. She was only sixteen winters, a year younger than Ragnhild and Unn. If Ursa lived, it would be with a livid scar on her cheek, disfiguring her pretty face. But like her sisters, she had chosen to become a shield-maiden and lead a life of adventure. Marriage held little attraction for her. The scar would enhance her reputation and strike fear into her opponents. Murchad sighed. These Norsewomen were so different from the Irish.

Ragnhild threw her hudfat over her shoulder and took Murchad's hand. As she led him down the beach, he smiled, anticipating the night of pleasure to come after so many at sea.

"Here," she said, halting some distance from the camp and dropping the sheepskin in the lee of a shrub.

Murchad gazed up at the clear, star-strewn sky and took a deep breath. Then he pulled her to him gently and found her lips with his, sending a warmth into his belly. She tasted of salt and ale. With one hand, she unbuckled his belt and let it fall. She tugged at his tunic and he raised his arms to let her pull it over his head. As she ran her hands down his sides, his flesh quivered beneath her palms.

They stripped off the rest of their clothes and burrowed together into Ragnhild's hudfat. It was a tight fit and their skin melded as they slid into the sleeping skin, sending a shiver of anticipation up Murchad's spine. His hand went behind her head, fingers burrowing into her hair and drawing her face in for another kiss.

"You are like Hervör, my shield-maiden," he murmured in Irish—their secret lover's language. "Fearless, expert, and beautiful."

"Just don't expect me to take up embroidery."

He chuckled at the thought of Ragnhild's battle-hardened hands wielding a dainty needle.

"We'll be home in two days, *a chroí*," Ragnhild breathed into his ear. "Åsa will welcome us with a royal feast, and she'll give us a feather bed of our own."

"It sounds perfect, *a mhuirin*," said Murchad, nuzzling her throat.

"No regrets?" she asked.

"No regrets," he said, and flung away the homesickness that nagged at his happiness.

CHAPTER 3

Skiringssal, Vestfold

Åsa and Sonja sat side by side on the bench outside
Skiringssal's doorway, watching Halfdan play on the court-
yard's hard-packed earth in the morning sunlight. Shrieking a
war-cry, the boy swung his wooden sword at the two queens,
who pretended to cower. At three winters old, Halfdan refused to
be parted from his miniature weapons, even when he slept.
Tromøy's blacksmith, Ulf, had made him a leather scabbard so he
could wear his sword on his belt.

Sonja clutched her six-month-old son, Rognvald, as if he were
made of Frankish glass. The little boy squirmed in her arms,
reaching a splayed palm toward Halfdan. "You can't wait to play
with your big cousin, can you?"

The boys were actually half-brothers, a secret Åsa would
never impart. As far as Sonja knew, her husband, Olaf, was Halfdan's half-brother, not his father. The truth was known only to
Olaf, Åsa, and the völva Heid.

Åsa had been devastated when Olaf married Sonja, though she only had herself to blame. She'd refused Olaf again and again, and she would still do so. After battling warlords who tried to dominate her, she could not bring herself to marry and give her power to a man, even Olaf. He was not like the others, but by law he would have authority over her, her people, her son.

Sonja stood half a head shorter than Åsa, her body lush rather than lanky. Her hair was silver-blond, nearly the same shade as Olaf's, and her eyes were the blue of the clearest summer sky. And unlike Åsa, Sonja was a consummate landswoman. While Tromøy's fields and livestock prospered because Åsa had recruited from Agder's farms for her hird, Sonja was one of them. She was álf-favored, and every creature flourished beneath her gentle hand. It was said flowers bloomed where she walked and crops sprang up beneath her feet.

She was the kind of woman Olaf deserved.

"Promise me you will foster Rognvald," Sonja said. "I could never trust anyone else."

"Of course, if you will take on Halfdan when the time comes."

"Agreed! Rognvald worships him already."

The thought of parting with her son gave Åsa's heart a little twist, but it was years away. Then Sonja would have everyone Åsa held dearest—Halfdan and Olaf. It didn't seem fair, though it was certainly fitting that Olaf would foster his own son. And Åsa would gladly take Rognvald into her hall when the time came.

A shadow fell across the yard. Åsa glanced up to see the brawny figure of Olvir, captain of her húskarlar, approach. "The ship is ready, Lady."

"We are ready, too," she replied, rising from the bench. She enveloped Sonja and Rognvald in a hug. "Come visit Tromøy soon."

"We will," Sonja promised.

"Heid, we're ready," Åsa called. She held her hand out to her son. "It's time to go to the boat."

Halfdan crowed in delight. The only thing he loved more than swordplay was going to sea. He all but dragged his mother down the trail to the harbor.

They made their way along the shoreline boardwalk, lined with traders' booths boasting exotic goods from far-flung lands, as well as more local crafts such as antler combs and finely woven cloth. A cacophony of tongues vied in the air as traders called out their wares.

Åsa had arrived with a load of soapstone and iron tools crafted in Tromøy's smithy. She was taking home spices, silks, and walnuts.

She followed her son down the dock to the ship, where Olaf waited at the head of the crowd. "Farewell, Åsa, Queen," he said, fixing her with his hazel eyes.

Åsa met his gaze. "Farewell, Olaf, King." Though their words were formal, the look they exchanged was intimate. Åsa broke eye contact as Halfdan yanked his hand from hers and scampered onto the ship. The deckhands greeted the little boy and secured him in a harness with a long line attached. Åsa insisted he wear it whenever they were on a ship. Halfdan seemed born with sea legs, but she had no intention of diving into the icy waters after her son.

Åsa boarded and went to the helm while Heid's apprentices helped the aging sorceress onto the ship, taking her shrill complaints with good humor. Once they were safely aboard, the crew cast off the mooring lines and the rowers took up their oars.

Åsa gripped the tiller, its carved serpent's head familiar in her hand. *Ran's Lover*, with thirty-four oars, had been her father's flagship. Now it was hers. Every strake in its oak hull brought back memories of childhood voyages.

As they left the dock, Åsa's gaze wandered back to shore and fastened on Olaf's shining head.

"Stop moping over that oaf!" said Heid as she settled herself on a sea chest in the stern beside Åsa. "We got what we wanted out of him. Now let him go. Olvir is a likely one to scratch an itch." Heid eyed the húskarl as he stood in the bow, coiling the mooring lines.

"There is far more between a man and a woman than the scratching of an itch!" said Åsa testily. "Not that you would know about that, with your völva ways, discarding lovers at a whim."

Heid's grin sagged and she stared into the distance. "But I do know about that," she said softly. "Though it was so long ago..."

Åsa stopped short. "I'm sorry. I had forgotten."

Long before Åsa had been born, raiders had murdered Heid's husband and child, and left her crippled for life. Though it had taken years, the sorceress had wrought a terrible vengeance on the men responsible—Åsa's husband, and Åsa's father.

Åsa felt the tiller, responding to the tug of the wind and current on the rudder as she steered the longship homeward. The mild land breeze whispered against her face, carrying the scent of woodsmoke. From her vantage point in the stern, she observed Olvir in the bow, bending down to show Halfdan how to tie a knot. The warm wind ruffled the warrior's shoulder-length brown hair and neatly trimmed beard. Olvir was handsome and fit enough, though his hair did not glint silver in the light. He was tall, but Olaf was taller.

The húskarl patiently put down the rope and followed Halfdan as he scampered about the longship. Heid's assessment was no doubt correct. Olvir would be a good lover, kind and considerate. Åsa imagined him smiling down at her, his arms about her waist. A small shiver coursed down her spine. But the blue eyes shifted to hazel, and in her imagination she gazed into Olaf's eyes.

It was no good. The poor man kept turning into Olaf—the only lover she'd ever known. She could not imagine another man. It would be unfair to Olvir, for whenever she was with him she'd be in Olaf's arms.

And it would be unfair in other ways. Olvir was not of noble birth. She could never take him as an equal. She was his queen and he could not refuse her, if she asked. He would be her—concubine. What would that do to his status with the men? Now he was their leader. But her special favor would create jealousy in their ranks. And if they had a falling out? What then? She could outlaw him, even have him executed if she wished. She would never know if he acted out of affection for her, or fear of her power.

No, Heid's suggestion would not do, not for a queen.

~

RAIDER BRIDE WENDED through the skjaergarden, the archipelago of rocks and skerries that provided a passage sheltered from the Skagerrak's seas. The rowers strained at their oars against the fickle currents and tide rips. Ragnhild, on the helm, kept a careful eye on Thorgeir, stationed on the bow, signaling hazards with a white flag.

Evening was not far away, and she steered *Raider Bride* into a cove she knew that was a half-day's sail from Tromøy. They would arrive the next day, around midday or early afternoon, well rested. Ragnhild was eager to see Åsa again, to show off her treasure and husband to the queen who had mentored her. She imagined Åsa's admiration at her accomplishments, of the awe she'd inspire among the húskarlar. True, she'd married Murchad instead of killing him, she'd lost several crewmembers, and hadn't achieved her goal of claiming her inheritance—but she'd survived her brother's treachery, gained a noble husband, and made off with a hefty treasure to boot. Not a bad outcome.

She could hardly wait to get to Tromøy.

The tide was low. They gathered shellfish and seaweed, and

feasted on it with the last of their ale. When they'd devoured the meal, Ragnhild looked to Murchad. "Tell us a story, *a chroi.*" The younger crewmembers chimed in their agreement. Though the entire crew loved Svein's stories, they knew them well, and Murchad's Irish tales were something none of them had heard. Each evening on the ten-day voyage from Ireland, Murchad had alternated with Svein to tell them a different story of the great Irish heroes. Ragnhild thought the Irish were a foolish bunch, constantly fighting over cattle and such, but the stories were entertaining, and it kept Unn's mind off her sister.

"Very well," Murchad said. "I have told you of Fionn mac Cumhaill and his warband, the fianna. Tonight I will tell you of his son, Oisin." The crew fell silent, leaning toward the Irishman, faces rapt. From her spot next to her sister, Unn turned her face to Murchad. Ragnhild was glad to see her distracted for a little while.

"Oisin's mother was turned into a deer and stolen by an evil druid, and Fionn raised their son alone to be a great warrior and poet. One day father and son were out hunting with the fianna. A beautiful woman with golden hair rode up on a magnificent white horse.

"The woman looked down from her horse on Oisin. 'I am Niamh of the Golden Hair, daughter of Manannan mac Lir, god of the sea. I challenge you to come with me to my home.'

"Fionn knew in his heart if Oisin went with her, he would never see his son again. But the moment Oisin looked into her eyes, he fell in love. In spite of his father's warnings, he mounted the white horse and rode away with Niamh."

The crew groaned, suspecting this was a bad decision.

"The enchanted horse took them under the sea to Tir na nOg, the land of youth. There they were married and Oisin was honored. He and Niamh had two sons and a daughter.

"Oisin was happy in Tir na nOg, but he missed his father and friends. After a few years, he told his wife he longed to visit

Ireland. Reluctantly, Niamh lent him her white horse and bade it take him to Ireland. 'But do not dismount,' she warned her husband. 'For if your feet touch Irish soil, you may never return to Tir na nOg.'"

The listeners sucked in their breath, knowing something would go awry.

"Oisin promised, and the white horse carried him swiftly across the sea to Ireland. He rode eagerly to his father's home, but found it had long been abandoned. He set off to find his father, and he came upon a group of men trying to move a giant boulder. They were having a hard time of it.

"The men greeted Oisin and asked him his business. 'I seek Fionn mac Cumhaill, and his warband the fianna.'

"The men answered, 'We have heard of the fianna in legend and story. It is three hundred years and more since the great Fionn walked the earth.'" Murchad paused as his audience gasped.

"Oisin was stunned. His heart filled with despair and he turned the white horse to ride back to Tir na nOg. The men went back to their work.

"But as he rode away, Oisin realized his horse had great strength. He could help the men without dismounting or touching Irish soil. Oisin rode back to the men, and instructed them to tie a rope around the boulder. He fastened the other end to his horse's harness and set the horse to pulling. But as the rope took a strain, the harness broke. Oisin fell from the horse and landed on the ground."

"No!" shouted one of the younger crewmembers, accompanied by groans.

"Yes," said Murchad. "No sooner had he touched the earth than Oisin began to age. He shriveled and shrank until he was no more than a bundle of leather and bones, and then he turned to dust.

"The horse ran off to Tir na nOg, and when she saw the horse Niamh knew her husband was lost forever."

A lump rose in Ragnhild's throat that nearly choked her. Would Murchad become homesick like Oisin, and leave her forever? She told herself it was a foolish thought.

But that night as they lay in their hudfat, she clung to him tighter than ever.

CHAPTER 4

Horns sounded a welcome as Åsa steered *Ran's Lover* into Tromøy's harbor. Folk had already gathered on the shore as the prow touched land. They rushed into the shallows to help the crew haul the longship high onto the beach. Åsa made her way forward and eased over the side, reaching back to pick up Halfdan before he could squirm over the gunnel. With her son in her arms, she hurried up the trail, leaving the unloading in Olvir's capable hands.

Brenna stood by the hall door beside her husband, Toki. "Welcome home, Lady," said the fóstra, taking Halfdan in her arms. Åsa gave the couple each a quick hug, then fled to the bower. She hurried to her chamber, where she flung herself on the bed and lay staring up into the ceiling's gloom.

Conflicting needs and desires roiled in her mind. She was young, with a long life ahead of her. The lonely years stretched out before her. Yet she couldn't give her power to a man. The law was clear, as she knew well. If she married, her husband would have the power of a king. After Gudrød, she couldn't let that happen. She would rule alone, and raise Halfdan to be a good king, like her father. If she must remain alone until her son was a man, so be it.

Her falcon, Stormrider, sat on her perch next to the bed. The peregrine lifted a foot and the copper bells on her jesses tinkled restlessly. Åsa reached over and untied the leather leash. She gazed into the falcon's dark eyes and felt herself drawn into their liquid depths. As she entered the bird's body, her vision shifted, waking to colors and detail no human could perceive. On the far side of the room, an insect crawled across the wall, leaving a glowing trail. As she watched its hairlike legs move, a predatory urge rose inside her.

She worked the bird's chest muscles and the powerful wings flapped, lifting her from the perch. She shot across the room, aiming for the open gable. The cool air drew her out into the limitless sky. Higher and higher she flew until, spent, she hovered.

Within the falcon's body, it was right to be alone—a solitary hunter without the gouging need for companionship. From on high, the world looked manageable. The steading was tiny, its inhabitants insects, the longships toys. The vast expanse of blue called to her and she winged out over the sea.

Far below, a sail surged on the shimmering sea. A longship, heading for Tromøy's harbor. She swooped down to take a closer look.

Sleek and graceful, its proportions proclaimed it a karvi, a smaller class of seagoing vessel. Her heart beat faster as she recognized *Raider Bride*'s blue-and-white sail.

It had been four months since Ragnhild had set sail to Ireland with her brother to avenge their father's death, and all that time Åsa had no word of her, not so much as a prophetic dream. Even the old sorceress Heid had no inkling of the shield-maiden's fate.

With relief Åsa spotted Ragnhild's tall, rangy form at the helm, the shield-maiden's hair bound in its familiar ratty braid. Åsa picked out Unn and two of her surviving sisters, and Ragnhild's three húskarlar—Einar, Thorgeir, and Svein. But *Raider Bride*'s ranks had thinned and several familiar faces were missing. Wounded lay on the deck, wrapped in their hudfat.

The falcon wheeled in the air and beat her way back to Tromøy to prepare for their arrival.

The lookout must have spotted the ship, for as Stormrider soared over the steading, Tromøy's warriors were already mustering on the shore. The falcon headed for the bower and flew straight in through the gable end. No sooner had the bird lit on her perch than Åsa sought her human form on the bed. From long experience, she sent her will coursing through the body, forcing it upright and stumbling out into the afternoon light.

"It's *Raider Bride*," she shouted. Nobody asked how she knew, but the warriors relaxed their stance. Garth, the stable boy, brought her horse, Gullfaxi, already saddled and bridled. Åsa mounted and rode down the trail at the head of the crowd.

Raider Bride neared shore. Tromøy's residents swarmed into the water to grab hold of the gunnels and drag the longship onto the beach. Shouted greetings filled the air as the voyagers leaped over the side to embrace their friends and families. They helped the wounded off with care. The injured lads disembarked with assistance, but Unn called for a board to carry the shield-maiden with her face bandaged. Åsa's heart thudded when she saw it was Ursa. The family had already lost their eldest girl. She hoped they would not lose another. The girl was pale and covered with sweat. Åsa bit back a surge of anger at Ragnhild, knowing that the crew had accepted the risk when they volunteered for the voyage. She hoped that Heid would be able to heal Ursa.

Ulf huffed up beside Åsa, watching as the voyagers disembarked. "I don't see Behrt."

Åsa's stomach twisted—she and the Christian warrior had formed a bond. Behrt had insisted on sailing with Ragnhild despite crippling injuries he'd sustained in battle. Åsa understood why he'd gone. Though Norse-born, Behrt had been raised in

Ireland and he never felt that he fit in here on Tromøy. The Irish had rejected him, but Ireland was his home and she couldn't blame him for wanting to return.

He'd made his choice, and now it looked like that choice had been the death of him. She had to accept it. Shaking off sorrow, she turned her attention back to the living. There was a stranger in their midst, a black-haired man who strode beside Ragnhild.

Maintaining a regal demeanor, Åsa sat her horse calmly while Ragnhild strode toward her, the dark stranger keeping pace beside her. He was the same height as Ragnhild, and well-muscled—a warrior. His shoulder-length black hair shone glossy as a crow's wing, his twinkling green eyes set in a handsome face. His chin was clean-shaven, though he sported a luxuriant black moustache. Judging by the lines around his eyes, Åsa guessed he had seen at least thirty winters, though there was no hint of gray in his raven hair.

He wore a short, close-fitting wool jacket and long, tight-legged woolen trousers tucked into soft boots. Over it all hung a mantle woven in a plaid of many colors, ranging from black and white to a yellow-gold and purple, clasped at the shoulder with a silver brooch. From his belt hung a sword with a jeweled pommel. A man of rank.

"Åsa, Queen," said Ragnhild, inclining her head.

Åsa nodded in greeting. "Lady Ragnhild, I am so glad to greet you and your crew. But here is someone I do not know."

Both women turned to the dark stranger. Many others were also eyeing him curiously.

"May I present Murchad mac Maele Duin," Ragnhild announced. Was there the slightest hint of defensiveness in her voice? "My husband."

Åsa's jaw dropped. A collective gasp escaped the crowd and everyone stared at the couple. Ragnhild—married?

A shocking thought struck her. "Is this…"

"The Irish king my father promised me to." Ragnhild's voice had a definite edge of defiance.

Murchad swept an elegant bow to Åsa. "King no longer, my lady," he said in perfect Norse.

Ragnhild gave him an affectionate smile that astounded Åsa. "Murchad gave up his kingship rather than annul our marriage."

The Irishman returned her fond gaze. "I could not bear to be parted from my wife."

Åsa struggled to grasp the idea that the man Ragnhild had set out to kill was now her husband. She shook her head as if it were a dusty quilt and recalled her queenly duties. "I'll not keep you standing after your long voyage. Let our people see to your ship and your wounded while you all come to the hall with me for the welcome mead, and you can tell of your adventures."

Ragnhild and Murchad bent their heads in thanks before following her up the trail to the longhouse. Brenna waited in the doorway with Halfdan, who squirmed out of her arms and dashed to Ragnhild. The shield-maiden bent and picked the little boy up. He stared over her shoulder at Murchad, his mouth forming an O.

"This is my son, Halfdan." Åsa dismounted and handed Gullfaxi's reins to the stable boy.

"Hello, little king," said Murchad. Halfdan buried his face in Ragnhild's shoulder.

The bearers arrived, carrying Ursa on her board, Unn and her two younger sisters walking alongside.

Åsa turned to Toki. "Please show Lord Murchad where he can refresh himself. I must see to Ursa." The steward escorted Murchad into the hall with the other men while the women followed Unn and her sister to the bower.

Heid met them at the bower door. She fixed Ragnhild with her piercing gaze. "So you have survived, shield-maiden."

"I have," said Ragnhild, setting Halfdan on his feet.

"I am glad to see it. I had no bad dreams of you while you

were away." The old sorceress turned toward Ursa. "Lay the girl here by the fire," she commanded. She knelt and peered at the injured girl, who moaned and tossed restlessly. Heid laid a hand on her forehead. "She's feverish." The völva peeled back the bandages from the wound. Åsa caught her breath at the ugly gash on the shield-maiden's cheek. She shot Ragnhild a frown.

Unn said anxiously, "I kept the wound as clean as I could, and dressed it with herbed honey and cobwebs."

Heid nodded. "You did well, Unn. I think your sister will live to tell this tale, though she won't be pretty anymore. But there is more to life than that. I will give her something to let her rest and we shall see."

Åsa gestured the other women back as Unn and her two younger sisters hovered over Ursa.

"You sisters can stay," said Heid sternly. "The rest of you will only get in my way. All of you, go."

As the women left the bower, Åsa put her hand on Ragnhild's shoulder and pulled her aside. "I can't believe you're married to the man you set out to kill."

Ragnhild beamed. "I love him."

Åsa shook her head. "You understand your marriage gives him power over you."

Ragnhild laughed. "It's not like that with us." She shrugged off Åsa's grip and swept Halfdan into her arms. They hurried to the great hall where the men were already gathered, Murchad among them. Ragnhild, carrying Halfdan, took her place beside him.

Servants had stirred up the longfire and lit the lamps, dispelling the gloom of the great room.

Åsa conducted Ragnhild and Murchad to the seats of honor next to hers. Ragnhild took her place, settling Halfdan on her lap. The húskarlar seated themselves on the benches, welcoming the crew of *Raider Bride* to their old places among them, while the other folk crowded in behind them, filling the doorway and spilling into the yard.

Toki tapped a keg of mead and Brenna marshalled the women to serve the newcomers. Heid hobbled in and took her own place near her queen. "The girl is sleeping and there's nothing more I can do right now. Her sisters will not leave her side. We can send them something to eat."

Brenna bustled in with the welcome horn of mead, trailing the aroma of honey behind her. She brought the horn to Åsa, who took it and rose. "I welcome you all back to Tromøy." She drank as the assembly cheered.

When the mead horn had made its rounds, Brenna took Half-dan, who had fallen asleep in Ragnhild's arms. Åsa settled back in her seat and turned to the shield-maiden. "Now tell us your tale. The last we heard, Ragnhild, you set sail to join your brothers in avenging your father's death."

"Indeed, I sailed with my elder brother Harald to Ireland, to take vengeance on the man who killed my father." Ragnhild smiled at Murchad. The Irishman's green eyes seemed to glow in response. "By doing so, I would prove myself worthy to take my odal lands in Gausel. But it was a trap. Harald had already made arrangements with Murchad to hand me over as wife in exchange for a substantial bride price, just as my father had planned."

Åsa stared at her. "We fought a war against your father to prevent that marriage. Warriors died for you."

Ragnhild smiled wryly. "What the Norns have woven come to pass."

Åsa glanced from Ragnhild to Murchad. "You believe you two were fated to be together?"

"So it would appear." Ragnhild laid her hand on her husband's. Åsa stifled a twinge at the gesture.

"And you are content to give him a husband's authority?" Åsa still had difficulty grasping that the shield-maiden had willingly accepted the fate she had tried so hard to elude.

"I am content. Murchad gave up his kingship to come with me

and reclaim my inheritance. Together, we will guard the seaways and protect Ireland from raiders."

To cover her shock, Åsa abruptly changed tack. "I see that some of your crew are missing and wounded, yet it sounds as if no battle occurred."

"When Harald betrayed me, the crew of *Raider Bride* got away. Harald pursued them, and though they fought him off, six were killed and several wounded in the battle." Ragnhild stood and raised her cup. "I drink the memory cup to those who are no longer with us. I name Hild and Jorun, shield-maidens who died with honor and have gone to Freyja's hall. Let us never forget them."

Åsa's heart squeezed. Hild and Jorun had been farm girls of no more than sixteen winters, full of mischief and courage. She joined the assembly as they drank in remembrance of each of them.

Ragnhild raised her cup again. "I also name Lars, Finn, Leif, and Gorm."

Boys no older than the girls had been. All gone so young. Åsa's mead went down hard with every toast.

After all had drunk to the departed, Åsa realized one had not been mentioned. "And what of Behrt, the Christian? How did he die?"

"He is not dead," said Ragnhild. "He has chosen to become a Christ-priest, and live in a monastery. He said he's found the place he belongs at last."

Another friend lost—but at least he lived. "I am so glad that he's found happiness. Of all people, he deserves it. But many of us here will miss him."

Ragnhild grinned. "He threatens in time to pay us a visit, and make Christians of us all."

"I don't know how much luck he will have with that, but he'll be welcome here," said Åsa. "Please, continue with the story."

Einar took up the tale. "After the battle, we eluded Harald, but the Irish captured us and imprisoned us in a cow-byre. They worked us like slaves." He looked to Ragnhild to fill in her part.

"During this time, Murchad held me captive on his island fortress," she said.

"I made you my queen, *a mhuirin*," Murchad protested. He spoke with the authority of a king. Åsa tensed, wondering if Ragnhild truly knew what she had gotten herself into.

"A prisoner all the same," Ragnhild said. "Murchad demanded custody of my crew from their captor, and arranged to bring them back to his own stronghold. But I didn't trust him. Instead I escaped with my crew and ship by night."

"And a good thing you did," said Murchad. "For I would not be alive and here today otherwise."

"We sailed away on *Raider Bride*," said Ragnhild. "But as we were leaving, Murchad's enemies attacked the fortress, and we turned back to help him."

"You saved my life," said Murchad. "You could have escaped and left me behind."

Ragnhild laughed. "I took you prisoner."

"I have always been your prisoner, *a chroí*."

Åsa caught the passionate look that passed between them and frowned. When Behrt had followed Ragnhild like a lost puppy, she had treated the Christian with disdain. Yet after all this—war, death, betrayal—the shield-maiden sat complacently beside the man she had vowed to kill.

Ragnhild continued. "Murchad's enemies pursued us and launched an assault on the nearby monastery. Harald arrived in his ship and joined the attack, though he had promised peace when he sold me to Murchad."

"An oath-breaker," said Murchad, suppressed fury hardening his voice.

Ragnhild shrugged. "What can you expect from my brother? But we came upon them by sea and attacked from behind. It so happened that Behrt had joined this very monastery, and he led the monks in defense, holding off the enemy while reinforcements arrived overland. Between us, we crushed the enemy forces. Harald got away—though not before I recovered my bride price from him." Ragnhild bared her teeth in a triumphant smirk.

Åsa caught her breath. "Is this the legendary bride price your father fought a war over? If so, you are wealthy indeed."

Ragnhild smiled. "It is!" A murmur arose in the room. "I have wealth, but no land of my own. I must raise an army to take Gausel from Harald."

"You are very set on taking this land," said Åsa.

Ragnhild raised her chin. "My mother left it to me, and Harald has no right to withhold it. It's mine and I will claim it."

Åsa recognized the set of Ragnhild's jaw. She seemed very sure of herself. "Just how do you plan to take Gausel?"

Ragnhild leaned forward, her face flushed with the warmth of the fire. "As we passed the Orkney Isles, we were attacked by Ivar, Harald's ally. They gave Ursa her wound, and the three lads. Murchad killed one of the ship's captains, but Ivar escaped. By now I'm sure he's gotten word to Harald that I am on my way home with *Raider Bride* and my crew. My brother will expect me to come to Gausel, if not now, then in the spring."

"That will be a bloody battle," said Åsa, her apprehension growing.

Ragnhild continued blithely, "I'll have to bring a strong force to take and hold Gausel. You can help me recruit, Lady. Maybe at the fall assembly?"

For a moment Åsa was speechless. The girl had no strategy. When she spoke, her voice hardened. "I've lost many good warriors for you. You need a plan before I'll help you recruit more lives for you to waste."

"If you remember correctly, I financed your warband," said Ragnhild.

That stung. Åsa's blood rose. "Yes, when you stole your father's hoard."

Ragnhild's face reddened. "I risked my life for that hoard. You've benefited from those riches. You needed the warriors as much as I did. If not for me, both you and this island would be Danish possessions."

Åsa bristled. "I rescued you the first time your father shipped you off to a forced marriage. Some who defended you lost their lives. Yet here you are, giving all your power to the Irish king."

Ragnhild said, "Murchad is a great warrior and a loyal husband. His cousin Niall and the Christ-priests objected to their king's marriage to a heathen. They demanded that he annul our marriage. Instead, he gave up his kingship to come with me."

"I have no regrets," said Murchad, though Åsa wondered if she detected a note of uncertainty in his tone.

"You had to give back your golden torc," said Ragnhild. "You should have seen it, Åsa. It was magnificent."

"That torc belongs to the king," said Murchad. "It is passed from one to the next. It was Niall's by right."

"Was I wrong to keep this, then?" A sly grin spread across Ragnhild's face. From her leather bag she withdrew a gleaming golden necklace that took Åsa's breath away.

Murchad blanched white. "*A chroi*, you have stolen the queen's necklace."

"Many riches from your country have found new owners in the north," she said complacently, displaying the three golden disks linked by a thick gold chain. An awestruck murmur arose in the hall.

Murchad rose and glowered at his wife. "Lady, that necklace belongs to the rightful queen of my people." His face had gone from white to purple. "It is a treasure intended for the rulers of my land. And now it is in heathen hands."

"It seemed all right in heathen hands when you gave it to me," Ragnhild retorted.

"Don't you understand what you have done?" he cried. "You've stolen one of the royal treasures of my people. You're no better than your brother—a thief with no honor!" The Irishman wheeled and stormed out of the hall.

A stunned silence fell over the assembly.

Ragnhild watched him go, open-mouthed. She turned to Åsa, but found no sympathy there.

"I'll not be recruiting more farmhands for you to waste, no matter how much gold you bring," said Åsa.

With a strangled sound, Ragnhild jumped up and ran out of the hall.

Åsa stared at the door. She'd done what she had to do, but still her stomach roiled. Was it worth losing a friend?

She looked around at the occupants of the hall. Most sat completely still, meeting no one's eyes. They were her people. She'd sacrificed so much to bring them together, to keep them safe. For them, she knew she'd give up everything.

Einar, Thorgeir, and Svein exchanged glances. As one, they rose from the bench and approached the high seat. Einar stepped forward and cleared his throat. "Lady, we ask your leave to go after her."

Though they owed allegiance to Åsa first and foremost, the three warriors had practically raised Ragnhild.

"Yes, yes, of course." Åsa waved them away.

She caught a glint of gold amid the rushes on the floor. The Irish necklace. Ragnhild had dropped it when she fled.

Åsa leaned over to retrieve it. The moment her hand touched the golden links, her fingers tingled, like tiny sparks that burned up her arm. She snatched her hand back.

"That thing reeks of magic," said Heid, a warning note in her voice.

The Irish gold had power. Åsa wondered if Ragnhild had felt it, too.

She picked the necklace up with the blade of her eating knife and tucked it in her belt pouch.

CHAPTER 5

Agder Forest

The blind wolf snuffled among the fallen leaves, tracking a mouse. Since losing his remaining eye, the wolf's sense of smell and hearing had become more acute than ever. He could scent the urine the rodent exuded in its panic, hear the scuttering of tiny paws in the bracken. The little mouse could not elude him. His stomach rumbled in anticipation.

There! Quick as lightning, the blind wolf pounced on his prey, trapping the mouse in his jaws. The wolf held the furry corpse in his mouth, resisting the urge to gulp it down.

He crept back to the cave that served as his den, burrowing into the bracken and brush he'd dragged in for bedding. Curling up next to the old man's body, he felt the slow beat of the heart, the barely warm skin, the halting breath. The wolf put his mouth up to the human's as if to kiss him, and pushed the mouse into the man's mouth. The frail shell could not sustain full consciousness, but the autonomic response kicked in and the old man sucked. Warm blood spurted down his throat, triggering him to swallow. The best the wolf could do was to keep him alive, keep them both alive.

When the human had sucked the little corpse dry, the wolf reclaimed the mouse. His stomach quivered as he finally let himself feed. Bones crunched with a satisfying crack as he bit down. He swallowed the furry body. The mouse would sustain him for the night, and tomorrow the wolf would hunt again.

He curled up beside the human, tucking his tail over his nose. It was a miracle that they had survived, both blind. After the witch had snatched his one remaining eye, he'd dragged the old man's body to this cave, and kept him alive on rodents and grubs through that horrible winter. With summer life had become easier. His hearing and sense of smell had sharpened. He was getting better at hunting. One day soon he might catch a hare, and its flesh would give him strength enough to take down a deer, perhaps restore him enough to reanimate his human host.

And then, blind or no, he would find her, the old witch who had taken his eye and left him for dead. He would find them all.

His vengeance would be terrible.

~

DUSK WAS FALLING as Ragnhild trudged down the trail. In the distance, Murchad's hunched figure strode along the beach. Pride forbade her chasing him, though her chest felt strangely hollow and a lump thickened her throat. She swallowed painfully and turned to her ship. Ragnhild climbed aboard *Raider Bride* and plunked down on her sea chest. Why was Murchad so unreasonable? Why wouldn't Åsa help her? It was so unfair. When she became Queen of Gausel, nobody could tell her what she could and couldn't do.

Raider Bride dipped. She looked up as Einar, Thorgeir, and

Svein climbed aboard. Ragnhild had never been happier to see the three húskarlar.

"That was stupid of me," she muttered.

"It wasn't the smartest thing you've ever done," Thorgeir agreed.

"I guess there's nothing I can do to set things right," she said, half hopeful that the húskarlar would have a solution.

"Not just now," agreed Svein. "Best to keep a low profile. Out of Åsa's sight would be the best."

"We can't move the ship without crew," said Ragnhild glumly. "Nobody will join us."

"Probably not," said Einar.

"Well, we'll just stay aboard."

"Good idea," Thorgeir said.

They each crawled into their hudfat in silence. A light drizzle began to fall. Ragnhild lay long staring up at the blurred stars, a heaviness in her chest that must be her heart turned to stone.

～

MURCHAD STORMED DOWN THE BEACH, his chest tight with rage. *I'm a fool. I gave up everything—my kingship, my home, my wealth—to follow a woman. She's proven herself no more than a thief. A raider, like all her kind.* In terms of Brehon law, he'd become a man who followed the buttocks of his wife over a border, and now his honor was reckoned by her value. He was adrift, the sole Christian in a heathen land, with no status of his own.

He was so angry with Ragnhild that he couldn't face her. He didn't belong here. He wished he'd never come, but he could see no way out. Perhaps a night alone, outdoors, would clear his head.

He'd followed his feet where they chose to guide him, and now he found himself a long way down the beach. He realized he had taken nothing with him but his cloak and his sword—no food, no water, not even a bed sack—and it was falling dark.

I will be like the monks who go into exile for Jesus, trusting in the Lord to guide my steps.

He was no stranger to fasting, and water was not a problem in this country, he thought ruefully as a steady rain began to fall. He would need shelter for the night.

He veered inland from the beach. The trees seemed to part before him, inviting him into their comforting protection. As he stared into the woods, a faint pathway appeared in the gloom where none had been a moment ago. A game trail, no doubt. The early autumn canopy shed the worst of the rain and the forest litter crackled, dry beneath his boots.

The music of trickling water beckoned in the distance. The sound grew louder as he followed the trail through the undergrowth, until he came to a spring bubbling from a rock, where he drank his fill. Nearby an inviting hillock promised a windbreak. With his knife, he cut saplings and wove them together to form a lean-to shelter in the lee of the hillock. He piled branches and leaves inside, making a snug nest.

Though he hadn't eaten since morning, he didn't feel hungry. It was full dark now, so he burrowed into his forest bed. The earthy scent of the leaves mixed with the astringent smell of pine, and the forest stilled save the hoot of an owl.

At some point he must have fallen asleep, for he dreamed that a tall, fair-faced woman came to him. There was a glow about her and he realized she was of the other world—a Ban na Sidhe—a faerie woman. Murchad's scalp prickled.

"Greetings, Lord," she said in a silvery voice. "You are far from home."

Murchad knew well to address beings of the other world with caution. Such things had comprised a part of his training by a master druid, though those lessons were kept secret from the

Christian priests. He'd never expected to use the knowledge, especially not in a foreign land.

"Greetings, Lady," he answered, respectful while letting his rank be evident in his tone. "Indeed, I am from a distant land, though we have your kind there."

"Perhaps you do." The spirit lady smiled at him. Her face was youthful, her body lithe. Her hair shimmered silver, falling over her shoulders. Gold and jewels twinkled beneath the fur collar of her finely woven red wool gown, bordered with intricate tablet weavings. A noble lady.

"What has brought you here?" he asked.

Her laugh rang out like a silver bell. "Why, you have come to me, and lay your bed against my hill."

He should have realized the hillock was a faerie mound. It had not crossed his mind that such things existed here.

"Your heart has been wounded," the fae woman said, a look of concern crossing her lovely face.

He smiled wryly. No doubt he wore his shame like a cloak. "Fool that I was, I let a woman lure me to this foreign land, and now I have lost everything."

The Ban na Sidhe smiled. "It may be that you have not lost quite as much as you think."

"What do you mean by that?"

"Perhaps this woman doesn't deserve you." The woman's words brought him up short. "She's betrayed you. By her actions, she's brought shame on you. You don't deserve such treachery."

Murchad sighed. How could he explain that Ragnhild drew him, calling to some ancient longing for a queen who led men in battle?

"I am such a one," the fae woman said, as if she'd read his thoughts. He stared at her, tall and proud. "Long ago, I was a warrior queen. My husband fell in a far-off land. I never married again. I took the power for myself and ruled for many years. I commanded armies and fought wars." Her voice softened as she gazed at him. "In life, I was feared by all. In death, I was put here, far from the living, and forgotten. I have been alone for a long time."

Murchad felt her loneliness sweep through him and suddenly he wanted to take her in his arms, to stroke her gleaming hair.

"Come with me. I have a feast prepared." She reached out her arms and the mound gaped open. Within, an eerie glow shone on a table set with silver plates and Frankish glassware. The aroma of wine and meat wafted out, making Murchad's mouth water and his stomach growl.

He clamped his jaw shut. He knew full well that if he touched the faerie food, he would become her prisoner.

No sooner had he formed the thought than the feast vanished.

"Talk with me, then," said the lady. "Long have I awaited someone worthy of conversation."

She held out her hand invitingly. What harm would conversation do? How good it would be to talk with someone who understood him.

Murchad placed his hand in hers.

"I am not of your kind," she said, gripping his hand firmly. "The rules of your land do not apply to me."

She stepped inside the hillock, drawing him into the dark maw of the burial mound.

The grave-glow cast a shimmer on a tent-shaped chamber of rough timbers. The walls were hung with rich tapestries, woven to depict a procession of warriors and horses and finely dressed women. An upright loom leaned against one wall, half-filled with an unfinished weaving. A gaming board was set up on a low table, two stools alongside.

The lady pulled him down beside her onto a feather bed covered by an intricately embroidered coverlet. Her fair hair shone on the pillow, the jewels sparkled on her breast in the glow.

As his head touched the pillow, an odor of must and decay prickled at his nose.

He bolted upright. The fine red gown was moldering, its tablet weaving falling to pieces. Out from the sleeves peeped finger bones, and the face, framed by the gleaming fall of hair, was a grinning skull.

Heart drumming, he scrambled off the bed and stumbled over something on the floor. Looking down, he saw a tangle of rags and bones. A human skull leered up at him from empty eye sockets. The queen's last companion.

He scoured the chamber for an exit, beating his fists on the walls, but the stout timbers held firm.

The chamber was impenetrable. There was no way out.

He was trapped in the mound with the dead.

CHAPTER 6

Ragnhild woke uneasily to a mild drizzle and the smell of boiling tar. She struggled out of her hudfat and joined the three húskarlar while they ate ship's rations of flatbread and dried fish around the fire, over which bubbled a cauldron of pine tar.

"We should go look for Murchad," she said.

"Give the man a little time," said Einar. "Even in a strange land, he can take care of himself. He'll come back when he's ready."

There was no arguing with their logic, but dread simmered deep in Ragnhild's stomach. What if he'd really left her? She knew he longed for Ireland, and had misgivings about staying here. "What if he's found a ship to take him home?"

"No ships can come or go without Åsa's knowledge. She has lookouts stationed all over the island. Let's ask the harbor sentry if any ships have sailed."

The sentry confirmed that no ships had departed since *Raider Bride* had arrived.

"Then he must be on the island," said Einar. "Come, we've work to do."

Ragnhild shoved down her misgivings and joined them in the repairs inevitable after a long sea voyage. They swept and scrubbed the decks, and rewove frayed ropes, recaulked seams that had worked open in the seaway and sealed them with fresh tar.

All day the work absorbed Ragnhild and soothed her, and when evening came she retired to her hudfat exhausted and fell asleep immediately. But that night she woke many times, worried about Murchad. She could understand his staying away for a day, but he was a stranger here, alone. He must be getting hungry by now, and the nights were cold. He didn't even have a hudfat.

Come morning, Einar took one look at her and said, "We should go search for the Irishman."

She nodded. The four of them set off silently down the beach. Ragnhild was glad to have her three húskarlar at her side.

The tide had long since washed away any footprints from the shore, but she spotted human tracks above the tideline and broken branches where someone had entered the woods. Svein found a faint trail of bent bracken and trodden grass and he led them along it, calling Murchad's name.

The only reply was their voices echoing in the forest.

On the flat, wooded terrain a hillock rose, overgrown with shrubs, so old that mature trees sprouted from it.

"Here," said Svein, calling them to a heap of leaves and pine boughs. "He made his bed here."

"He must have gone on, though I don't see any trail," said Thorgeir, peering into the wood. They searched the area but there was no further sign.

Ragnhild eyed the hillock, a wave of nausea washing over her. There was no sign of a struggle and yet, a shiver ran down her back. She leaned down, touching the ground where her husband had lain. Cold. He was long gone. The hairs on her arms prickled.

"Come, let us look further," said Thorgeir.

They wandered the forest all morning, calling Murchad's name in vain. Ragnhild's apprehension grew as the day wore on. How could a man simply vanish?

At noon Einar called a halt to the search. "If he doesn't want to be found, then leave him alone."

"But he could be sick, or hurt," said Ragnhild, pacing and twisting her braid around her hand.

"Then you'll have to swallow your pride and go to Åsa," said Einar. "She and Heid may be able to discover what's happened to him."

"But will she help me?" Ragnhild wrung her braid.

"She won't refuse to help Murchad. He's a guest of her hall."

Ragnhild hurried up the trail. She'd barely slept since her husband's disappearance, leaving her dizzy with worry.

She found Åsa in the dairy, a place the queen had always found solace. She was massaging a grass-wrapped brick of gammelost, the air redolent of the cheese's sharp scent.

"Lady, I beg your forgiveness," Ragnhild blurted. "I need your help."

Åsa sniffed the cheese. "I already gave you my answer."

"Murchad is missing."

Åsa set down the cheese and stared at her. "Missing?"

"We've heard nothing of him since he stormed out of the hall. We've searched everywhere, but his trail vanished in the forest. I thought he'd come back, but it's been too long. He took no provisions, no weapons, not even a hudfat."

Åsa's expression changed to one of concern. "Where did you lose his trail?"

Ragnhild described the hillock where Murchad had made his bed. "We tracked him to the spot where he spent the night and then—it was as if he'd vanished."

"I will go investigate," said Åsa as she doffed her apron and strode off for her chamber, Ragnhild scurrying along behind. The queen sat on her bed, reaching over to loose Stormrider's jesses. Ragnhild took the watcher's place on the stool beside the bed and looked on while Åsa eased back against the pillows and closed her eyes. After a few long breaths, her body went still and the falcon roused. With a couple of powerful flaps, Stormrider lofted off her perch and winged out through the open gable of the roof.

Ragnhild slumped on the stool, twisting her braid around her hand. There was nothing to do but wait.

~

ÅSA SOARED out over the forest. Her keen falcon's vision spotted the Irishman's sign, a broad ribbon of crushed leaves and bent twigs running through the woodland. She glided in among the trees and followed the trail through the woods to the mound Ragnhild had described. This was no natural hill. Here was the grave of one who had been buried far from the living, where they could cause no harm.

The Irishman's trail ended beside the mound just as Ragnhild had described it. Åsa lit on the ground beside it, examining the litter of leaves and pine boughs. Traces of his sweat and strands of his raven hair glowed brightly where he'd bedded for the night. But then after? The trail led nowhere. It was true that a master woodsman could conceal his sign from other humans, but not from her falcon's vision.

She lofted up from the mound and circled the area. Traces of forest animals were everywhere, but they were smaller and more delicate than a man's. No, he'd gone no further than this mound.

That meant he must be inside it.

Her skin went clammy beneath the feathers. For this she needed help.

She winged her way back to the bower.

~

ÅSA FLOWED into her body and blinked in the bower's dim light. Ragnhild was still perched on the stool, her shoulders rigid with anxiety.

Åsa broke the news as gently as possible. "I couldn't pick up his trail leaving the haugr. He must be inside."

Ragnhild leaped to her feet. "We have to dig him out!"

"Wait!" Åsa croaked, struggling to rise. "It's not that simple. We don't know what's in there. If we try to dig him out, it might kill him. We need to consult Heid."

Ragnhild's eyes were wild. She grabbed Åsa by the arm and hauled her out of bed and dragged her to the door.

They found the old sorceress sitting on a bench outside the hall, her ravaged face turned up to the weak autumn sun.

The wrinkles of the völva's face deepened, furrowing her brow as Åsa told her what she'd discovered. "Are you certain he's in there?"

"I can find no trail leading away from the mound. He has to be inside."

Heid got to her feet. "If he's been in there this long, we have little time." She shouted for her cart and her acolytes.

Heid hobbled to the bower chamber she shared with Åsa and Halfdan. From the shelves that lined the room, she filled her pouch with herbs and dried roots. Crabbing her way to the door, she snatched up her iron distaff and shambled into the yard, where the stable lads scurried to hitch the horses to the wagon and her acolytes gathered around it. They hoisted their mistress into her cart, settled her on the cushions, and tucked a blanket around her while Heid slapped at their hands impatiently.

The völva shook the reins, and the horses set off down the trail, her apprentices trotting alongside. Åsa and Ragnhild followed, as did nearly everyone on the steading. When they arrived at the beach, Einar, Thorgeir, and Svein joined them.

Ragnhild guided them down the beach to the place where Murchad had entered the forest.

"Here," she panted, indicating a break in the undergrowth.

The apprentices helped Heid down from the cart and parted the brush for her. The mist hung heavy among the trees, muffling any sound. Leaning heavily on her staff, the sorceress shoved her way into the forest and hobbled after Ragnhild as she guided them to the mound.

"Get me up there," Heid commanded. Her acolytes scrambled onto the grassy hillock, hauling her with them. "Have a care!" she shouted at them. "You'll pull my arms from their sockets."

Eventually the old sorceress was settled on her cushion atop the haugr. Her apprentices handed up the iron distaff and placed it in her hand. Heid reached into the leather pouch on her belt and brought forth a dried mushroom the color of blood, its cap covered with pale warts. She broke off a tiny pinch of it and popped it into her mouth.

Her apprentices formed a circle around the base of the mound and began to chant the vardlokkur, the mysterious song calling the spirits in a language lost to mankind. Åsa and Ragnhild joined their voices in the chant.

Within a few minutes the old sorceress collapsed on the mound. She began to speak, her rusty voice intoning words tantalizingly familiar, yet none that could be understood. From her rising tone she was arguing with someone. She began to shout. At last she uttered an unearthly shriek and beat her distaff on the ground three times. Then she went limp.

The women kept up the vardlokkur, eyeing each other with concern. Eventually the old sorceress groaned and roused. The apprentices broke off the chant and swarmed up the mound to assist their mistress.

When Heid had been revived, seated on a stump with a cup of spring water, she fixed Ragnhild with a piercing gaze. "Well, girl, you've done it this time. An ancient queen sleeps in this haugr. She's taken your Irishman as a companion. She's working her will on him. Soon she will possess him forever."

Ragnhild's face burned red. "Just tell me how to get him back."

Heid said, "Someone has to take his place."

CHAPTER 7

"I'll go," said Ragnhild.

"The draugr is my kin," Åsa said, "and has taken a guest of my house. I will go."

"He's my husband," said Ragnhild.

Heid eyed the shield-maiden speculatively. "He must be replaced by a person of equal rank, someone who will intrigue her. You are of royal blood, and a warrior. You just may fit the requirements. But it has to be done soon, for a human can't survive long inside a mound. If it's not too late already."

Ragnhild nodded and stepped forward. Åsa opened her mouth as if to protest but Heid gripped her arm with a claw-like hand. "Let her try."

"Tell me what I must do," said Ragnhild.

"You must spend the night beside the haugr alone, just where Murchad slept. Make it known that you are willing to take the Irishman's place. The mound will open, and if the draugr deems you worthy, she will take you and let him go."

"As simple as that." Ragnhild's throat was dry. Her chest tightened as bile rose up to choke her. *He'll go free, and that's the last time I'll see him. And I'll be buried alive under a mound of dirt, trapped in the dark, prisoner of the undead forever.* With a shudder, she took a deep breath and pushed the image away. *It has to be someone. It should be me. This is all my fault.*

The sorceress put a bony claw on her shoulder and spoke in low tones. "There's a chance that you can free the Irishman and yet escape yourself."

Ragnhild swallowed. "How?"

"You must decapitate the mound dweller with your sword. If you succeed, you will have cut off her power over both of you. But your opportunity will be short, and this ancient queen is crafty and powerful. You'll have to outwit her."

The knowledge that she could kill the draugr with cold, hard steel comforted Ragnhild. The chance was slim, but it gave her courage.

As evening fell, Ragnhild returned to the mound alone, carrying her hudfat. Her freshly sharpened sword hung at her side. *Don't think, just act. It's no different than going into battle.* But battle made her blood race, not run cold.

She planted her feet firmly and faced the mound. "I am Ragnhild, daughter of Solvi, king of Solbakk," she declared. "I offer myself in exchange for the Irish king."

Her only answer was night sounds of the forest. Crickets, frogs, small animals rustling in the undergrowth, the patter of a light rain on the leaves.

Ragnhild wrapped herself in her hudfat and lay down, and forced her breath to slow and deepen, not allowing herself to think of the ordeal ahead. Though she did not sleep, her mind drifted and stilled.

Late in the night, light touched her eyelids and they flickered open. Beside her, a doorway gaped in the mound like a monster's maw. A faint light glimmered within.

"Come," called a smooth, silky voice. Female, yet somehow that made it scarier.

A shiver ran down Ragnhild's back. She rose, gripping her sword hilt, and stepped into the mound.

The eerie light revealed a tall, slender woman with a cascade of silver hair. She stood beside a bed on which Murchad lay, propped on bolsters. Ragnhild caught her breath at the sight of her husband. He was so still, his face a deathly white. She strained to see and thought she detected a faint rise and fall in his chest, but it could be a trick of the light.

"Murchad!" cried Ragnhild. In one stride she reached the bed and took hold of his arm. His eyes opened. "Murchad, I'm here to free you." He stared at her as if he didn't recognize her, his arm hanging limp in her grasp. She rounded on the ghoul. "Let him go."

"Perhaps he does not wish to leave. He seems happy here with me."

Ragnhild stared at her husband. His eyes were clouded. A faint smile played about his lips. She shook him, but he didn't react. "I demand you release him."

"I can't make him go if it is not his will." The haugbui looked at Murchad. "Lord Murchad, would you like to go with this woman, or stay here with me?"

"Here with you," he chanted.

Ragnhild's heart plummeted, but she raised her chin in defiance. "I don't believe that. You've put a spell on him, taken his will. I demand you set him free."

"But then I would be all alone," said the queen.

Ragnhild swallowed. "I will take his place."

"Tell me why you would make a better companion than this king?"

Ragnhild tore her gaze from Murchad and glared at the haugbui. "I am as great a warrior as he. I am far-traveled and skilled in seamanship and battle."

"But he is a handsome man. How can you replace him?"

Ragnhild panicked, her mind blank. Then the völva's words came to her. "I am of your own kind. We understand each other."

"This man could tell me tales the like of which I've never heard."

"Yet his very foreignness will eventually leave you lonely."

The woman sighed, and ran her hand over Murchad's raven hair. He smiled vaguely at her touch and a chill ran down Ragnhild's spine.

"How do I know you will be good company?" said the ghoul. "How would we pass the time?"

Ragnhild glanced around the room in desperation. Her eyes fell on a gaming board set up on a small table in the corner. "I play hnefatafl."

"Very well," said the haugbui. "Let us play for him."

Ragnhild's heart sank. She had never been very good at the game. Her brothers had always beaten her. She wished Åsa were here. Åsa could probably even beat Harald. But it was up to her.

The haugbui moved toward the table, then paused and looked at Ragnhild. Her eyes glinted like a wolf's in the eerie light, raising Ragnhild's neck hairs. The ghoul took a seat at the table.

Ragnhild swallowed. She tried not to look at the bundle of rag and bone on the floor as she stepped over it to take her seat.

"Forgive me if my game is a little rusty," chuckled the draugr, gesturing toward the pile of bones. "My last opponent has been gone for a long time."

Ragnhild shivered. The air was musty and thin. She took small breaths, hoping there would be enough for both her and Murchad to survive the game.

The gaming pieces were exquisitely carved in the image of warriors, the white from walrus ivory and the black from dark-stained wood. The draugr plucked one of each color from the grid-carved wooden board and put them in a linen bag. She shook the bag and held it open. Ragnhild reached in and drew a piece—white.

She sucked in a breath of relief. White was the king's color. Fashioned from a piece of ivory taller than the rest, the king held the center square, surrounded by his twelve húskarlar. Twenty-four black pieces were arrayed in wedge formations along the outer edges of the board, leaving the four corners open. Ragnhild must get her king from the center throne square to one of the corner refuges while her opponent tried to capture him.

Though Ragnhild had fewer men than her opponent, she had some important advantages. Her king was much more powerful than the other pieces. He could only be captured when the enemy surrounded him on all four sides. The húskarlar of either color could be captured when flanked by only two enemy pieces, or by a single opponent who trapped them against the edge of the board. And Ragnhild had only to get her king safely to one of the corner squares to win, while black must potentially block all four corners.

The queen played first, quickly moving in to surround Ragnhild's king, while Ragnhild scrambled to block her.

Ragnhild controlled her panic and focused on one side of the board, knowing that was a winning strategy. She offered up a piece for sacrifice, tempting the queen to take it and enabling Ragnhild to strengthen her position and open a pathway out of the center for her king. But the queen didn't take the bait and instead threatened Ragnhild's king.

Hard as Ragnhild tried to focus on a strategy, it seemed as if her opponent was always a move or two ahead, as if she knew what Ragnhild intended. Perhaps it was because a haugbui did not need air, which seemed to be in short supply.

The draugr eyed her speculatively. Ragnhild knew she should be forcing the queen's play, but her head felt muddled and she kept yawning. She knew she must end the game quickly.

Ragnhild hurried her pieces to secure the corners, but her opponent countered every move, as if the draugr could read her mind. The attackers closed in, restricting Ragnhild's movements, forcing her to make moves that were not to her advantage.

Ragnhild caught a glint of tooth as the queen grinned in triumph. Looking down at the board, Ragnhild gasped when she saw her blunder. In trying to block the black pieces, she'd also trapped her own king, who could not jump his own men, nor the black pieces. Her king could not move without putting himself in check.

"You've lost!" cried the queen triumphantly.

Ragnhild's throat clogged with despair. Now she would go into the darkness, and Murchad with her.

Then she remembered Heid's words. Ragnhild loosened her sword in its scabbard and waited as the haugbui bent over Murchad.

Ragnhild drew Lady's Servant and lunged.

But the creature jerked out of the way, laughing. "Ah, shield-maiden, do you think I am defenseless? I, who waged war and led men in battle? Now I will take you both!" She ripped a sword down from the wall and swung at Ragnhild.

For all her frail appearance, the wraith was fast. Her sword-blow had a ferocious strength that caught Ragnhild off guard and her own stroke missed its mark.

Ragnhild's head swam, as if she were drunk. She swung again in desperation and missed again. The draugr grinned and closed on her.

Ragnhild took careful aim, and targeted the blow to cleanly sever the queen's neck. But the haugbui dodged, laughing.

How could the ghoul be so quick? As if she could read my mind. Ragnhild's legs trembled and she sank to her knees. Fireflies swarmed in her vision against the darkening air. Then she fell.

CHAPTER 8

Åsa waited with the others, gathered around a beach fire near the place Ragnhild had entered the woods. Though Åsa had provided food and a keg of ale, no one spoke as they watched the stars sparkle in the glossy black sea.

At every rustle or twig snap, Åsa looked back toward the woods. Though she knew there was nothing she could do, she hated sitting here, helplessly waiting.

"She's a brave girl," murmured Heid. "Will you forgive her if she survives?"

Åsa sighed. "If I can do it and save face."

"Will you help her take Gausel?"

Åsa considered. "It would be worth it to deal with Harald once and for all. He's a threat to Tromøy as well as to her, and having her as an ally in her own kingdom would benefit us. But she needs to come up with a better plan before I'll help her find any more warriors to kill off."

Heid looked at her pointedly. "What about the necklace?"

Åsa said nothing, though her hand strayed to the leather pouch at her waist.

"If the shield-maiden survives, you should make her return it to Ireland."

"I'm sure you're right," said Åsa, avoiding the sorceress's eyes.

"You're not thinking of keeping it?"

Åsa didn't answer.

Heid retired to her tent where her acolytes had made up her collapsible bed. Åsa rolled up in her hudfat beside the fire, but she didn't sleep.

Ragnhild can take care of herself. Murchad is her husband, after all. She'll have to sort it out. But thoughts kept nagging at Åsa. *The haugbui is my kin. My responsibility. How can Ragnhild stand against her?*

She'll be fine. She'll arrive in the morning with the draugr's skull, hauling Murchad along beside her. He'll be sheepish for getting himself in such a position. Rescued by his wife, a young girl.

But these thoughts did not let her sleep. She opened her leather belt-pouch and pulled out the Irish necklace. The golden links winked in the firelight, the metal warm to her touch. She could feel the power of it vibrating beneath her fingertips, tiny sparks surging up her arms. No wonder Ragnhild had kept it. She wondered again if the shield-maiden was conscious of its power. Perhaps not. Ragnhild did not embrace magic. She only believed in what she could see and touch. She probably told herself it was the gold she was drawn to.

Åsa slid the necklace back into the pouch. When she managed to doze, her dreams were troubled by visions of a grinning corpse standing over Ragnhild and Murchad, their bodies lifeless and cold. The images sent her bolting awake.

At last she gave up on sleep and crawled out of her hudfat. She coaxed the campfire's embers back to life and hung the soap-stone pot full of water on the iron tripod over the campfire. Then she seated herself on a drift log by the fire, waiting for the sun to emerge from the sea.

As the sky lightened, Heid struggled out of the tent and

plopped down beside her with a groan. The völva's crippled spine never let her sleep well.

"No sign of them yet," said Åsa.

The sorceress nodded. "Give her time. Where are those useless girls?" she said querulously.

Two of her apprentices appeared beside her, yawning. The cauldron was steaming and they hurried to prepare their mistress's morning brew, a concoction of willow bark and herbs that enabled the old sorceress to function.

Åsa's stomach was too unsettled for her to eat breakfast. She paced the beach while the others finished. "It's been long enough. I'm going in."

"Very well," Heid grumbled, but she did not argue. That worried Åsa even more.

She set off into the wood alone. When she arrived at the mound, she found Ragnhild's hudfat empty at the base.

Åsa inspected the hillock carefully. There was no sign of the ground having been disturbed. She drew a deep breath and closed her eyes. The air crackled with power, a presence. A resistance.

She unsheathed her sword, Gudrød's Bane. She struck the blade on the mound three times. "I am Åsa, queen of this land." Her voice quavered. She cleared her throat. "This haugr is in my domain and I demand you open for me."

Nothing happened.

Åsa rapped on the mound three times more and drew in a deep breath, summoning her galdr power. "I command this grave to open." Her voice resonated, clear and strong.

Again, nothing.

Åsa fumbled in her belt-pouch until she touched the necklace. She held it a moment, letting the power burn up her arm. She drew her hand out, gripped her sword with both hands, and beat it against the hillock with all her strength, shouting, "All who dwell here are subject to my will. You will open to me."

All was silent for a moment. Then a groan emanated from the mound and a ragged hole opened, emitting an eerie glow.

"Come, daughter," called a silky voice.

Åsa's scalp prickled and she took a deep breath. Gripping her sword hilt, she stepped into the hole. She whirled as the opening closed up behind her.

Within was a timber-walled room furnished much like Åsa's own chamber. All the familiar things lay to hand for spinning, weaving, cooking. With a shudder, she realized one day she would be entombed like this.

As her eyes adjusted to the gloom, she made out two forms on the bed. Ragnhild and Murchad, side by side, their arms crossed over their chests, eyes staring, faces pale as corpses. Her heart clenched.

The haugbui stepped toward her and her eyes flicked up. "Welcome, daughter."

This creature bested Ragnhild.

The ghoul chortled. "I took the shield-maiden easily."

"You hold my people captive," Åsa said sternly, raising her sword. "I will have them back. You will not deny me. I am the reigning queen of our line."

The haugbui smiled at her. "Only I can wake them. If you kill me, they will sleep forever."

Åsa lowered Gudrød's Bane. "Tell me what you demand in return for my people."

"If I give them to you, I will be all alone. Will you take their place?"

"I cannot while I rule. My duty is to my people."

The haugbui sighed. "Long have I been neglected. Once I was a mighty queen, just as you are. Like you, I ruled alone. I gave up all happiness to keep my power."

"You were buried deep in the forest, far from the living, for good reason," said Åsa. "You are a threat to those who live."

"Perhaps. But know this, daughter. I hold the fortunes of this kingdom and all who dwell here in my hands. Should you do me harm, the hamingja of your hall and your family will die with me."

Åsa shuddered to think how far this ghoul's power reached. Halfdan's image flashed through her mind.

"Yes, even your son, the boy with strong hamingja, like yours. I can take his luck and doom his future, as I did your father's."

Åsa stared at her. "That was Heid's doing..."

The haugbui sneered. "Did you think that pathetic old witch had the power to bring about your father's downfall?"

Like a fly caught in a spider's web, Åsa struggled against panic. Could it be true? Had Heid not brought about her father's destruction, as she'd claimed? Could this ghoul have been responsible? She shook her head to clear her thoughts. "Wake them."

"Why do you want them back? They represent the happiness you've lost." The ghoul smiled down on Ragnhild. "She married a king, and gave her authority to him. But you," she turned her gaze on Åsa. "You'll never give your power to a man. You'll rule alone forever. You're like me."

"I'll never be like you," said Åsa.

The mound queen grinned. "You already are, daughter."

Dread formed in Åsa's stomach. She turned her gaze to Murchad and Ragnhild.

"I'll play you for them," said the queen, gesturing toward the tafl board. "If you win, you all go free. If I win, I will keep these two."

"Very well," said Åsa. She gritted her teeth as she stepped over the litter of bones on the floor and took a seat at the table.

The queen held out the linen sack and Åsa reached in. Her heart sank as she drew out the black piece. White had the advantage. She would have to outwit the draugr to win.

Again her hand slipped into her belt pouch and touched the

Irish gold. The power shimmered up her arm to her heart, filling her with confidence.

The draugr's head snapped toward her. "What do you have in that pouch, daughter?"

Åsa jerked her hand out. She ignored the question and made her move.

Both queens opened with conventional plays, quickly claiming key squares in their bid to control the board. Åsa moved to seal off all four corner refuges while the queen worked to disrupt her opponent's formations and clear a path for her king. They offered pieces up for sacrifice, trying to lure each other into disadvantageous moves. But the wily draugr queen did not take any of Åsa's lures, and she constantly made moves that spoiled Åsa's plans—as if she could read her mind.

The haugbui *could* read her mind. The realization came on Åsa like a war-arrow. She must guard her thoughts. But how?

Stormrider's mind could process two thoughts at the same time. The falcon could watch a mouse while calculating the distance of a tree she must avoid. Could she manage that kind of dual thought in her human mind? She had to try.

Åsa stifled the thought before her opponent caught it.

The draugr threatened one of Åsa's pieces with her king. Åsa's hand slipped into the pouch and touched the necklace for an instant, willing her mind to split into two while she studied the board. She brought her hand back to the table and moved the piece out of harm's way while thinking how she couldn't afford to lose any more pieces. It was a decoy move, and Åsa lured her opponent away from her true objective of clearing a path across the board for a future attack.

Åsa fought to maintain the dual strategies, keeping her focus and the draugr's on one side of the board while she secretly built her forces in the opposite corner. She made sure those moves seemed like desperate bids, always forming the conscious thought that she was afraid of losing warriors. The draugr cleared a pathway for her king and Åsa seemed to put up a feeble resistance, all the while opening the way across the board for her distant pieces.

The queen took the bait, seeming confident in reading Åsa's thoughts. In twenty moves, Åsa swept three pieces across the board and surrounded the haugbui's king.

"Checkmate," said Åsa quietly.

The haugbui's face bore a look of disbelief and suspicion. "How did you do that?"

"I see you are not accustomed to this game," Åsa said dryly. "Nor to a falcon's mind."

"You hid your true thoughts from me," cried the queen. "That's cheating."

"No more than you prying into my mind and using my own thoughts against me." Åsa brought Gudrød's Bane to the haugbui's throat. "Now, awaken my friends."

The queen stared at her for a long moment. Her eyes flicked again to Åsa's belt pouch. Åsa jerked Gudrød's Bane to get her attention.

"If you send me onward, daughter, the hamingja of our ancestors dies with me and doom will fall on your house. The land spirits will turn against you and your heirs. Crops will fail, livestock die, folk fall ill."

Åsa bit back her fear. She couldn't sacrifice Ragnhild and Murchad, not even for Halfdan's future. She squared her shoulders and poked her sword under the haugbui's chin. "Nevertheless, wake them, or I'll send you to Helheim forever."

The queen locked eyes with her, raising Åsa's neck hair. "I will release them on one condition."

"What is that?" Åsa felt her apprehension grow, but she was desperate.

"You must honor me as befits a dís of our family. You must sacrifice on my mound on the holy days. If you do this, the hamingja of our family will grow greater than ever it was. I swear I will lie easy in my grave and trouble the living no more."

Åsa quailed at the thought of returning to this mound and making sacrifice to this evil creature. Yet what choice did she have?

"Very well."

"Do you swear on your son's life?"

Åsa's heart went cold. "That I cannot do. But you have my word and I will keep it."

The ghoul stared at her and Åsa feared she would insist on the oath.

Then the queen heaved a sigh and shrugged. "Very well." She leaned over the figures on the bed and began to croon a song that sent a shiver down Åsa's spine.

Ragnhild and Murchad groaned. Ragnhild sat up first, blinking. Murchad joined her.

Åsa grabbed the haugbui by the hair and held her blade to the queen's throat. "Open the mound."

The draugr heaved another sigh and raised her arms. The mound rumbled and quaked. The wall timbers split open to reveal a doorway. "Farewell, daughter. Remember your promise."

Murchad and Ragnhild stared around the chamber, bewildered.

"Go," Åsa cried. "Hurry! It's closing." She grabbed Ragnhild with one arm and Murchad with the other and lunged for the narrowing gap, jerking them along behind her.

She tumbled through the opening and yanked the two with her just as the mound closed. The three of them fell in a heap on the ground, breathing hard.

Heid and her apprentices were waiting, along with Ragnhild's húskarlar. They stared, open-mouthed, at the three who lay reeking of the grave, mound dirt still clinging to them.

Ragnhild struggled to a sitting position. She threw her arms around Murchad and hugged him hard. "Please, don't ever leave me again, no matter how wrong I am."

Murchad held her but did not reply. He turned to Åsa and bowed his head. "Lady, I thank you for rescuing us."

"You are a guest of my hearth," she said in a shaky voice. "Your safety is my responsibility."

The three húskarlar helped them to their feet and dusted them off.

"Welcome back to the land of the living, shield-maiden," said Heid, looking them over. She nodded at Murchad. "Irishman." The sorceress gave Åsa a sharp look.

"Let's get away from this place," said Einar.

They slowly made their way through the forest to the shore, the three húskarlar assisting the mound queen's victims. Åsa noticed that Ragnhild kept a firm grip on Murchad's arm. She'd never seen the shield-maiden cling to anyone. Murchad himself looked pale but steady.

They arrived at the campsite and Thorgeir coaxed the fire back to life. Åsa flung herself onto the driftwood log. Murchad bowed before he took his seat on the log beside her.

Ragnhild slumped down next to him. "Lady, please forgive me," she blurted.

Åsa nodded. "Now that we're all safe, perhaps we can start again."

"Thank you, Lady." Åsa marveled to see tears glistening in Ragnhild's eyes. "I've decided to give up on Gausel," said Ragnhild. "It's not worth the risks."

"*A chroí*, how can you say that?" Murchad exclaimed. "It's all you've ever wanted."

"No," said Ragnhild. "You are all I've ever wanted. And Åsa, and Halfdan, and all of you. I'd give up anything for you."

Murchad smiled at her. "Spoken like a true leader."

"Now that you understand, maybe I can help you," Åsa said

briskly. "We should be able to recruit your army at the next assembly. We have all winter to come up with a plan of attack."

"Thank you, Lady!" Ragnhild threw her arms around Åsa. Then she settled back and accepted a cup of ale.

Murchad bolted upright and stared at his wife. "Where is the necklace?"

Ragnhild's eyes flew wide. "I...in all the confusion..."

Åsa gave him a level look. "It is in my care."

Storm clouds gathered in Murchad's eyes, but her tone allowed no further discussion.

When they had rested, they set out for home. Heid gestured Åsa over. The old sorceress fixed her with a searching look. "What did you promise the haugbui?"

Åsa shuddered. "I have promised to sacrifice to her at the blót."

Heid inhaled sharply and shook her head. "You must be very careful with this draugr."

"I know."

～

THE BLIND WOLF'S sharp ears picked up the crashing in the brush. Something big. He crept toward the sound, keeping low. His keen nose quivered as it scented the deer. Blood. It was wounded and had escaped its predator, for now. The wolf's heart beat hard. If he could get to it first...

Silently he followed the blood trail through the forest. The animal was still moving through the brush, but by the sound, its movements had slowed. The wolf hurried along, nose to the ground.

The wolf felt a thud beneath his sensitive paws, then all was still. The deer had fallen, and not far away. In the distance voices shouted. Men. In spite of their weak senses, they would find their kill soon. There wasn't much time.

The wolf crept toward the deer. A stag, by its musk. He could hear the antlers thrash against the ground. The hunters' voices drew near. The wolf crouched on his belly. How to approach?

He crept closer, sniffing. The scent of blood was strong and now sticky under his paws. The thrashing slowed as the stag bled out. Then the wolf heard the death rattle in the deer's throat as it drew its last breath.

In a flash the wolf darted in. He located the sternum. Snarling, he ripped his teeth into the deer's chest, chewing through bone and sinew. Blood flooded his mouth and he sucked it down but never paused until he reached his goal—the heart. He felt the organ in his mouth and bit down.

The shouts of the men were close now. With all his strength he wrenched the stag's heart free.

Carrying it with a soft mouth, he loped away. His coat snagged on the underbrush, picking up burrs, and thorns pricked his paws, but he kept moving.

After he'd put some distance between himself and the kill, he allowed himself to slow to a more careful walk. His paws stung. They were bleeding, but that would not matter for long. Soon he would rest.

He found his way back to the cave where the old man lay on his pallet. The wolf approached and set the heart over the human's lips. With his powerful jaws, he squeezed the remaining blood from the organ into the old man's mouth. At first the human choked, but in a moment he swallowed.

His breathing strengthened. He gulped the blood greedily, then suckled and chewed. As his strength returned, he gripped the heart and bit off a chunk. He gobbled it down.

When he'd fed, he dropped the remains of the heart on the cave floor. The wolf snapped it up and tore into it. As the wolf gnawed, the man's voice split the air, sharp as a fang.

"Hrafn."

CHAPTER 9

Tromøy

The autumn equinox approached, and folk began to arrive from the hinterlands for the álfablót, the sacrifice to the ancestral spirits who protected the folk and livestock.

From his vantage point on the hilltop, Murchad sat his borrowed horse and watched the procession of freeholders herding livestock and driving carts laden with wool and grain. Olvir and his húskarlar were at the gate, collecting a portion from each farmer.

Murchad was surprised at how many folk there were—there must have been more than two hundred people—and children. Their cries rang in the air, echoing off the burial mounds.

They raised their tents in the fields and a lively market sprang up that reminded Murchad of a saint's feast day at home. In Ireland it would be Michaelmas, and all the farmers from miles around would flock to the monastery to sell and trade and pay their tithes to the abbot, who would bless them and pray to the saints for peace and plenty through the winter months.

Murchad shivered at the thought of the coming northern winter. The shortening days with their threat of darkness and cold, living confined in a strange land among people he barely knew, made him long for home. But he'd chosen his path and for now there was no way out of it. He tried to think of spring.

Heid drove her cart down the trail, her apprentices following on foot. Åsa rode beside her on Gullfaxi, Stormrider stoically gripping her shoulder.

Murchad steered his horse next to Ragnhild, mounted on Hofvarpnir. Behind them, Jarl Borg, Einar, Thorgeir, and Svein rode horses resplendent in gilded tack. After them marched the warriors of Tromøy, nearly one hundred strong.

The shield-maiden Ursa walked beside her sisters. She had fully recovered from her injury, and proudly displayed the jagged scar on her cheek that made her fearsome to sparring opponents.

Bringing up the rear, Brenna led Halfdan by the hand among the women and children of Tromøy. The children chattered with excitement while their dogs frolicked about the fringes, barking joyously.

Åsa halted the entourage below the burial mounds where her forebears lay—or the memory of them. The great hill she'd raised to her father and brother stood empty, for their corpses had burned with the old hall.

The sorceress reined in alongside her, and allowed her apprentices to help her down from the cart with a minimum of fuss. Åsa dismounted and took her place beside the völva at the base of her father's haugr.

The hubbub of arrival began to die down, and the folk left their campsites and stalls to gather before the mounds where Heid and Åsa waited, surrounded by Heid's apprentices. When all had assembled, the women raised their arms and gave voice to their magical songs to summon the spirits.

Toki led a goat to Åsa and Heid. Two of the apprentices took hold of the animal's halter, stroking its head, and gave it a drink of a calming potion. The goat stood quietly, spellbound by the singing as the drug took effect. Åsa drew her sacrificial knife swiftly across the goat's throat while an acolyte knelt and caught the blood in a brass bowl. Still singing, the apprentices lowered the dying animal onto the grass.

Murchad knew his own ancestors had once made such sacrifices, and realized what a blessing it was that Ireland had converted from its bloodthirsty, pagan ways. These sacrificial killing methods were kinder than the everyday slaughter that took place in the farmyards both here and in Ireland. He knew these Norse to be good people, but they had not been enlightened. Perhaps after he and Ragnhild returned the necklace to Ireland, he would bring Behrt back here and help him bring them to the light.

Åsa accepted the brimming bowl from the acolyte, while another handed her a bundle of fir twigs. She plunged the twigs into the blood and spattered the mound, beseeching the ancestral spirits to bless them and help them through the winter— much as the Irish prayed to the saints and angels. Åsa dipped the twigs again and sprinkled the crowd. Murchad winced away as the folk crowded in to receive a drop or two of the sacred blood.

Heid and Åsa sacrificed another goat and a hog, then Toki and his men carved up the meat and set it to simmer in huge soapstone cauldrons for the evening feast. The folk returned to their stalls and commenced trading, raising a clamor as they bartered their wares.

Brenna and the other women led the children to a grassy spot where the newly arrived children had already declared a mock war. Halfdan drew his wooden sword and charged down on them with a battle cry, followed by the rest of Tromøy's youth and all their dogs. Soon the clacking of wood and excited shouts

73

arose as a major battle ensued. Murchad felt a tug in his chest as he watched Halfdan.

"The boy will make a mighty king," said Ragnhild. "He has strong hamingja."

Murchad gave her a quizzical look. "Hamingja?"

Ragnhild frowned. "It's like—luck, I guess. But more than luck. It's also strength, skill, ability. It's passed down in families. Halfdan gets his hamingja from his ancestors. A person can lend his hamingja to others, but it can leave him, too." Murchad was still mystified and it must have shown on his face, for she shook her head and took his arm. "Let me show you the market."

She led him through the stalls where women laid out their linen and wool cloth on rough wooden tables, a metalsmith displayed copper and bronze brooches and harness fittings while a bead-maker set out glass beads in vivid crimsons and indigo. A comb-maker had a selection of grooming implements carved of antler. Ragnhild exclaimed over his wares. "Look, his combs have cunning little cases riveted on!"

"Yes, Lady," said the comb-maker, "your comb will stay clean no matter how bloody the battle. And see, here is a loop so they can hang from your belt."

"I'll take one! And one for my husband as well." She reached into her bag and brought out a handful of silver.

Murchad sucked in his breath as he recognized crosses and other ornaments of Irish workmanship.

The comb-maker brought out his folding scales and weighed the silver. He lifted a finely wrought gilt cross from the scale and brought out his knife.

Murchad winced as the cross lost an arm. The merchant added the defiled ornament back to the scale and handed Ragnhild her change.

Murchad forced a smile as she strapped the comb onto his belt, her eyes shining.

At every booth, the people bowed their heads to Ragnhild. When she introduced Murchad, they bowed to him too. But their respect came from her status. Here he was just the husband of a famous shield-maiden.

Åsa wandered among the farmers, stopping to talk with families.

"Most of our warriors came from the farms in the hinterlands," Ragnhild said. "They joined Åsa's hird in hopes of a better life. Many of them will see their families here for the first time in months. With any luck, Åsa will recruit new warriors here. There look to be plenty of the right age. Our winter task will be to whip young farmers into passable fighters by spring."

That evening the families gathered around fires for their evening meal. As he settled on a bench among Åsa's household, Murchad felt a bit more at home amongst these strange, stoic people. They were taciturn, compared to Irishmen, and while they had music, it did not lift him to his feet with joy. The tales they told around the fire at night were different, their heroes grimmer, their honor that of one who never surrendered even in defeat.

Murchad regarded Ragnhild, the warrior woman who led men into battle. She'd been his wife for a few months. She was so different from the women from his country. It was part of the attraction, yet he wondered if they would ever understand each other.

From the darkness, a few young people emerged to kneel at Åsa's feet and place their hands on her sword blade, pledging themselves to her. Murchad watched as she questioned each one, asking about their family, their training, before bestowing an arm ring.

He eyed Åsa's belt pouch. He knew she kept the necklace there. He hated the thought of the royal treasure in the hands of a Norsewoman, a Fin Gaill.

Åsa had risked everything to save them from the fae queen. He and Ragnhild owed her their lives. Perhaps the necklace was best in her care for now. It was impossible to return to Ireland this time of year, with the storms raging on the sea. He had all winter to persuade Åsa to relinquish the necklace. In the spring, he would insist Ragnhild take him to Ireland on their way to Gausel and restore it to its proper place.

For all her youth, Åsa was a wise queen. So much wiser than his countrymen, who were always feuding, taking heads and burning monasteries at the least provocation. He doubted that the kings of this land were much different, but Åsa was. Here on Tromøy, she had created a special world where peace reigned. She had proven herself strong enough to keep it.

His heart swelled with admiration for the young queen. He could well understand Ragnhild's devotion to her.

He barely realized his own intentions before he was on his feet and approaching the high seat. Åsa looked at him in surprise. The crowd hushed as he went to one knee as he had seen the others do.

~

Åsa watched in astonishment as the Irishman knelt before her.

"Lady, my wife has sworn to you, and now I offer you my oath of loyalty."

She quickly recovered from her surprise and recognized the opportunity. Smiling, she laid Gudrød's Bane across her knees.

As the others had before him, Murchad placed his hands on the blade and raised his eyes to hers. "I, Murchad mac Maele Duin of Cenel nEoghan, swear to serve you, Åsa, Queen, to defend you with my dying breath."

A wave of sympathy swept over her. Murchad was an outsider here, far from home. It must be so hard for him, once a king, now dependent on others. She remembered how she had felt in Gudrød's hall, alone and friendless, with no power. How could she make him feel accepted?

"I thank you, Lord Murchad. I gladly accept your oath. Please rise."

Murchad stood. Åsa rose as well, raising her drinking horn in salute. "This man is now one of us."

The warriors cheered their approval, banging their ale cups on the boards. Murchad smiled and swallowed his ale.

Åsa began to reach for an arm ring, but then stopped. She needed to give him something special. "I wish to reward you, Murchad. I have rings of silver, but what would be a suitable gift for a king?"

His face lit up. "Lady, I ask you for a horse. An Irishman without a horse of his own is a cripple."

"Very well," said Åsa. "Tomorrow you shall have your pick from my herd."

Murchad's beaming face told her she had succeeded in granting a heartfelt wish.

After the festivities quieted and everyone had wandered off to bed, Åsa rose from her hudfat and dressed quietly. She buckled her belt around her waist, with the pouch that held the necklace, then took up her knife and bowl. She paused to look on Halfdan sleeping in his cradle, his tiny arms flung wide, the rabbit skin kicked aside.

From her bed, Heid roused. "You're going to the queen's mound, aren't you?" the old sorceress rasped.

Åsa drew her cloak around her and put up the hood. "I gave my word."

"Are you going to let that ancient ghoul control you for the rest of your life?"

"If I don't keep my vow, she'll take my family's hamingja, as she did my father's."

"Is that what she told you? Ha! It's easy for her to make that claim. You well know that I brought about your father's downfall." When Åsa offered no reply, Heid muttered, "Perhaps one day you'll find the strength to break her hold."

"Perhaps."

The völva's voice softened. "I would go with you."

"I know you would." Both knew the journey was far too taxing for the crippled sorceress.

"At least take someone along," said Heid. "Wake that lazy shield-maiden."

"No, I won't expose anyone else to the haugbui again. She is my responsibility."

The sorceress offered no further argument. "Don't trust her."

"I won't. Keep watch over Halfdan until I return."

"May Freyja protect you."

Åsa shivered and pulled her cloak close as she stepped out into the night. The moon, near full, shone bright in the sky.

She made her way to the chicken coop and grabbed a hen, tucking it under her cloak before it could make any noise.

Silently she walked down to the beach, following the shoreline until she came to the spot where they had entered the forest. She swallowed hard and stared into the trees. The moonlight laid down a shining trail. A chill ran down her spine and her hand strayed to her belt pouch. She didn't reach inside, but she felt the reassuring shape of the necklace through the leather.

Squaring her shoulders, she stepped into the forest. The foliage appeared to part before her. She followed the moonlit trail, toward the sound of trickling water in the distance. As she walked, the water seemed to take on a voice of its own, calling her. Dread welled up with every step.

All too soon, the mound hulked among the trees, dappled by moonlight and shadow that moved with the wind.

Åsa stopped and faced the haugr. Taking a deep breath to still her fears, she began to keen the vardlokkur while she drew the hen from under her cloak. The bird roused and struggled. Åsa pulled her knife from its sheath and in one smooth motion struck off the chicken's head. Blood spurted, steaming in the cold. She sprayed the blood over the mound, chanting all the while.

An answering voice emanated from within.

When the hen was bled dry, Åsa laid the dead bird at the foot of the hillock, concluding the spirit song.

"Come, daughter."

A shock ran through Åsa as she recognized her mother's voice. Her mother had been dead for many years.

"Come, talk with me, child." It *was* Gunnhild's voice.

The mound gaped open, emitting a faint glow. The dim light shone on familiar items: a loom with a half-finished tapestry, the gaming board on its table, a trunk carved with battle scenes. In this light, it could have been Gunnhild's chamber as Åsa remembered from her childhood.

"Come, daughter, I have much to teach you. So many things I had no time to tell you while I walked the earth."

A longing rose up in Åsa, for her mother, for someone who understood her burdens. She took a step toward the light.

"There is so much you do not know. Come to me."

Åsa took another step toward the mound.

A woman's form appeared in the gaping hole, shining with a silver light. She beckoned with a welcoming smile. "Ah, what a queen you will be when I teach you to rule."

Åsa stopped abruptly. A chill ran down her neck. The voice had taken on a gloating tone. The grave mound gaped like a maw.

This was not her mother's chamber. If she entered, she would never come out.

Åsa's hand slid into the pouch and touched the necklace. She felt sparks sear up her arm. "I am a proven queen," she declared. "I already know how to rule."

"You are pitiful," the draugr mocked. All resemblance to

Gunnhild dropped away. "Ruled by your heart, you are weak. I will teach you to be strong, to stand alone." The haugbui reached toward her. "Come!" she commanded.

Åsa turned and fled.

CHAPTER 10

T he morning dawned chill and overcast. Murchad waited with the horses already saddled. He grew more worried as the time passed. Perhaps Åsa had forgotten her promise.

At last she appeared, looking pale and haggard. She had obviously not slept well the night before.

With a sigh, she pulled herself onto Gullfaxi and led the way to the horse pasture. "You may have your choice of any of these. They are varying ages and stages of training."

Murchad cast his eye over the herd in delight. They were fine looking animals, about the same size as the Irish ponies he was accustomed to, but shaggier. Among them, a black stallion about four years old caught his eye. The way the horse carried himself, the deference of the other animals, made it stand out. Here was the mount of a king.

When he pointed the animal out, Åsa nodded her approval. "I see you have a good eye. Svartfaxi is a spirited mount, one that I think you can do something with. He's been broken to the saddle and bridle, but he needs a firm hand. I believe you can provide such."

"That I can," said Murchad. "I thank you, Lady."

When Murchad took hold of Svartfaxi's halter and looked into the horse's eye, he knew he'd found a kindred spirit. He understood how Ragnhild had felt about Brunaidh, her only friend among strangers in Ireland.

"I'll leave you to get acquainted," said Åsa with an understanding smile.

~

ÅSA ARRIVED at the burial mounds as men set the hazel poles in the field and roped off the law circle, defining a boundary beyond which no weapons could pass. Åsa's high seat stood in the center of the circle beside a chair for Jarl Borg, who served as lawspeaker for the district.

Heid sacrificed a cock and blessed the circle with a spattering of blood. Fighting weariness, Åsa entered the hallowed space and took her seat. This had been her father's place, and his father's before him. She felt their strength rise up in her, dispelling her fatigue.

Jarl Borg stood to declaim the laws. At each assembly, the lawspeaker was required to state one third of the laws. By the end of the year, the public would have heard the entire legal code. Though he was in his seventies, the old warrior's memory was perfect and his voice carried strongly across the fields.

Jarl Borg finished and took his seat. Åsa pulled her wool shawl closer and prepared herself to hear the first dispute of the day.

The litigants approached, two farmwives. Åsa had seen these two before. They were neighbors, widows both. They seemed to have nothing better to do than to accuse each other of witchcraft, and worse. Åsa mentally rolled her eyes, while smiling at the two women.

"Greetings, Hana, Erna. What brings you before this assembly?"

"Greetings, Lady." Hana was thin, but she stood tall in her undyed wool apron dress and linen shift, clean but much-mended. Simple bronze brooches clasped the straps, no beads strung between them. She clutched a shawl of brown wool to her throat against the morning chill and glared at Erna, who was dressed almost identically. "She's taking the milk from my cow, Blossom."

Åsa took a deep breath and kept a straight face. "Where do you keep Blossom?"

"She's in her stall in my house. She grazes in the pasture of my steading."

"And can you see Blossom most of the time?"

"Yes! I never take my eyes off her. She's not giving as much milk as she used to. And Erna's stealing it!"

Åsa smiled, calling on her patience. "If you can see Blossom nearly all the time, how is Erna managing to take this milk?"

Hana turned her stare on the assembly, obviously enjoying the suspense. "Magic," she said in a hoarse whisper that nonetheless carried through the crowd, eliciting a murmur.

Åsa suppressed a sigh. "And what kind of magic did Erna use to steal Blossom's milk?"

Hana lowered her voice even more. "She used a milk-rope."

The crowd gasped. This was a well-known form of milk-thievery, but Hana explained the process with glee. "By night, Erna lays a rope at Blossom's feet, and leads the rope to her own house. Blossom's milk flows along the rope all night, and in the morning, Erna pulls it back into her house. And there is little milk left for me, her rightful owner."

The crowd murmured in sympathy.

"I did no such thing!" cried Erna. "She's lying. Ask her to prove it."

"Have you seen this magical rope?" said Åsa. "Perhaps brought it here before us?"

Hana frowned. "No, but I know what happened. Blossom's always been a good milker."

"That cow is older than the hills," shouted Erna indignantly. "It's a miracle she gives any milk at all."

"It's true, Hana, you've had Blossom a long time," said Åsa.

"That I have. But I've taken good care of her."

"I'm sure you have, Hana," said Åsa gently. "But even the best care cannot prevent old age. Is it possible that explains why Blossom is giving less milk?"

Hana hung her head and grumbled something incomprehensible.

"What was that?" Åsa prompted.

"I can't afford a new cow." Hana choked out the words.

Here was the real problem. If Blossom stopped giving milk, it would be a great loss for a poor widow like Hana. Åsa knew what she must do. "Blossom is a fine cow," she said gently. "I know she has served you faithfully for many years, and you have cared for her well. Perhaps it is time to send her to Asgaard, where she can be young again. Such a fine cow deserves to serve the gods."

Hana looked at Åsa fearfully. Would the queen take her only cow, and leave her with nothing?

"What if I send a boy home with you, with a bred heifer, and he brings Blossom back to me for the winter nights' sacrifice?"

Hana's voice came out in a strangled sob. "Yes, Lady."

"And we'll forget all this about Erna taking your milk?"

"Yes, Lady."

"Very well." She turned to one of her warriors, a farmer's son. "Sorli, you pick a good milker for Hana and take it back with her when the assembly is over." Åsa made a mental note to tell the boy to inspect Hana's steading, and make sure she had enough help.

"Yes, Lady."

The onlookers pounded their weapons on their shields in

approval. The two women returned to the crowd, though they did not meet each other's eyes.

Next, two farmers approached the law circle, each surrounded by their friends and kin. Åsa's house guard flanked the antagonistic parties, ensuring tempers would not get out of hand. Though weapons were not permitted within the law circle, violence sometimes erupted.

Åsa sat up tall and fixed each man with her gaze in turn. She took a deep breath and summoned her galdr training to give power to her voice.

"State your names," she commanded.

The man to her right stepped forward. He was smaller than the other man, and of lighter build. Åsa guessed he was near forty, perhaps a decade older than the other. "I am Jokul Ulfson," he stated, glaring at his opponent.

Åsa turned to the scowling man beside him. "State your name."

"I am called Onar Thorson." Onar was a strapping man in his prime, under thirty years of age. His biceps bulged and his forearms were like oak roots. He towered over Jokul, but the smaller man returned his glare defiantly.

"What brings you before me today?"

"This man has failed to return my sister, Helga's, dowry, though they were divorced in the spring," said Jokul.

Åsa recalled the divorce. Onar's wife had declared herself separated from her husband in front of the court, and he had not contested it.

"I have returned his sister's dowry." Onar turned and glared into the crowd. Åsa followed his gaze to a woman, whom she recognized as his former wife. The woman kept her gaze averted from Onar, a glint of fear in her eyes.

"How much is the dowry in question?" Åsa asked.

"Seven milk cows. And I sent them along with Helga when she went back to her family," said Onar.

Seven cows was a handsome dowry. Jokul and his sister were prosperous to provide such wealth. Åsa looked at Jokul. "Is this true?"

Jokul scowled at Onar. "Four of the cows died before they reached our farm. We demand replacements."

"They died because of your sister's neglect," retorted Onar.

According to the law, the livestock's welfare was the wife's duty. Åsa wondered if Onar's statement had any truth to it. Before she could formulate a question, the argument rushed on.

"She left you because you did not provide enough fodder for the cattle," said Jokul. "That is why they died."

Onar spluttered. "I provided her with plenty of good, cleared land to grow enough hay for all the livestock."

Jokul snorted. "Land there may have been, but you gave her no help with the haying, and no field hand to help either. One woman can't do that all herself."

This was a good example of how a successful farm required the contributions of both the husband and the wife. If either of them failed to keep up their end, the place suffered.

"It sounds as if your farm was a sorry place, ill-kept and ill-run by both husband and wife," Åsa said, then sat back and watched both men. She had presided over law courts for the past several years, and learned to listen closely. If she watched the adversaries' reactions, the answer would come clear. Guilt or innocence were often evident in the claimants' posture and tone, in their facial expressions. In this case, Jokul looked determined, while Onar scowled in defiance. Åsa's gaze went to Helga, who kept her eyes fixed on the ground, her face carefully expressionless. She was of an age with her brother, slightly built but wiry.

"My sister runs our farm very well," Jokul insisted. "I provide her with all she needs to do so, unlike her former husband."

Onar bristled. "I gave her what she needed. She was too lazy to make use of it."

Åsa watched Helga cringe without looking up. She wondered

if Onar had raised his fists to his wife. Wife beating was outlawed, but Helga did not look as if she had the courage to bring a complaint.

The case was deadlocked, each man's word against the other. Time for the testimony of others. "Since you both claim this to be the other party's fault, do you have any witnesses to verify your claims?"

Since Onar was the accused, he brought the first witness. He called a kinsman named Gisli.

"Onar is as good a farmer as ever ploughed a field," said Gisli. "He takes care of his livestock and his fields."

Gisli was of a size with Onar. Åsa noted that his hands, big as ham hocks, lacked the work-roughened skin of a farmer. There was no dirt permanently embedded in their creases. Perhaps they were more familiar with the sword than the plow.

Next was Jokul's turn. His witness was a neighbor, an aging man with hands chapped by work and etched with dirt, his face creased and brown from long hours in the field. He spoke in mild tones, but there was a ring of sincerity and knowledge when he praised the way Jokul and Helga tended their crops and animals.

The men continued to bring forth witnesses all morning, in equal number, all of whom attested to their party's fastidious animal husbandry. Frustration mounted with the deadlock. Voices rose, faces reddened, fists were shaken.

Åsa hurried to resolve the case before it disintegrated into violence. "Since you are equally supported by witnesses, and it is impossible for me to determine the truth or falsehood of what occurred, I propose you split the difference. Onar will supply two healthy cows to Helga, and she and her family will drop their claim."

Åsa hoped the two men would accept her solution. But the voices grew louder. Both men crossed their arms over their chests and set their jaws.

Then, red-faced, Onar shouted, "Holmgang!"

Åsa's color rose. Though litigants had the right to call for a duel, she had managed to avoid such bloodshed recently.

"Holmgang!" the crowd echoed, eager for a fight. "Holmgang!" Their cries escalated, reverberating off the mounds.

Jokul looked ill. The crowd left him little choice. Though Onar clearly outmatched him, honor demanded that he take the challenge or be branded a coward forever. His face was milk-white but he took a deep breath and cried, "Holmgang!"

Onar smiled in triumph and a black cloud settled in Åsa's stomach. She had little doubt Onar had come today determined to settle the dispute with a duel, where he had the advantage. If he won, as he looked certain to do, he would not have to provide healthy cattle. If he killed Jokul, he could take Jokul's farm, and Helga. It was grossly unfair, but the law was clear on this matter. He had the right to settle the dispute by combat. Åsa had no choice.

"Very well, holmgang," Åsa said. "The duel will be fought at dawn three days hence."

The assembly beat their weapons on their shields. They were always glad of the prospect of bloodshed. Jokul swayed on his feet. It took real courage to stand up for his sister against a man so much younger and stronger. But now he was forced into sacrificing his life—for four cows.

Åsa caught sight of Ragnhild. She was glaring at Onar. Åsa shook her head in warning, trying to catch Ragnhild's eye, but the shield-maiden stepped out of the crowd.

"I will be Jokul's second," Ragnhild declared.

A murmur arose from the crowd. To offer to fight in Jokul's place would have been an insult. But offering to be his second put Ragnhild in a place to protect the man. It was rash, but it evened the odds. Better than leaving Jokul to be backed up by a farmer more familiar with a scythe than a sword.

And better than Onar slaughtering Jokul. Åsa breathed a sigh of relief.

The next four cases were divorces, all uncontested. Divorce was a simple matter of declaring the marriage dissolved before the assembly. It was common at the fall assembly, for couples who proved incompatible wanted to separate before winter's confinement.

Evening fell and the threatened rain held off. Åsa took her place among her household at the campfire while Murchad told one of his Irish tales. She found these stories haunting, of impossible love and heroic sacrifice. She looked around the circle—the others were silent. "Tell us more about Cu Chuilain." The younger crew members chimed in their agreement.

"Very well," Murchad said. "Cu Chuilain was the son of the sun god, Lugh, and he trained under the warrior woman Scathach. When Cu Chuilain went into battle, a frenzy came upon him that made him invincible, and he recognized neither friend nor foe."

"A berserker," said Ragnhild. A shiver ran through the hird. Many of them had fought the ferocious warriors who had been indoctrinated by the outlaw Hrafn. Though they had vanquished the berserkers and burned their bodies, the horror lived within each of them.

"Be that as it may, tonight I will tell you how Cu Chuilain single-handedly defended Ulster from the army of Mebdh, queen of Connacht," said Murchad. His lilting voice held the crowd spellbound. Even Heid listened raptly.

"Mebdh was jealous because her husband, Ailill, possessed a white bull beyond compare. Actually, this bull had originally been in Mebdh's herd, but he did not want to be owned by a woman and so he moved to Ailill's herd."

"Foolish bull," murmured Ragnhild.

Murchad smiled at her. "This meant Mebdh's husband had greater wealth than she, and their marriage was no longer one of equals. This could not stand."

"This is very important in an Irish marriage," said Ragnhild.

"In my wedding contract with Murchad, I claimed as property *Raider Bride* and the steading of Gausel, neither of which I actually possessed at the time. Murchad loaned me ten cows in order to make our marriage one of equals. Anything less would have prevented me from being queen."

Murchad smiled. "I could never have allowed that to happen, *a chroí*. But you do owe me ten cows. As for Mebdh, the queen tried to negotiate the loan of the only animal that could match it, the great brown bull of Ulster. But negotiations went awry, and Mebdh raised an army to come against Ulster and take their bull by force.

"Now the men of Ulster were unable to fight, for a curse had been laid on them to suffer birthing pains whenever their time of greatest need came upon them."

"I'm sure they deserved it," said Ragnhild. "I can think of a few men I'd like to lay such a curse on." The shield-maidens laughed, though the men were silent.

"Indeed they did, for the men of Ulster had forced a pregnant sorceress to pull a chariot in a race, and it was she who cursed them."

"That's a fitting curse," said Unn. "Irishwomen must be very tough."

"They were in ancient time," agreed Murchad, "but Norsewomen are tougher."

The shield-maidens murmured their approval and Murchad took up his tale again. "Cu Chuilain was only a boy at the time, and so he was not affected by the curse. He challenged the heroes of Connacht to single combat. One by one, he defeated Connacht's best men until the Ulstermen's curse wore off. Though Cu Chuilain was sorely wounded, his father, the god Lugh, healed him. When their labor pains finally eased, the warriors of Ulster came against Connacht."

"So, who won?" said Ragnhild.

"Nobody. They fought to a draw, then decided to let the bulls fight it out. The brown bull of Ulster defeated Connaught's white bull, and scattered his body parts all over Ireland, where they can still be seen to this day. But before he died, the white bull gave the brown bull his death wound."

"And so it was all for nothing," Einar mused.

"Not quite," said Murchad. "Cu Chuilain caught Queen Mebdh in an undefended position. Though he could have killed her, he spared her life, and in gratitude she gave him her daughter for a wife. There was peace between Connacht and Ulster for seven years."

Ragnhild snorted. "That's a long time for Irishmen to get along."

"Indeed, you know my country well," said Murchad.

The tale ended, they all rose to go to bed. Åsa stopped Ragnhild as she was entering her tent. "Onar is no farmer," she warned.

"Neither are his friends," Ragnhild agreed complacently.

Murchad regarded his wife with stormy eyes. "I don't like you involved in this."

"Then it's a good thing you have no say in the matter." Ragnhild ducked into her tent, followed by a frowning Murchad. Åsa shook her head. It promised to be a less-than-friendly night for the couple.

CHAPTER 11

On the morning of the duel, the sun shone with a warm autumn glow. Jokul and Onar met on the shore, surrounded by a great crowd. Ragnhild and Onar's second, the thuggish Gisli, stood beside small skiffs in which they would row the duelists to the rocky holm. No more than an islet, it had been the traditional place of holmgang since time immemorial. Only the two antagonists and their seconds were allowed on the holm, though the islet was close enough to shore that the fight would be clearly visible to the crowd.

Jokul's face was very pale but his jaw was firm. Helga stood in the crowd, red-eyed. Onar was surrounded by his friends who laughed and slapped him on the back. The two men brought axes to the fight. Åsa was not surprised at the choice. Swords were so expensive that it was unlikely a farmer would own one. Every steading had an axe or two. They made a brutal, effective weapon. Onar's axe was a long-shafted weapon forged for battle. Jokul wielded a workman's axe, designed for felling trees, not men. Its sturdy shaft came to Jokul's shoulder and the wedge-shaped axehead showed wear, but the edge shone bright in the sun. A well-cared-for tool.

Ragnhild watched Onar the way a cat eyes its prey. A faint smile played on her lips, and every now and again her hand twitched toward her sword hilt.

Murchad stood beside Åsa, his green eyes raging beneath knitted brows. Åsa shrugged. Ragnhild had never meant to have anyone worry over her. She put a hand on his shoulder. "She'll be fine. You know she can take care of herself."

Murchad met her gaze and nodded.

Åsa joined Heid to sacrifice a cock and sprinkle the combatants with blood, the apprentices chanting a warding spell to prevent any magical influence on the duel's outcome. That done, they stepped back into the crowd to watch.

Jarl Borg stepped forward to state the rules of the holmgang. "This is the law of the clenched fist," he said. "Each man will have three shields. When the last shield is shattered, each man will keep fighting. Biting, kicking, and scratching are forbidden. Punching and hair pulling is allowed. If one of the fighters steps off the island into the water, he is considered to be in flight and he loses the battle. The duel continues until first blood is spilled. If one duelist is killed or incapacitated, his second may continue the fight. If Jokul wins the duel, Onar will give him four cows. If Onar wins, Jokul's claim will be satisfied and Onar will owe him nothing. But if one duelist is killed, his family will not be entitled to wergild, and all he possesses passes to the winner. If either man fails to abide by these rules, he will be outlawed. He will have until sundown the next day to flee into the forest, or be hunted down and killed."

As Jarl Borg recited the rules, Jokul grew paler and his hands trembled. But at the end, he set his jaw and agreed to the rules of combat. Helga looked ready to cry. If Onar killed her brother, she would have no choice but to be his concubine, or have nowhere to live.

THE FOUR GOT into their skiffs and Ragnhild and Gisli rowed the combatants out to the holm. When they landed on the islet, Ragnhild hopped out and steadied the boat while Jokul climbed onto the slippery rocks and got his footing. Once the duelists were safely ashore, Ragnhild and Gisli secured the skiffs and took their places behind the principals, holding the three shields each man was entitled to. As seconds, their job was to watch the fight carefully and ensure the rules were followed.

Ragnhild met Gisli's eyes over the rim of the shields she held, sizing him up. She hoped he would cause some trouble. Lady's Servant had drunk no blood lately.

Jokul accepted his first shield from Ragnhild and stepped forward to meet his foe. Onar rushed at the farmer, axe held high, and Jokul froze.

"Duck!" Ragnhild cried. Jokul flinched away from the blade as it whizzed past his head. Onar's momentum carried him past Jokul. Both men whirled to face each other.

Ragnhild's warning seemed to have awakened Jokul from his trance. He blocked Onar's next attack with his shield, following up with a sturdy blow from his own axe that sent Onar staggering. Hope bloomed in Ragnhild's chest. Perhaps the farmer would survive.

The two men traded blows, hacking each other's shields to splinters. Jokul's shield was first to fail. He caught the new one Ragnhild tossed and before he could regain his balance, Onar struck. Jokul staggered and Onar swung his axe again. But Jokul had recovered. He caught the blow on his own shield and delivered a counter blow, catching Onar on the arm. A red weal appeared in the fabric of his sleeve.

"First blood!" Ragnhild called out. The fight was over. She was relieved that Jokul had survived and won.

But as Jokul lowered his axe and shield, Onar charged. Ragnhild shouted a warning and Jokul dodged. Onar's axeblade missed his head but tore deep into his shoulder. The force of the blow knocked him off his feet. As Jokul lay stunned and bleeding, Onar advanced on him, weapon raised for the kill.

With a shout, Ragnhild drew her sword and stepped between them. "You're a dead man, Onar!"

Onar's eyes widened at the sight of the shield-maiden's blade leveled at him. He whirled and dashed past his stunned second. Onar shoved his boat off the islet and dove in. He fitted the oars and rowed hard toward the far shore, away from the shouting crowd. Ragnhild and Gisli dropped to their knees, working furiously to staunch Jokul's bleeding.

As the crowd screamed for his death, Onar reached the far shore. A few folk were running toward him as he beached the boat and fled into the forest.

Ragnhild and Gisli carefully loaded the wounded Jokul into his boat and rowed him to shore. Helga emerged from the crowd to claim her brother.

Åsa declared, "Onar has lost the duel thrice over, by first blood, by attacking his opponent after the duel was called, and by fleeing from the island. He is outlawed. After sundown tonight, anyone may kill him on sight. I award all his property to Jokul and Helga. Heid and her apprentices will tend Jokul's wounds."

Heid stared into the forest after Onar. "I fear this may not be the last we hear of that evil man."

～

THE EXCITEMENT of the duel had got the blood up among the younger folk, and many more lined up to join Åsa's warriors. A dozen boys and girls in their teens presented themselves over the remaining days of the assembly, their parents eager for them to join Tromøy's hird. Åsa gulped and took them all.

"We haven't had a single experienced warrior appear," said Murchad.

Ragnhild shrugged. "We'll take what we can get and make the most of them."

"But these are all striplings," the Irishman exclaimed.

"They're young now, but next spring they'll sail with us to take Gausel." Ragnhild lowered her voice.

"How are we going to feed them?" Murchad grumbled.

"Fish more, hunt more," said Ragnhild. She patted her purse. "We'll buy grain from Vestfold if we have to."

~

SOLBAKK, Rogaland

SIGNY WAS RELIEVED on many fronts. Her morning sickness had receded, though she was growing uncomfortable now in her sixth month of pregnancy. She welcomed the cooler weather. Harald had returned, but without Ragnhild.

"She's safely married to the Irish king," was all he'd say.

Ragnhild, married? That didn't sound right. The shield-maiden had fought a war against her own father to escape that marriage. Signy just could not believe her sister-in-law would give in without a fight. A big one.

Bit by bit, Signy ferreted out the truth from Harald's crew—how he'd betrayed his sister into the hands of the very man they'd set out to kill. Signy was appalled at the thought of brave, brash Ragnhild now little better than a prisoner through Harald's treachery.

But Ragnhild had somehow escaped and reclaimed *Raider Bride*—and attacked Harald in a battle between two Irish factions. Faced with overwhelming forces, Harald and his crew had fled.

Signy was glad Ragnhild had managed to win her freedom and regain her ship. Though Harald said nothing, she understood he expected his sister to try to take Gausel in the spring. Signy's stomach was unsettled by more than her pregnancy. By law, Ragnhild was entitled to her inheritance, but Harald insisted on keeping it from her. He was in the wrong, yet he held all the power in the situation.

There was little Signy could do for her sister-in-law except pray. It was good that her advancing pregnancy precluded any form of intimacy with her husband. It gave her an excuse to avoid him without letting her feelings be known.

～

Agder Forest

FROM DEEP WITHIN HIS TRANCE, Hrafn sensed a presence in the forest. He reached his mind out to the wolf, who caught the man's scent on the air.

Find him. Bring him to me.

The blind wolf loped off, tracking the smell of fear that hung heavy in the air. Every inch of ground hereabout was familiar to him and he ran quickly.

A rustle in the brush told him he was getting close. He slowed his pace to a creep, moving silently through the undergrowth.

His keen ears picked up ragged breathing. He closed on the man where he cowered in a thicket. When the wolf was near enough to feel the human's hot breath on his nose, he suddenly rose, snarling. The human shrieked and burrowed into the thicket. The wolf advanced, growling. The brush rattled as the man scrambled to his feet.

The wolf darted in for a nip. The human screamed in terror and stumbled out of the thicket. Long branches snarled around his legs and he fell with a huff, then scrambled up in a panic. His breath came in rasping gulps.

Snapping his jaws at the ankles, the wolf herded the man

toward his master. The human was so terrified he fell again. This time the wolf sank his teeth into the buttocks with a satisfying chomp. He couldn't help drooling a little. The man screamed and wrenched away, leaving a scrap of cloth in the wolf's mouth. He spit it out.

Hrafn heard the panicked crashes grow nearer and smiled.

"Save me!" The man thudded down beside Hrafn, panting.

"Welcome," said Hrafn. His voice, so long disused, screeched like a rusty hinge.

With a growl, the wolf sat. The man caught his breath. Hrafn could actually hear his heart thud.

"I am Hrafn. The wolf is mine. He will not harm you unless I tell him to. Tell me your name."

"I am called Onar," he choked.

Hrafn honeyed his tone with sympathy. "And tell me, Onar, how came you to these forsaken woods?"

"I've been outlawed."

Hrafn's hopes flared. An opportunity. He reached out with his mind, and took hold of the man's thoughts. Onar's breathing and heartbeat calmed.

Yes, an opportunity.

CHAPTER 12

Tromøy
November, AD 822, Slaughter Month

With the full moon, the Winter Nights feast was upon them. In Ireland, they would be celebrating All Hallow's with masses said for all the saints and bonfires to ward off the fae.

For the Norse, it was the start of winter and all the preparations that must be made for survival. Murchad watched Toki and his crew slaughter the livestock not deemed fit to survive the winter. The yard smelled of butchery and everything was slick with blood. The preparations gave Murchad a chill at the thought of the northern winter to come. Already the ground was frozen. In Ireland, the rains and wind storms would have begun, but the cattle could find grazing all winter on his emerald isle. Here the only feed for the animals was the fodder they put by, and so a large percentage of their herd had to be slaughtered.

The entire settlement turned out to preserve the meat, salting it or hanging it in the smokehouse over a smoldering fire for weeks until it was dry and chewy. Fish were dried and smoked as well. Apples and root vegetables were buried in the ground, the granaries full, and the dairy reeking of cheese. By spring, food would be scarce.

Unlike the álfablót earlier in the season, only the farmers who lived close by braved the sleet and gales of Slaughter Month to travel to Tromøy for Winter Nights. They arrived on horseback, for the ground was too muddy for carts yet there was not enough snow for sleighs.

Once they'd been ferried over from the mainland, they gathered beneath the sacred tree beside the hall while the sleet pelted them and the wind howled. These Northmen seemed impervious to the weather as they watched Åsa and Heid sacrifice the animals that had been selected for this occasion.

The scent of cooking meat and wet wool mingled with the woodsmoke and rose into the hall's high ceiling. Everyone gathered on benches while Heid's apprentices served horns of ale. Åsa rose and led them in a toast first to the gods, then to the dísir and the álfir. Murchad grimaced as he thought of the queen in the mound. No wonder they felt they had to appease these spirits.

After a sufficiency of ale, Thorgeir rose and declared, "One day, Thor's great hammer, Mjölnir, went missing." The listeners cheered in approval and Murchad settled back, anticipating a good story. "The god of mischief, Loki, borrows Freyja's falcon cloak and flies off to find the hammer. He discovers the thief is the Jotun, Thrym." Thorgeir paused and looked at Murchad. "The Jotnar are the mortal enemies of the gods. Loki, who is himself half giant, bargains with Thrym for the return of the hammer. But the Jotun drives a hard bargain. In exchange for Mjölnir, he demands the goddess Freyja as his wife.

"When Loki comes back with the news, Freyja is so furious she flings her golden necklace, Brisingamen, to the ground, causing an earthquake." Murchad remembered that Ragnhild had called the queen's necklace Brisingamen. He had also heard the story of how Freyja had paid for the necklace, by sleeping with the four dwarves who made it.

"The gods realize that Freyja is not a willing bride. How could they get Mjölnir back? After much discussion, the god Heimdall says, 'Since it's your hammer, Thor, you should go get it.'

"Thor scoffs at the idea. 'Gladly, but the Jotuns will never let me in their gates.'

"Heimdall gives Thor a fiendish smile. 'They will if you are the bride.'

"The gods fall silent, staring at Heimdall as Thor turns red. Heimdall continues, 'Imagine Thor, dressed and veiled as a bride, in Freyja's place. Loki could go along, disguised as her servant.'

"Thor is outraged at the thought of dressing up as a bride, but he's desperate to get Mjölnir back.

"'All right, I'll do it,' he says.

At this point Thorgeir bowed to Åsa, who handed him her shawl. The stocky warrior draped the finely embroidered wool over his head and minced around the longfire, hand fluttering in the air while his audience roared with mirth. Murchad laughed so hard he gasped for breath.

"Thor and Loki arrive in Jotunheim, Thrym gets suspicious when the bride drinks three barrels of ale." Thorgeir grabbed a horn from Einar and guzzled the contents, letting the ale dribble down his beard, "and eats an entire ox.

"Loki explains, 'Freyja is so excited about the wedding that she has not eaten for eight days.'

Thorgeir glared around the room. "Thrym worries about his bride's blazing, bloodshot eyes. Loki says, 'Freyja is so excited about becoming your wife that she hasn't slept for eight nights.'

"At last Thrym is convinced, and the ceremony takes place." Thorgeir perched himself on the end of the bench, crossing his legs daintily. "Thrym brings in Mjölnir and places it in the bride's lap to ensure her fertility." Amid hoots of laughter, Ulf rose and carried his blacksmith's hammer over and laid it in Thorgeir's lap. "Thor grabs his hammer and smashes Thrym and all the wedding guests." Thorgeir leaped up, hammer in hand, and whirled it about him while the audience dodged, laughing.

When the tumult died down, people brought out instruments —bone flutes and what looked like a lyre, strung with horsehair, jaw harps, and a few skin drums. While the wind howled outside, they feasted and sang, and told outrageous lies about each other. Thorgeir rose and launched into a story about how he'd caught Svein sneaking off to practice embroidery. The audience erupted into laughter at the picture of the ham-fisted warrior plying a delicate bone needle.

Svein rose, and Murchad held his breath. In Ireland, such an insult would demand a fight to the death.

The beefy húskarl staggered over and grabbed Thorgeir about the middle, dragging him off his feet. Thorgeir fell to the floor, but Svein himself was so drunk he fell on top of Thorgeir, who grinned and kissed him on his bristling beard, yelling, "Sweet cheeks!"

Murchad's mouth fell open. He watched in amazement as the two burly warriors tussled in the straw, shrieking insults while the crowd cheered them on. Finally the two lay still, laughing, and one of Heid's apprentices brought them a horn brimming with ale. They sat up and shared the drink. Murchad wondered if he'd ever be so comfortable among these people. The Irish, with their prickly pride, would never be so playful.

Murchad glanced up at Åsa on her high seat, smiling down on her people. He thought of what that seat had cost her. He knew her story, of how she'd avenged her father's and brother's murders by killing her own husband in a duel over her son. He shuddered at the idea that a king would sacrifice his own child to the gods for victory in war, yet he knew his own ancestors had been just as ruthless. In some ways his people still were, their ferocity restrained beneath a thin veil of Christianity. They still took the heads of their enemies, burned and sacked monasteries of their rivals. No, the Irish were not gentler than the Norse. Just different.

~

ÅSA PAUSED in the doorway to her chamber. Stormrider, hooded, dozed on her perch. Heid snored in her bed across the room. Halfdan slept peacefully in his bed.

Heid sat up in her bed. "Are you going to sacrifice at the queen's mound tonight?"

Åsa shivered. "If I give her another chance to lure me in, she might succeed. It was so close last time, using my mother's memory. But if I don't go, she'll take my good fortune as she did my father's."

"Bah!" Heid snorted. "Could she really? She's lain quietly in her mound for ages. She's never made her presence known before. That old witch claims powers she doesn't possess. I was responsible for Harald's downfall." The sorceress turned her face to the wall and burrowed into her quilt.

Åsa sighed. The völva would never admit that anyone had more power than she, but the haugbui had shown herself adept at saying whatever her victims were most likely to believe. Who was telling the truth? Åsa shook her head. Her terror of being captured by the ghoul and dragged forever into the mound far outweighed her fear of the loss of hamingja.

She took one last look at Halfdan and crawled into bed, pulling the covers up to her nose. She lay fretting for a long while before falling into a restless sleep.

In her dream, she ran through the forest, fear clutching at her heart. The full moon flashed through the bare trees, branches snagged her hair and tore at her clothes. She slipped and fell, picked herself back up and ran on. A light shimmered through the trees ahead and she made for that, fighting her way through thorns and tangles. She entered a clearing and stopped, panting. Before her brooded the queen's burial mound. And on top stood the queen, shimmering silver in the moonlight.

"Daughter." Her voice resonated, setting up a vibration that shook the earth. "Daughter, you have betrayed me. You will pay, you and yours will pay."

"I'm sorry," Åsa shouted. From her cloak she pulled a terrified hen. "I'll sacrifice—here, I've brought you a sacrifice."

The haugbui laughed. "It's too late for that. You didn't come. Your fate is sealed. Ill will befall those you love, and you will be alone forever, alone as you have left me. Too late…"

Åsa woke in a sweat, her throat dry, her heart pounding. The queen's words echoed in her head.

Heid touched her shoulder. "What is it?" she croaked.

"I dreamed of the queen in the mound. She cursed me!"

"Bah!" Heid said. "It was just a dream." But the sorceress's worried look belied her tone. "Go back to sleep." She turned and hobbled toward her bed.

Åsa reached out and found the pouch, hanging from her bedpost. Fumbling inside, she touched the necklace. With a sigh of relief, she welcomed the vibration that surged up her arm and steadied her heart.

Clutching the golden links, she slept.

～

SNOW FLEW, and Onar settled into the cave deep in the forest.

It had been so long since Hrafn had spoken to another human that often he forgot and lapsed into long silences. This seemed to suit Onar just fine. He never asked questions, rarely initiated conversation. Gradually, Hrafn coaxed out the man's story, of the duel and his escape into the forest.

"They took everything from me," said Onar.

"We are both wronged, you and I," said Hrafn. "By the same

people. But we will get revenge, and you will regain all you have lost."

Onar said nothing, but Hrafn knew he was thinking it was the ravings of a madman. How could an outlaw and a blind old man take vengeance on the powerful queen of Tromøy and her sorceress? Hrafn didn't argue.

At night when the man was sleeping, Hrafn reached into Onar's mind as he did the wolf's, and found it cluttered and confused. An easy place to plant suggestions.

Next morning, Onar ventured out into the snow-clad forest, returning with a straight sapling as tall as he was. He spent the next few evenings stripping the bark, cutting off the branches and smoothing the knots. Finally he sharpened the tip into a spearhead.

He and the wolf set off hunting. Between the wolf's keen senses and Onar's skill with the spear, they managed to hunt down a small deer. Onar dragged the carcass back to the cave, where he skinned and butchered it. He spitted the choicest pieces of meat on a sharpened stick and cooked them over the fire.

Hrafn's mouth watered. "I've missed the smell of cooking meat." He gobbled the charred bits with relish.

Onar smoked the rest of the deer meat over the fire. He scraped the hide clean and hung it over the cave entrance to keep out the snow and rain.

With his axe he felled a small pine tree and spent evenings making himself a pair of hunter's skis. He carved footbeds, pierced with holes for deer hide lacings. One ski was as long as he was tall, for gliding. The other was a third the length of the first, its bottom covered with hide, fur side out, for traction. He used this one to kick off, propelling himself in the hunter style. His spear served as a ski pole.

During the long winter evenings Onar made snares and fashioned a bow and flint-tipped arrows. The daylight hours were short, and whenever the weather permitted he spent them hunting with the wolf. He also ran a trap line, catching hares and other small creatures.

With the regular diet of rich meat, Hrafn's strength grew. He spent more time wandering in the younger man's thoughts. It gave him a sense of freedom and power he had lacked for a long time. Onar had become accustomed to sharing his mind with Hrafn and appeared to take the old man's thoughts as his own.

One evening, as Hrafn rummaged around in Onar's mind, a sudden dizziness overcame him. The world tilted at a crazy angle. He thought he might vomit as he struggled to regain his balance. Shapes flashed and moved.

The world righted itself. Soft light resolved into fire and the rough cave walls came into focus. Shock seared through him. *I can see. For the first time in two years, I can see.*

He was looking through Onar's eyes.

He stared at the wolf's black pelt, its pointed ears. And a shrunken, feeble old man lying on a filthy pallet. A fury burned in his breast, hotter than before. *Look what they've done to me. But my spirit is not feeble. They haven't won.*

When Onar went hunting, Hrafn rode along in his mind. The old man reveled in the vigor coursing through the younger man's limbs as he skied, his keen sight and strength when he hefted the spear.

Though Onar never spoke it aloud, Hrafn came to know the younger man's deepest desires, and promised to get them for him. "If you help me, you will take your revenge. You will kill Jokul and regain not only your property, but his. I will make you a powerful man, a jarl. And Helga will be your slave."

Hrafn felt Onar's heart thud, and knew he had the man, inside and out. It was time to send him out to complete the plan.

"Bring me the boy."

CHAPTER 13

Tromøy

Winter Nights passed. The weather turned foul, keeping everyone indoors. The bower hall rang with chanting while Heid and her nine apprentices practiced the vardlokkur and galdr spells. The other women who slept in the bower busied themselves elsewhere, and no man dared come near.

Åsa spent her time with the völva and her apprentices, weaving a battle-flag for Ragnhild: a Valkyrie on horseback, shield raised, spear leveled. The figure was woven in black and white wool against a blue background.

As Åsa and Heid worked together at the loom, the völva remarked, "I wish you would get rid of that necklace."

Åsa touched her pouch, feeling it gleam within. She quailed at the thought of parting with it. It was the only protection she had against the queen's curse. "Yes. I will."

"There is more to that necklace than just magic. It's hidden, but I can feel it. You should send it with Ragnhild and Murchad, and let them return it to where it belongs."

"Mmm," Åsa murmured, keeping her voice noncommittal.

To her relief, the sorceress let the subject drop. "I've decided to begin training my successor."

Åsa looked at her, stunned. "Your successor?"

"Someone must be qualified to take my place. I won't live forever."

The aging sorceress's words sent a chill down Åsa's spine. She hoped they weren't prophetic. "Have you made a choice?"

"Yes, Vigdis is a likely candidate. She's smart, fearless, and already adept at healing. She has a strong voice for galdr."

Åsa ignored the hollow feeling in her gut. "Is this her wish?"

"She's told me she wants to follow the völva's path."

"She's a good choice, but what do her parents say?" Vigdis was high born, and her normal path after two years of training would be to become a jarl's wife.

"The girl is eighteen. Her parents have no say in the matter. Besides, they have other daughters to marry off to allies. I've agreed to accept two of her younger sisters as soon as I have a vacancy." Heid's apprentices must always number nine, the holy number. Many of them left to marry after a year or two of training, and so places became available nearly every year.

"Very well," said Åsa, trying to quell the uneasiness that roiled within.

∾

SNOW HAD BEEN FALLING SOFTLY all day. Onar uncovered his skiff where he'd hidden it amongst the trees. He dragged the little boat down to the beach and launched it, then rowed across the narrow channel to Tromøy. He pulled into a tiny, isolated cove where he dragged the skiff ashore and waited while the flakes continued to drift down. His tracks gradually disappeared beneath the snow.

Toward nightfall, a familiar figure came walking down the beach toward the boat. Dag, a man Onar had known for years. Onar emerged from the trees, holding his knife at his side.

"Onar?" There was shock in Dag's voice. "You shouldn't be here. I won't tell, but you should go. If they catch you, man..."

Onar grabbed his old friend and slashed Dag's throat. Terror in his eyes, Dag clutched at his neck as the blood welled between his fingers. "You're not Onar..." whispered the dying man.

Onar dragged the corpse into the woods where he covered the body with rocks, then set about obscuring the bloody trail in the snow, smoothing his work with a pine branch.

He hiked up to Dag's hut, where the fire was still burning, and made himself at home.

~

THE WEATHER CLEARED and it was time to concentrate on transforming young farmers into warriors. Åsa focused on the training, glad to be outdoors and active. As queen, she was the primary battle commander, and took her place in the training field, but she thanked the gods that Jarl Borg was still hale despite his seventy-some years. Though she had gained confidence from winning several battles, and she trusted her seasoned warriors like Olvir and Ragnhild's three húskarlar, no one had the leadership know-how of the old jarl.

Each trainee had spent the past weeks making a wooden shield covered with leather, rimmed with iron and mounted on an iron boss from the smithy, and a simple blunt spear shaft carved from ash. When their training was complete, Ulf would rivet an iron spearhead on their shaft. Spears were the most common and cheapest weapon, and their long reach made them the most effective in a shield wall.

Jarl Borg lined them up in the practice field and strode up and down their rank, hands clasped behind his back, fixing each with his keen gaze. "Yesterday, you were farmers." His voice still carried across the field despite his years. "Today you will become warriors. Though you have never stood in a shield wall, you are already tough, your muscles hardened from long hours of field work. Perhaps you have never wielded a weapon in war, but you know how to handle an axe for cutting wood, and a scythe to harvest barley. Today you will learn to reap men."

The old jarl spaced experienced warriors among them to demonstrate proper form as they learned to overlap their shields to form a wall and thrust their blunted sticks at an invisible opponent from behind locked shields.

Murchad did not join them, but rather watched from a distance as Jarl Borg drilled the recruits. Åsa thought perhaps the Irishman wanted to get a feel for their tactics before he participated, but he began to disappear for long hours. This behavior made her uneasy, and she sent a man to follow Murchad.

Her spy reported back, "He rides out on his horse. Should I follow him?"

"No." Åsa decided he needed his solitude. Part of the adjustment, perhaps. He had been a battle commander in Ireland. Maybe he was too proud to serve under Jarl Borg.

After a week of practice, Jarl Borg formed the recruits into two lines and set them to attacking each other, trying to pry apart the opposing shield wall by jabbing their spears at heads and swinging them low to sweep the feet out from under the defenders.

Murchad still watched from the sidelines, or disappeared on his horse. Åsa saw that people were beginning to notice. In the evening, when everyone gathered on the benches of the great hall for ale and a meal, Jarl Borg was heard to mutter about men who were afraid to stand in a shield wall. Ragnhild colored at this remark, but Murchad seemed not to hear. His attention was focused on a project, braiding long strands of leather. Everyone's hands were busy this time of year, mending harness and tack, patching clothes, sharpening weapons and tools.

~

WHILE THE ADULTS PLAYED WAR, so did the children. They had their own practice field nearby, and they made war every day, wooden practice swords and shields clacking, high-pitched war cries incessant. Murchad spent much of his time watching them. Three-year-old Halfdan was the most active, stronger than many older than him. He was the natural leader.

"That boy has strong hamingja," Ulf observed as he took a break from the smithy to watch the children. "Like his mother and his grandfather."

"Ragnhild tried to explain this word," said Murchad, "but I can't say I understand it. It means...luck?"

Ulf thought for a moment. "It also means destiny. You can lose your hamingja—like Åsa's father did when Gudrød killed him." Ulf scowled. "That witch Heid had a hand in that." Then his expression softened and his eyes seemed to stare into the distance. "I remember Åsa's father when his hamingja was strong. He won every battle. Things that were impossible for other men came easily to him. He was unstoppable when he was young."

Murchad nodded. "I think I understand." As he watched Halfdan play with the other children, the longing for a child of his own rose inside him. He knew Ragnhild continued to drink the herbal brew Heid prepared to keep her from conceiving. Pregnancy would spoil her plans.

CHAPTER 14

From the forest's verge, Onar watched the children play. One stood out from the others, hair black and shiny as a raven's wing. The queen's son. The queen who had outlawed him, who'd taken his land. Hrafn promised to get it back for him when he brought the boy. And Helga. She would be his slave. His mind ranged over what he would do to her.

But that man, Toki, was always watching the boy. He stood in the way.

Over the course of several days, Onar watched them from his hiding place among the pines. Each night he returned to Dag's hut.

One morning the old steward set off on skis, pulling Halfdan on a sledge. They entered the forest. Onar followed, keeping his distance, silent on skis.

Toki glanced back uneasily, as if he knew he was being followed. Onar froze behind a tree trunk. The steward peered into the forest, then, satisfied, resumed his trek. Onar paralleled their course cautiously, careful not to rustle the dry branches.

At last Toki stopped. He unlaced his skis and began to gather fallen wood, stopping to cut off side branches with his axe.

Halfdan jumped off the sledge and ran in circles, brandishing his wooden sword. The child ran right up to Onar's hiding place. He froze, mouth open, and stared at the outlaw.

Onar burst from cover. Toki whirled in surprise, swinging his axe, but Onar stepped inside the swing, grabbed the old steward by his beard, and drew his hunting knife across Toki's throat.

Screaming a war-cry, the boy charged Onar and bashed his leg with a wooden sword hard enough to bring him to his knees. He tackled the child, wrapping his arms around him. The boy shrieked and Onar managed to cram the brat's mitten in his mouth. Halfdan kicked, hard. That would be a bruise. He grabbed the churning legs with one hand while tucking the boy's head under his other arm.

He laid the struggling boy on the sledge, pinning him with one hand while he grabbed Toki's ropes with the other. Halfdan landed another kick on Onar's face that made him see stars, but he managed to hog-tie the thrashing child and bind him to the sledge. Onar struggled to his feet and set off once more through the forest, pulling the sledge toward his skiff. The boy bucked, emitting muffled shrieks. The lad had a temper.

Onar heaved the sledge, with the bound and kicking boy, into the skiff. He took up oars and rowed across to the mainland, where he beached the boat and unloaded his cargo, then hid the skiff under the pine boughs once more. Donning his skis, he set out through the woods, towing the sledge.

When they arrived at the cave, the old man and the wolf lay as if sleeping, but Hrafn roused when Onar pulled the sledge inside. The boy lay quietly now, but his face was red and he eyed his surroundings with fury.

"Well, child," Hrafn rasped. "Welcome to my hall. I'm an old friend of your mother's." To Onar, he said, "Untie him from the sledge, but keep him bound hand and foot."

Onar took the mitten out of the boy's mouth, and Halfdan shrieked, "You're a bad man! You hurt Toki!" Then he took a deep breath and emitted a high-pitched scream that went on and on. The old wolf howled, and Onar's sensitive ears rang.

"Perhaps he's hungry?" Hrafn suggested.

Onar offered the boy a piece of dried meat. Halfdan stopped screaming and sucked in a threatening breath. Onar hastily stuffed the meat into the boy's mouth. Halfdan thrust his head forward and bit down on Onar's fingers. Hard. Panicked, Onar tried to jerk his hand away but the brat clamped his jaws firmly.

"He's going to bite them off!" Onar cried.

"Don't be such a baby," said Hrafn. "Surely a big man like you can handle a little child."

"He's no child. He's the spawn of Loki."

"The boy has spirit, as well he should. Remember, he's destined to become a mighty king. Now see to his needs."

As Onar tried to extricate his fingers, his eyes met Halfdan's and he quailed at the murder he saw there.

At last the boy's jaw slackened, and Onar was able to slip his hand away. The child spat out the meat and shouted, "I want Mama! I want Brenna!"

Hrafn put a soothing note into his voice. "Yes, son, I know you do. But you shall have to wait."

Halfdan let out a blood-curdling shriek. "No!" He drew in a huge breath that filled the men and the wolf with dread. Then he opened his mouth and screeched. "Mama! Brenna!" He shrieked on and on. It was hard to believe such a tiny child could scream so loud, and so long. Surely his little body would collapse. But Halfdan seemed driven by an inhuman energy. The cave echoed with his shrill cries and the men covered their ears. Even the wolf put his paw over his head in a futile attempt to hide from the shrieks.

"Give him to the wolf," Hrafn gasped. The wolf cringed, but he allowed Onar to lay the bound, exhausted boy next to his belly. The child continued to scream while the men and wolf quivered in pain.

Gradually, the cries lost momentum. They diminished into a half-hearted grizzle.

Halfdan buried his tearstained face in the wolf's pelt, whimpering.

In an instant, he was asleep, and a blessed silence fell. Both men and the wolf breathed a sigh of relief.

~

"WHERE'S HALFDAN?" Åsa asked.

"He's with Toki getting wood in the forest. They haven't returned yet," Brenna replied as she bustled about the hall, getting ready for the evening meal. She glanced at the low sun. "It's getting late."

"Yes, it is," said Åsa, her voice rising in alarm. "I'm going to look for them." She might be just an over-protective mother, she thought as she hurried to the bower where Stormrider drowsed on her perch. Åsa undid the falcon's jesses and slipped into the bird's body. Stormrider roused, flapped her wings, and lofted out through the smoke-hole. She soared toward the forest, the falcon's keen sight picking out the sledge tracks.

The trail ended in a bloody mess in the snow. A body lay crumpled in the center of the crimson stain. The peregrine's heart thudded as she flew down for a closer look. Her stomach lurched when she recognized Toki.

Åsa let the predator's mind throttle her emotions, enabling her to investigate the scene. There was no saving Toki. By the whiteness of his face and the amount of blood saturating the snow, he'd bled out some time ago.

She circled the area, searching for any sign of Halfdan. All she found were more sledge tracks, leading away. Her heart beat harder. He could be alive. She followed the trail to the water's edge. The tide was high now, and she couldn't tell if a boat had been beached there recently, but the tracks ended abruptly at the tideline.

She soared across the narrow waterway to the mainland, and there the tracks reappeared in the snow, leading deep into the forest. She glided through the trees, keen falcon's vision picking out the faint sign of sledge runners in the dim light.

The trail ended at a cave in the rocky hillside. Wisps of smoke escaped the hide flap over the entrance. She lit in a tree, as close as she dared. A tiny moan came from the cave, and she recognized Halfdan's cry immediately.

Åsa exhaled. He was alive. She stifled the overwhelming urge to swoop into the cave and attack the kidnappers, knowing she'd lose the fight and forfeit the advantage of surprise.

By now it was getting dark. She needed to head home and muster a force.

She flew into the bower and reentered her body. Brenna was sitting by the bed, her kindly, plump face furrowed with worry.

Åsa didn't want to tell Brenna that her husband was dead, murdered, but she had no choice.

"Toki has been killed," she said, as gently as she could. Brenna's face crumpled and Åsa put her arms around the older woman. "Halfdan's been taken, on Toki's sledge, then by skiff to the mainland. The kidnappers are holding him in a cave. He's alive, for the moment, but I must go after him. I'll send a party to bring Toki home."

Åsa released the sobbing fóstra and hurried to the hall. She found Ragnhild and Murchad in the private chamber off the main room that Åsa had given over to them. They followed her into the hall and gathered the rest of the warriors while Åsa told them what had happened.

"I need four men and a sledge to bring Toki back here. Please ask Einar, Olvir, Thorstein, and Svein to get ready to cross over to the mainland with us to go after Halfdan."

When Åsa returned to the bower to get ready, Brenna had

dressed and was prepared to follow them. Åsa didn't want her to see the grisly murder scene. "Let them bring him back to you," she said gently. She knew that right now, keeping Brenna too busy to think was the best thing. "Will you please organize what will be needed?"

Brenna nodded, her breath rasping in her throat.

Åsa squeezed her hand gently and tried to still the panic that rose in her own chest. Halfdan! This was her fault. She'd lost their hamingja. If only she'd sacrificed to the haugbui when she had the chance, Toki would be alive and Halfdan safe.

It was too late now. She armed herself and settled Stormrider on her shoulder. By the time she returned to the yard, four men waited with a sledge to bring Toki back. Murchad, Ragnhild, Einar, Olvir, Thorstein, and Svein stood beside them, armed, their hudfat bundled.

The völva was also there, her horse-drawn sleigh already loaded with her tent and bed, the horse hitched up, her apprentices ready.

"I'll be needed," Heid said shortly. Åsa knew better than to argue.

The war party tossed their hudfat bundles onto the völva's sleigh. They strapped on skis and set off by torchlight, following Åsa through the forest to the murder scene.

Everyone stood silent for a moment, shocked by the sight of Toki's body. Åsa stared at the kindly steward she'd known all her life, guilt and sorrow overwhelming her.

"Time to mourn him when we have Halfdan back," said Heid.

They wrapped Toki in blankets and laid him on the sledge, securing him with hide lashings. The four men departed, towing him back to the hall.

Åsa turned to the others. "I couldn't see inside the cave. We don't know what we're facing, or who. We need to cross to the mainland and make camp some distance away. We can't let them know we're there."

They made their way across the island to the landing. For once, Heid's horse pulled her sledge onto the raft without coaxing, as if it sensed this was no time for drama.

Dawn was filtering through the clouds by the time they had crossed to the mainland and made a cold camp in the forest.

"Get some rest," Åsa said. While her apprentices set up Heid's tent, Åsa took the sorceress aside. "I'll take Stormrider and try to discover who has my son, and what kind of force we have to overcome." She retired to Heid's tent and lay on the camp bed. The völva seated herself on a stool beside the bed to keep watch.

Åsa slid into Stormrider and flew out of the tent. She winged across the forest, following the trail that was so clear to her falcon's eyes.

From the air, she sighted a lone figure skiing along, armed with a hunter's spear and bow, towing Toki's sledge behind him. The man lifted his face and with a jolt she recognized the outlaw, Onar.

She flew to the cave and lit in the top of a tall pine.

The hide flap had been pulled aside to let in the weak morning light. With her falcon's sight, she stared into the gloom. In the shadows lay an emaciated old man, wrapped in furs.

A shock of recognition flashed through her.

Hrafn—alive.

And his wolf. What she saw made her falcon's heart falter.

The wolf held Halfdan firmly between his paws, his huge jaws slavering over the boy's head. Åsa's heart lurched.

Then she realized Halfdan was laughing as the big tongue flicked across the boy's raven hair. The wolf was grooming him.

Suddenly, Halfdan looked up at her. "Mama!" he cried, holding his arms out to her. She froze. Of course he'd recognize her. He had seen her enter Stormrider many times.

From his filthy furs, Hrafn stirred at the sound. His empty eye sockets stared at her and he grinned. "Greetings, Åsa, Queen.

Your son and I are making friends. If you want him to live, send me the witch—she must come alone."

Panic gripped her. She wanted to soar down and pluck her son out of the wolf's clutches—but she knew her falcon's body could never wrest him away, or carry him to safety. With a resolute flap of her wings, she lofted into the sky and flew back to the camp and straight into her tent, where she dove into her body.

Åsa bolted up, startling Heid, who drowsed on her stool by the bed.

"It's Hrafn. His wolf has Halfdan," she gasped. "He saw me!"

"How could he see you? I plucked out his one good eye," said Heid.

"Halfdan recognized me. But Hrafn stared right at me and called me by name."

"If his wolf is blind, then that old coot's blind as well. He should be dead. Somehow he's managed to survive in the wild, without his sight." The völva shook her head. "That took great skill. Fueled by even greater hate."

Heid's words sent a shard of ice into Åsa's heart. "He knows I've found him. We've lost the advantage of surprise."

"We've lost nothing," said Heid. "If his other senses have been developed to this degree, it's unlikely that an armed troop could have approached his lair without him knowing. As long as he has the boy, he holds the power. What does the old bastard want?"

Åsa hesitated for an instant, tempted not to answer. She couldn't lose Heid. But this was her son at stake. "He wants you."

Heid sighed. "As I suspected." She hoisted herself up from the stool.

Åsa stared at the old sorceress. "I can't trade you."

"For your son? Of course you can." Heid drew her cloak over her crooked shoulders, pulling the hood up over her grizzled hair. Leaning on her iron staff, she lifted the tent flap and hobbled out.

Åsa leaped out of bed. She secured Stormrider on her perch, then hurried after the sorceress. "You can't go."

But Heid crabbed her way resolutely to her sleigh. "You told me that wolf had ahold of the child. Hitch up the horse," she ordered. The stable hands scurried to obey. Heid's apprentices helped her into the sleigh, tucking her furs around her. Then they donned their skis.

"Stay, girls. I go alone," Heid said.

"We can't let you do that, mistress," protested Vigdis.

"You can't disobey my orders," Heid growled. "Vigdis, you're in charge." She picked up the reins and shook them, setting off with bells chiming.

Åsa shot Ragnhild a glance. The shield-maiden caught her look and strapped on her skis. Åsa quickly donned her own skis, belted on her sword, and slung her father's war horn over her shoulder.

"Ragnhild and I will follow her," said Åsa. "The rest of you, stay far enough back that hopefully Hrafn won't sense you, but close enough that you can hear the war horn if I call you. If you hear three blasts, come quickly. A word of warning. I spotted Onar in the forest with Toki's sledge. If you come across him, you know the law." Olvir nodded grimly. An outlaw lived under a perpetual sentence of death. Now, it looked like Onar had committed murder, and justice would be served. They all knew that once Halfdan was secured, they would hunt Onar down.

Åsa and Ragnhild set off into the forest, skis whispering across the snow. Sunlight glimmered through the trees, revealing the trail. No new snow had fallen since the kidnapping, and the sorceress's sleigh clearly followed the sledge's track. It was easy skiing on the hard-packed snow.

When they got close to the cave, Åsa halted in the dense cover of the forest. "You stay here, and listen for my horn," she said to Ragnhild. "I'm going to take a look." She set off on her skis, cutting off from the trail and getting ahead of Heid. Through the trees, she glimpsed the old sorceress driving her sleigh along the track, horse hooves tromping and sleighbells ringing. Heid made no secret of her approach.

Åsa reached the cave before the völva, and stationed herself behind a tree near the entrance. The flap was still open to the weak winter light. Within, Halfdan had fallen asleep, his black hair gleaming against the wolf's pelt. Hrafn was no more than a pile of rags in the corner. But as the sleighbells sounded, the old man roused and sat up in his furs.

Heid pulled the sleigh up in front of the cave entrance. Her horse snorted and stamped her hooves at the scent of the wolf.

"Greetings, spawn of Loki," said Heid.

Hrafn broke into a grin. "Welcome, daughter of Hel."

CHAPTER 15

"I am here," said Heid. "Let the child go."

Hrafn cackled. "Come down from that sleigh first."

Heid sighed in exasperation. "Don't be a fool. What is it you want?"

"What do I want, hag?" mused Hrafn. "I want a warm bed in a dry hall. Good food. Ale and mead."

"You had all that, you idiot, you had it twice, and twice you lost it through your own treachery. Åsa will never give you a third chance."

"This boy will get me all of that when I raise him to be a mighty king."

Halfdan had awakened. He began to whine. The wolf held him down with his enormous paws and ran his tongue over the black hair.

From her hiding place, Åsa held her breath. Her hand slipped into her belt pouch to touch the necklace.

The instant her fingers contacted the gold, Hrafn aimed empty eye sockets in her direction. An icy jolt shot down Åsa's spine and she jerked her hand out of the pouch.

"That's right, little queen, I know you're there." Hrafn sank back into his furs. The wolf's tongue retracted from Halfdan's hair, and the animal bared his teeth. His fangs gleamed against the raven hair. The boy's little head just fit between the slavering jaws. Åsa shuddered.

Heid huffed. "I think you've made your point, old man."

"Come here, witch," Hrafn demanded. "I want to hear you die."

"Let the boy go first," said Heid.

"I can't do that."

"If I get down from this sleigh, you'll have us both."

"It seems we're at a standoff."

The crippled völva and the blind sorcerer remained frozen, physically unable to attack each other. The wolf held Halfdan between his great paws.

"Oh, let him go! He's just a little boy," cried Åsa. She wanted to rush out and snatch him away, but she knew the wolf's jaws could crush her son's skull before she reached him.

"The world is not always kind to little boys," said Hrafn.

"Nor girls," retorted Åsa.

"This child has a destiny," said Heid.

"Yes he does. He needs a strong mind to guide him and teach him to wield his hamingja, and that mind is mine," said Hrafn. "I'm not a fool. If I let the child go, my life is forfeit. I'll keep him here, and teach him what I know. Åsa, Queen, hear me. I will be your son's mentor. He will take the place of the king I lost, and when he grows up to rule Tromøy he will restore me to power."

Åsa shivered at the memory of Hrolf, Olaf's half-brother, whom Hrafn had groomed to be king. He'd ruled Tromøy once, with cruelty and terror, until Olaf had killed him and Åsa had taken over the kingdom.

"You can't raise a child in a cave," Heid said.

"Oh, yes I can. All I need is to get you out of the way, hag," said Hrafn.

"Fine. I'm ready to travel that road," said Heid.

"Yes, you are," said Hrafn. "And woe to me if I'm the one to send you on that way and bear your curse forever. No, it won't be by my hand that you die."

Åsa held her breath, waiting for one of them to act. Each wanted the other's death, yet feared to be the one to take it and the eternal malevolence it carried.

From the forest an arrow whirred and slammed into Heid's back. The völva slumped forward, reins still clutched in her hands. Her horse whinnied in panic.

Onar skied in, plucking another arrow from his quiver. Quicker than thought, Åsa drew her knife and threw it, impaling the outlaw in the throat. He collapsed to the ground, a pool of blood spreading onto the snow.

The wolf snarled. Halfdan screamed.

Åsa kicked off her skis and raced into the cave, drawing her sword.

The wolf clutched Halfdan firmly in his great paws.

Clutching a flint knife, the old sorcerer scrambled behind the boy and grabbed him. "If you come any closer, your son is dead!"

Åsa stopped short, heart in her throat.

Halfdan began to cry. "Mama!" Her hand slipped into the pouch and clutched the necklace, feeling the power surge up her arm.

Snarling, the wolf opened his jaws and bit down.

On Hrafn's throat.

The wolf got to his feet, the old man clamped in his jaws. He shook his quarry like a rag doll. Hrafn opened his mouth in a scream but no sound came out.

Åsa rushed to her son and snatched him away. She ran outside just as Ragnhild arrived. The shield-maiden grabbed the bridle of Heid's terrified horse before it could bolt while Åsa brought out her horn and sounded it three times.

Ragnhild spoke soothingly to the horse, settling it down. Åsa set Halfdan on the sleigh beside the völva and climbed in. The old sorceress was slumped forward, the arrow lodged in her shoulder blade. She breathed, shallow and rasping, eyelids fluttering in a white face.

Blood had soaked through the sorceress's cloak. Åsa carefully cut the shaft of the arrow, then cut a strip from Heid's linen shift to bind the wound.

"Make sure they won't walk again," Åsa said, nodding toward the two corpses.

Ragnhild drew Lady's Servant and beheaded Hrafn and Onar, then jumped into the sleigh and took the reins. They set off toward camp.

The blind wolf loped along behind.

∿

Back at camp, the apprentices clustered around the sleigh. They gently lifted their injured mistress out and carried her into her tent. Åsa climbed down, Halfdan clutched in her arms. The little boy wriggled out of her grasp and ran to the wolf, who swiped his huge, bloody tongue over the child's hair.

Åsa wasn't ready to let her son out of her sight. She picked him up and carried him to the völva's tent. The wolf followed and lay down outside.

Heid lay on her camp bed, cradled with pillows and bundled in furs, her face paler than milk. The arrowhead and her bloody clothes lay discarded on the ground.

"She lives," said Vigdis. "I need to get her warm."

A brazier was lit inside the tent and Vigdis heated stones in it. When they were warm, she tucked them into the furs around her mistress. She set a small soapstone pot to boil. From her pouch she drew herbs and cast them into the boiling water.

While the brewing herbs filled the tent with a comforting aroma, the apprentices linked hands and began to sing a vardlokkur, beseeching the álfir and dísir to come to Heid's aid.

When the concoction was ready, Vigdis cooled it with a handful of snow and dipped a clean linen cloth in the pot. The women kept singing as she gently pulled back the furs and washed Heid's wound. The völva moaned and writhed but didn't regain consciousness.

"The arrow doesn't seem to have penetrated to her lung. We need to stay here tonight. My sisters and I will keep watch over her. In the morning we'll see if it's safe to move her." Vigdis looked Åsa up and down. "There's nothing more you can do here. You're exhausted, Lady. You must rest."

"Very well," said Åsa, knowing Vigdis was right. Halfdan was already asleep in her arms. She rose and carried him outside. As she passed the cook fire, Olvir held out a bowl of stew. The scent made her knees weak, and she realized she hadn't eaten all day.

Beside her, the blind wolf sniffed the air. "Some for the wolf, too," she said, sitting down on a stump and accepting the bowl. When Olvir looked askance at the bloody maw, she said, "He saved Halfdan's life."

Olvir dished up a second bowl and set it down for the wolf. He sucked it up in one gulp and rooted around as if wondering where it had all gone.

Ragnhild appeared and Olvir dished up a bowl for her. She carried it off to Murchad. Their voices rose in a soft murmur.

Åsa was almost too tired to bring the spoon to her mouth. Halfdan roused at the scent of the stew and she fed him a few bites. At last she rose and carried him to her hudfat. The wolf followed. Åsa laid a pelt on the ground for him. He circled three times and lay down, curled up with his tail covering his nose.

In the morning, Heid was still unconscious and pale, but her breathing was more regular. Vigdis decreed that it was safe to transport her home. The three apprentices lifted their mistress into her sleigh and donned their skis.

Åsa put Halfdan into the sleigh next to Heid, climbed in, and took up the reins. The apprentices, Ragnhild, and Murchad skied alongside and the wolf loped behind.

Ragnhild looked up at Halfdan. The little boy's cheeks were rosy from the cold and his eyes glistened. "He seems no worse for his adventure."

"He's a true king in the making," agreed Murchad.

~

TOKI'S BODY lay in the cold brewhouse. Here he would stay until they could build a pyre for him and send him to the gods in fitting style. Brenna had washed the blood away and dressed him in clean clothes. With the blankets covering his savaged throat, he looked like he was sleeping. But his face was too white, and Toki, who was never still, lay far too quietly.

Brenna had not left his side. Åsa took her hand. Guilt weighed her down like a sack of rocks. "I'm sorry, Brenna. He was a good man. The best. I can't imagine life here without him."

Toki's funeral was an all-day affair. They built an enormous pyre and Brenna laid his prized possessions with it—his carving knife, the whetstone he used to keep it sharp, and a soapstone cauldron. As the body burned and his spirit rose with the smoke, the women sang him into the afterlife.

Vigdis and Åsa sacrificed a sow to Freyja. "Goddess, please welcome Toki in your hall to cook for the Einherjar who fall in battle every day and rise each evening to feast together."

Toki's work was taken over by his assistant, Hogni. He was an able young man and had trained under the old steward since he was a child gathering firewood. Hogni and the rest of the crew prepared a great feast for the population of Tromøy.

While they waited for the meat to cook, Brenna, dry-eyed but gray-faced, insisted on serving the funeral ale. Åsa accepted the horn from the old fóstra and stood, hoisting it in a toast. "Toki has always been a quiet, steady voice in the background of our lives. Now that he's gone it seems part of the world is missing."

As the pyre burned down, the folk toasted the old steward and shared their memories of him.

~

HEID SLEPT FITFULLY for two days. Vigdis kept the wound clean and the fever down with wool cloth soaked in a willow bark infusion. Åsa took turns with the apprentices keeping watch over the sorceress, crooning the vardlokkur unceasingly until their throats were raw.

Vigdis dipped a linen rag in broth and held it to Heid's lips. Involuntarily, the old sorceress sucked on it. "It's not enough," Vigdis fretted. "She's too frail to go long without nourishment. She needs to wake soon."

The weary apprentice was as pale as her mistress. "Get some rest," Åsa said. "I'll keep watch." Vigdis reluctantly agreed and shuffled off to her sleeping bench.

When she was alone, Åsa slipped her hand into the leather pouch and touched the Irish necklace. As the power seared up her arm, she placed her other hand on Heid's chest. Her hand vibrated, growing warm.

The völva's eyelid twitched. Åsa kept her hand on the sorceress's chest. Heid took a rattling breath. Her eyes jerked open, fixing Åsa with a piercing gaze.

"What have you done?" Heid demanded.

"Saved your life," said Åsa.

"Be careful…that Irish gold is not a friendly power."

Åsa returned her stare. "I can handle it."

A bony claw snaked out and grasped her arm. "Where is Halfdan?" Heid's voice was faint but her eyes demanding.

"Shhh. He's all right." The völva loosened her grip and lay back, closing her eyes. "Vigdis! She's awake," Åsa cried.

Vigdis came running, followed by the rest of the apprentices, who crowded around the sorceress's bed.

"Give me air!" Heid commanded. The women hurriedly backed away. "Now, help me up."

The apprentices automatically moved to help her, but Vigdis stepped in. "Not yet," she said firmly.

"Do as I say," said Heid. Faint as her voice was, it held power.

Vigdis stood firm. "Mistress, you must stay in bed."

The völva scowled. "Then get some men in here to carry this cursed bed into the bower hall. Loki knows what you have been getting up to while I wasn't there to supervise."

Vigdis's expression softened. "Very well. If you promise to stay in bed."

"Just get me in there."

An apprentice scurried off and returned leading four burly men, their eyes wide with apprehension at entering the women's forbidden domain. They hoisted the bed, sorceress and all, and lugged it toward the door.

"Careful, you oafs! I'm not a bale of hay. One more bump and I'll make your peckers fall off."

The big men tiptoed through the door with the bed, while the apprentices scurried alongside.

As soon as they were inside the room, the bearers set the bed down and headed for the door.

"Not here, you fools! Closer to the fire. No, not that close! Are you trying to scorch me?"

While the big men jockeyed the bed, the apprentices tucked blankets and plumped pillows. At last the sorceress was satisfied. She lay back on the pillows, her face as white as goose down.

"Leave us," said Vigdis, and the men hurried outside in relief. She fetched some broth and brought a spoonful to the völva's mouth. Heid turned her head away, mouth firmly closed. "Mistress, you must eat."

"Let me," said Åsa. "You need to rest too. I'll make sure she gets it down." She turned to Heid. "Won't I?" she said in a voice that brooked no argument. Vigdis heaved a sigh and handed her the bowl.

Heid grinned up at her. "How can I deny an order from my queen? I'll eat if you tell me everything that happened." The sorceress opened her mouth and let Åsa spoon some broth in.

"Onar's arrow hit you in the back," said Åsa. "You were prepared to trade yourself for Halfdan."

"That boy has a destiny," said the völva. "From him will come the king who will one day unite this land and put an end to all the wars." Åsa had heard this prophecy before. It was the reason Heid stayed on Tromøy to watch over Halfdan.

"Hrafn threatened Halfdan," said Åsa, "but the wolf turned on Hrafn and killed him instead. Since, then, the wolf has never left Halfdan's side."

"The creature abandoned the old sorcerer and switched his allegiance to the boy," said Heid with satisfaction.

Åsa's eyes widened. "Did you have something to do with that?"

Heid scoffed. "Nonsense. How could I? I was unconscious. The boy's hamingja was stronger than the old man's, and it drew the wolf to him. Halfdan has great power, young as he is." She shook her head. "I'm sorry for Brenna."

Åsa's shoulders sagged. "It was my fault. Halfdan was kidnapped and Toki murdered because I broke my promise to the haugbui."

"Don't be foolish. It was none of her doing. That ancient ghoul had no control over Hrafn. And she's not powerful enough to take away your hamingja, nor Halfdan's, no matter what she told you. The boy's alive, isn't he? That proves it."

Åsa doubted that the haugbui was as powerless as Heid claimed, but she was unable to argue with the völva's logic.

She shook her head. "Have it your way. Now, keep your side of the bargain. Finish the broth."

"I will," said Heid. "But you must promise to send that Irish necklace away."

"You owe it your life." *And Halfdan's too.* If it wasn't Heid's power that saved her son, then it might have been the necklace. She felt its comforting presence in her belt pouch.

She silenced Heid by bringing the spoon to the völva's mouth.

CHAPTER 16

Jól, December, AD 822

As the winter settled in, Heid regained her strength and resumed her duties. Her querulous voice emanated from the bower hall, bullying her apprentices at the same volume as before.

Åsa called Ragnhild, Murchad, Jarl Borg, Svein, Thorgeir, Einar, and Olvir to a council of war. The völva barged her way in uninvited.

"Ragnhild, have you developed a plan for taking Gausel?" Åsa asked.

The shield-maiden nodded reflectively. "I have given it much thought and have some ideas. All the waterways to Gausel pass by Solbakk. It's impossible to approach by sea without Harald's knowledge. But there are other ways to get to Gausel, out of sight of Solbakk." She looked at Einar. "We have the knowledge to work out another approach."

"That's a good start," said Jarl Borg.

Murchad spoke up. "We will take the necklace back to Ireland first."

"Good idea," said Heid.

Panic rose in Åsa at the thought of giving the necklace up. If she did, she'd be defenseless against the haugbui. For a moment, she could find no words.

Fortunately, Ragnhild objected. "It's too risky to go to Ireland before we secure Gausel. After we establish ourselves, we can plan a voyage to Ireland. For now, we'll leave the necklace here with Åsa."

Murchad's face reddened. "I can't leave a treasure of my people in foreign hands." He turned to Åsa. "No offense, Lady. I know it's safe with you."

"I don't understand why you're so eager to return it to your ungrateful countrymen," said Ragnhild. "They deposed you, remember? You owe them nothing. Besides, the necklace is far safer with Åsa than with us on this voyage. With all the risks we'll run and the battles we'll have to fight, there's a great chance that it will end up Harald's war prize and never be returned to Ireland."

Åsa cleared her throat. "Ragnhild is right. I will keep it safe for you while you win Gausel and establish a secure foothold."

The others murmured their agreement. All but Heid.

Murchad's eyes were stormy, but he said no more. Clearly, he realized he'd get no further at this time. Åsa's shoulders relaxed and she quickly ended the meeting before the subject could come up again.

Training resumed in the yard. Murchad still made no appearance, and Åsa worried. She knew what it was like to be among strangers. Ragnhild threw herself into training the recruits and barely seemed to notice her husband's absence.

After a week of drilling in rigid shield walls, one morning Borg shouted, "Break up!" The experienced warriors pulled their shields away from their neighbors' and charged the opposing line, leaving the new recruits on their own. Instantly, the orderly rows disintegrated and side fights erupted, with all the confusion of real battle. The recruits recovered quickly and dashed into the melee.

They were hard at it when an eerie shriek split the air and Svartfaxi hurtled into the fray, Murchad clinging to his back, armed with a javelin-length stick and shield. Screaming Irish battle cries, he lashed down on the foot soldiers with his stick. In a few moments he'd knocked four recruits off their feet and galloped away, leaving the experienced warriors thrusting their poles at thin air.

Jarl Borg raised a shaggy eyebrow and watched with interest.

Murchad wheeled his horse and swooped in for another attack. Though he owned a chain mail brynja and helmet, the Irishman wore only his battle jacket and tight-fitting trews, like a berserker. He rode bareback in Irish style, gripping a single, braided leather rein attached to the top of the horse's noseband and led back over the horse's forehead through a ring on the brow band.

"That rein," Åsa said to Jarl Borg. "That's what he's been working on in the evenings. Look, he's maneuvering without reins—using his legs and the butt of his spear to direct the horse. He must have been training that horse all this time."

"I think we can learn a thing or two from this Irishman," Jarl Borg murmured thoughtfully. "Flexibility is the key to success. All the formations in the world turn worthless when disaster strikes."

"His fighting style could be very useful in the right circumstances," Åsa agreed.

That evening when they gathered in the hall, Jarl Borg approached Murchad. "I'm very interested in your techniques. Would you be willing to teach them to us?"

"I would," said Murchad, his green eyes glowing with satisfaction. He raised his voice. "None of you Norse know how to fight on horseback. I can beat you all at that."

"Except me," Ragnhild said, raising her chin.

Murchad met her challenging look. "You learned from the best. But you've never beaten me, *a mhuirin*."

"That's because I've never tried—but I'll bet I can."

"I'll take that bet."

"You've spent weeks training your horse," said Ragnhild. "And you have a special way with them."

Murchad shrugged. "No more than any Irishman. But to make the wager fair, I will help you train your horse."

In the morning, the practice yard was cleared of snow and the warriors gathered around the rim. Ragnhild and Murchad appeared on their horses, carrying practice sticks. Neither wore armor. Ragnhild rode her horse, Hofvarpnir, named after the mount of the messenger goddess Gna, a horse that could fly and walk on water.

"This should be interesting," Jarl Borg said to Åsa. She wondered how Murchad's lingering anger at Ragnhild over the necklace would affect his performance. This promised to be a grudge match between the couple.

Murchad and Ragnhild walked their horses toward each other, murmuring encouraging words to their mounts. Murchad waved his practice spear slowly over Svartfaxi's head so that the horse could glimpse the pole in his peripheral vision. He brushed the stick over Svartfaxi's ears, tapped the horse lightly on his neck and shoulder, all the while murmuring praise and encouragement. Hofvarpnir watched with suspicion, ears flicking. Ragnhild patted the horse's neck and let her sniff the stick, then mimicked Murchad's actions.

Gradually Murchad and Ragnhild approached each other. When the horses were within spear's length, Murchad reached his pole out and tapped Ragnhild's gently. He showed nothing but pure patience. Ragnhild tapped his shield in return. The horses nickered, but they remained calm.

"Well, this is a bit dull," said Ursa. "When are they going to fight?" She and several other young warriors wandered off.

Ragnhild and Murchad continued slowly over the next few days, approaching each other on horseback at a walk, tapping their sticks on shields and flanks. Murchad did not appear upset in any way, but rather displayed infinite patience with the horses and his wife. Ragnhild's focus was absolute, letting nothing interfere with her concentration.

Over the next several days, their mounts' gaits evolved from a walk to a canter. The horses grew accustomed to Ragnhild and Murchad trading blows with wooden swords and hurling javelins. Murchad brought in a few foot warriors, who shouted and waved weapons until the horses could enter an infantry melee without fear, though they would never charge a shield wall. He hung bloody rags from the saddle, so their mounts could become accustomed to the scent of blood.

Murchad had Hogni bring a goat into the ring and slaughter it while they practiced. The horses shied at the death-cries, nostrils flaring, but Ragnhild and Murchad managed to calm them. Once the horses had settled down, they circled the goat's carcass, treading through the blood.

Finally Murchad deemed their mounts ready for the match. Åsa announced it at the evening meal. Soon everyone in the hall was laying wagers on Ragnhild or Murchad. The shield-maiden was the favorite, but some had noticed Murchad's skill with horses and laid silver on the long shot.

In the morning, the two of them appeared on opposite ends of the practice field, wearing their helmets and armor. Murchad rode Svartfaxi bareback, with his single rein. He carried a shield and a light javelin, his practice sword on his belt. Ragnhild rode Hofvarpnir with a Norse saddle and stirrups, dual reins in one hand, bearing a heavy spear shaft the same length as the one her husband held, as well as a practice sword. They drew rein, facing each other across the field.

Jarl Borg gave them a few moments to settle, then rose and shouted, "Charge!"

They kicked their horses into a canter and hurtled across the field at each other. Murchad held his javelin cocked over-arm while Ragnhild gripped her spear under her arm, tight to her body. Åsa tensed, waiting for Murchad's repressed fury to surface.

As they closed, Murchad flung his javelin at Ragnhild. She dodged it while reaching out to jab him with her longer spear. She made contact with his ribs as he swept past.

"Murchad's throw was good, but she has better reach and more control with that long spear," the old jarl observed.

They wheeled their horses, Murchad's mount responding to the pressure of his legs alone. He drew his sword and charged Ragnhild. She dropped the tied reins across Hofvarpnir's neck, directing the horse with her legs while she held her opponent off with her spear—until he managed to break it in half with a sharp blow from his practice sword. Åsa caught her breath as Murchad swung his blade, but Ragnhild got her sword up to meet it. They hacked away at each other, neither gaining the advantage. Though Murchad's attacks were strategic and forceful, Ragnhild evaded his blows with lightning reflexes, and the wild courage of her counterattacks enabled her to score a few hits.

Murchad's extra time training Svartfaxi paid off as the horse responded nimbly to his shifting weight and leg pressure. Ragnhild's stirrups provided her the leverage to deliver harder blows to her husband, gave her better balance, and enabled her to brace against his onslaught, but she let the reins rest on Hofvarpnir's neck during battle and resorted to leg pressure to handle the horse.

They traded blows, Murchad dodging Ragnhild's heavy sword deftly while scoring light hits on her. As the fight went on,

Åsa tensed, reading the frustration in the set of Murchad's shoulders as he jabbed at his wife in vain. Ragnhild's blows were becoming sloppy. They were both getting tired. One of them might make a mistake—a mistake that could result in serious injury.

Then Ragnhild swung her sword in a clumsy arc. Murchad's block came an instant too slow and her sword hit his arm with numbing force. His hand opened and it looked like he would drop his sword, but at the last moment his fingers grabbed the hilt.

Murchad's face whitened in pain and fury. He swung his sword at his wife. This time it was she whose guard was down and eyes went wide as Murchad's sword flew at her head.

Åsa watched the Irishman jerk the sword back just before it hit Ragnhild's head. The force flung him forward on Svartfaxi's neck and the horse sidled, snorting in alarm.

Ragnhild clutched Hofvarpnir's reins, eyes wide in her blanched face.

Jarl Borg was already on his feet to end the match. The tension drained out of Åsa as her respect for Murchad's skill and endurance rose.

Jarl Borg strode onto the field, applauding. "I call a draw. You've demonstrated both methods have their advantages. If you combined Murchad's techniques with the use of saddle and stirrups, you would be unbeatable."

Ragnhild and Murchad looked at each other, aghast at what had nearly happened. They both slid off their mounts and led them to the stables in silence.

After their match, Murchad and Ragnhild had no trouble recruiting twenty of Tromøy's best horsemen to fight from horseback, including Åsa, Olvir, Einar, Thorgeir, and Svein. Ursa insisted on being included. "With this face, I'd better become a famous shield-maiden."

The couple trained together, but they seemed distant toward

each other. Åsa wished she could think of a way to break the invisible wall between them.

Gradually, Murchad and Jarl Borg brought the cavalry and the infantry together. The horsemen practiced ambushing unmounted warriors, skirmishing and then scattering before their victims could form a cohesive attack. The infantry learned to quickly form shield walls that sent the horses sheering off. They practiced attacking horsemen, trying to drag them from the saddle.

~

AS THE WINTER SOLSTICE APPROACHED, training stopped and all of Tromøy prepared for the long Jól holiday of feasting, drinking, and sports.

The pond had frozen deep enough, and the Norse cleared it of snow. They strapped cow bone skates to their boots and took to the ice, playing games that gave them strength and skill.

Skates were new to Murchad and at first he refused to participate. He didn't need to make a fool of himself and lose what respect he'd gained.

"Afraid of a few bumps and bruises, old man?" Ragnhild teased him, coming off the frozen lake to catch her breath on the log where he sat.

Shooting a glare in her direction, he said, "Very well, show me."

With a fiendish grin, Ragnhild strapped a pair of carved cow bones to his shoes and pulled him to his feet. She handed him a spear and demonstrated, digging her spear point into the ice and propelling herself along.

Murchad gamely dug his own spear tip in and shoved. As he lifted his spear, he wobbled, windmilling his arms wildly, and sprawled onto the ice. Laughing, Ragnhild helped him up. "It takes a few tries to get the hang of it. But you fall like an expert!"

Murchad kept trying, falling so often that day Ragnhild had to help him hobble back to the hall. In spite of the pain and humiliation, he forced himself onto the ice the next morning. After a few days spent mostly sliding on his butt, he succeeded in keeping to his feet for a short time.

The Norse, who learned to walk and skate at the same time, showed their Irish guest no mercy. Even the farmers were skilled at skating, and they were all much younger than him. Their games were rough and every time he managed to stay on his feet a few moments, one of them would barrel into him and send him crashing onto the ice, with a chuckled "Sorry, old man!" as they whizzed by.

Murchad woke each morning so bruised that Ragnhild had to help him out of bed, yet he insisted on returning to the ice. "You think it's funny, all you Norse. The day will come when I'll make you sorry."

Murchad had always excelled at games. He set his jaw and kept at it, picking himself up time and again. *I may be older than most of them, but I'm also wilier.*

As he found his balance, he continued pretending to flail and stumble on the ice while he systematically began to take his revenge on each of his tormentors—tripping one with a well-placed spear, body-slamming another, always with an apologetic laugh. Soon he was the one administering the bruises, and the Norse began to give him a wide berth.

~

HALF A DOZEN WARRIORS dragged the great Jól log into the hall and laid it on the longfire where it would burn throughout the twelve-day festival. Ulf carved its bark with runes. The women sang over it while Åsa kindled the fire with a piece saved from last years' Jól log.

Heid marked the eve of the solstice, when the veil between the worlds was thin and Odin led the spirits of the dead on the wild hunt. The living gathered in the hall where the longfire blazed and all the lamps were lit against the dark. Stories of the dead were told in hushed voices. That night, they left the great hall empty, the boards laid with a meal and the sleeping-benches vacated so the dead could have one night among the living. Those who normally slept in the hall bedded down in the guest house.

Brenna now slept in the bower with Åsa, to help her forget that Toki was no longer with her. Åsa lay listening to the fóstra's even breathing, thinking about the queen in her mound, waiting for the sacrifice that would never come. What new mischief would the haugbui make? Fear rose in her chest, threatening to choke her. She kept her hand on the necklace all night long, letting its power soothe her.

When morning came, she shook off her fears and dressed hurriedly. Today was the quest for the oath boar. She threw open the door and joined the crowd gathered in the yard. Eager dogs strained at their leashes while the hunters sharpened their boar spears. As soon as the sky lightened, the party set off into the silent forest where branches dripped with frigid mist.

The dogs picked up a scent and raised a ruckus. As soon as they were unleashed they crashed into the snow-laden undergrowth. The hunters followed, spears at the ready.

The hounds began to give tongue, chasing their quarry through the brush, then suddenly stopped. Åsa glimpsed the boar as it stood at bay, black against the snow, snout low to the ground, ears laid back. The creature clashed its tusks to sharpen them.

It pricked up its ears and rolled its eyes, then took two steps toward its tormenters. The dogs leaped, their powerful jaws latching onto the boar's ears. The boar thrashed its head and charged, dragging the dogs through the snow.

Olvir forced his way into the mob. He grabbed the boar by its rear leg and wrenched it onto its side. The creature flailed and bellowed while Einar came forward and lashed the hind legs together. Murchad darted in under the thrashing tusks to grip the forelegs while Svein tied them.

They bound writhing beast to a sledge while Heid's apprentices forced a calming potion down its throat. The four men towed the trussed boar back to the hall, excited dogs and hunters following in their wake.

By the time they reached the hall, the drug had begun to take effect. The húskarlar untied the boar and manhandled it into the hall. The hunting party stomped in after them, shaking snow from their cloaks. The boar's tusks gleamed in the firelight and, despite the calming potion, the red eyes shone with hate. Cheers rang in the rafters as the warriors paraded the staggering creature around the longfire.

One by one, each of Åsa's warriors and jarls laid their hands on its quivering hide and renewed their oaths to her. Even Murchad swore the pagan oath.

Åsa filled the silver-chased drinking horn with mead, and rose to circle the fire in blessing. She toasted the gods, and the nobles passed the great horn around the room, drinking it dry. The kitchen staff stepped forward to fill everyone's cup, and everyone rose and shouted, "To Åsa, Queen, long may she rule!"

Now Åsa handed out gifts to the oath takers: silver rings, horse harnesses, fine armor and weaponry. To Murchad she presented a gilded bridle that would look fine flashing against Svartfaxi's dark hide. To Ragnhild, she presented two of the captured Danish ships. "They'll need work, but they're seaworthy and battle-tested."

Ragnhild rose. "I thank you, Lady. A better gift I could never dream of. The steading of Gausel is my inheritance, but my brother, Harald, withholds it from me. I ventured to Ireland to prove my worth, yet Harald tricked me and left me behind, a prisoner. Long have I dreamed of taking what is mine, yet still my brother holds it. Now, with my husband at my side, I will claim my home at last. I hope that many of you will volunteer to sail with me in the spring." Ragnhild approached the seething boar and laid her hands upon its bristles. The great room was silent except for the Jól fire's crackle. "I swear by the gods that I will take Gausel, or die trying. Who will sail with me in the spring?"

A cheer rose up from the benches and many volunteered to join Ragnhild's crew.

After the roar died down, toasts were made to the memory of departed kinfolk. They drank to Toki, to Helga, and all those lost. Åsa toasted her mother, her father, and her brother Gyrd.

The húskarlar led the oath boar back outside the hall where they tethered it beneath the enormous ash tree. The citizens of Tromøy gathered to watch their queen perform the sacrifice to the female spirits who watched over them, the dísir.

The boar stood quietly now, under the full effect of Heid's herbs. Åsa unsheathed her ceremonial knife and approached the animal, crooning the chant. She knelt and placed her hand gently on the boar's throat to locate the artery, then drew her knife over it swiftly. She eased the animal to the ground as Vigdis stepped in to catch the spray of blood in a brass bowl. Åsa took the brimming bowl and anointed the worshipers.

The women of Tromøy sang the vardlokkur to call the spirits while the men formed a protective circle around them. Heid mounted the seidr platform and seated herself in her chair of prophecy. She raised her voice in prayer to the spirits to let her see the future of Tromøy and its people.

She closed her eyes and fell silent for a long time. When the sorceress opened her eyes, her gaze went first to Åsa.

"I see success in your undertakings in the new year, Lady," she said. "There will be new happiness for you. But there is also danger. There is something left undone, and it will come back to haunt you."

Åsa shivered at her words of warning. Could they refer to the queen in the mound? Her hand strayed to her leather belt-pouch, where the golden necklace lay solid and potent beneath her touch.

Heid turned to Ragnhild. "You, Lady, have hard battles ahead of you, and their outcome is far from certain. Be careful, for in gaining what you desire, you may lose what you hold dear."

Ragnhild's smile died on her lips and she sobered. "I will be declaring war on my own family," she murmured to Murchad.

"I know how much that hurts, *a chroi,*" he said.

That evening they feasted, and afterward the company entertained themselves with new riddles and old legends until late into the night.

After everyone had stumbled off to bed, Murchad slipped away from the festivities to celebrate Christ's Mass in his own way, alone beneath the trees.

In the bower, Åsa lay awake, thinking of the queen waiting in her mound.

~

Solbakk

SIGNY WAS SAMPLING the Jól ale when she felt the water run down her leg. Panic filled her, but she calmed herself and called to her women.

"The baby's coming," she said.

Old Katla, her ancient fóstra, hobbled over, a gleam in her faded eyes. Signy relaxed and a feeling of security descended. The old woman had delivered all of Solvi's children, and raised them after their mother's death.

The other women clustered around, babbling excitedly but

taking hold of Signy with sure hands. They led her to the bower and bustled about in preparation.

Harald burst in. The women stared at him disapprovingly. Male intrusion was frowned upon in the birthing room.

Brushing past the women, he knelt beside her bed and clutched her arm as if his grasp could keep her alive. A worried boy looked out of the fierce warrior's face.

Signy smiled reassuringly. "I'm in good hands."

"What if—what…" He couldn't say it.

Old Katla sidled up and put a bony hand on his shoulder. "You must leave us, Lord."

"Promise me one thing," Signy said.

"Anything." Desperation burned in his eyes.

"Promise me that if it's a girl, she'll be called Ragnhild."

Harald's jaw dropped in consternation. The worried boy vanished and the warrior scowled. "I'm not naming our child after my—enemy!"

"It's proper to name the first girl after your sister. And you may not always feel as you do now. Promise me," Signy said in a honeyed tone. She winced as a contraction took her unawares.

Harald looked wildly around at the women, who waited expectantly. "Very well!"

Signy sighed as the contraction eased. She patted his hand. "Now go. We have work to do."

The women hurried him out of the room as the next contraction took her.

CHAPTER 17

Solbakk

T he infant girl wailed as the women washed her. They dried
her and wrapped her in fine linen cloth, then a wool blanket, and handed her to her mother.

Signy took her daughter and cooed until the baby stopped
crying. "You must behave with dignity before your father," Signy
said. The child had survived nine nights, and today she would be
presented to Harald, for him to accept her or reject her to be cast
out in the woods.

The ritual was little more than a formality. This girl was their
first child, and there was no question that Harald would accept
his daughter. Still, Signy's heart beat fast and she clutched her
baby close as she followed her women out the bower door.

They entered the great hall, crowded with her husband's
sworn men, and the bonders and jarls who owed him homage.
Harald sat upon his high seat, eyeing his wife as she carried their
daughter toward him.

As she reached the high seat, Signy stopped before her husband. She unwrapped the child's coverings and laid the baby naked on his knees. "Husband," she said, "our daughter has survived nine nights. She is healthy and whole. I ask you now to accept her, to sprinkle her with water and give her a name."

Harald stared down at the little girl in fascination. She blinked up at him and smiled, flinging her tiny arms.

The local sorceress stood beside the high seat, holding a bowl of water from the holy spring. She cleared her throat and gave Harald a discreet nudge.

He woke from the spell his daughter had cast over him, dipped his fingers in the bowl and sprinkled the baby with water.

The child blinked as the water hit her face, but she didn't cry.

Harald smiled. "I accept my daughter. Let her be called..." He looked over at his wife, her gaze expectant. He scowled. "...Ragnhild."

The baby smiled, and Harald gazed at her in utter enchantment.

The völva took the seat of honor. While the women chanted, she cast herbs onto a brazier and inhaled the fumes deeply. Her head lolled as the trance came upon her.

Signy tensed.

The völva's eyes flew open. She sat straight up and fixed the baby with a stern gaze. "This child has a great destiny," she declared. "She will be the mother of kings, and her progeny will do great deeds."

Signy exhaled. Her eyes met Harald's and they exchanged a smile.

❧

Tromøy

After Jól, Åsa drove her sleigh to the winter market in Skiringssal. She was glad to be out of the dark hall and in the clean, bracing winter air. Beside her, Halfdan slept in Brenna's arms, and Olvir led a contingent of men driving sledges loaded with soapstone quarried from the hillsides of Agder, smelted bog iron, finely woven and dyed wool, and axeheads, speartips, tools, and fittings produced in Ulf's smithy.

The wolf loped along beside the sleigh. Halfdan had aptly named him Fylgja, since he followed the boy everywhere. In spite of his blindness, Fylgja had no trouble keeping up and his sense of smell and hearing drew him unerringly to his tiny master's side.

The winter night had fallen by the time they arrived at Skiringssal, and they found their way to the hall by torchlight. Åsa spotted Olaf waiting at the door, blond hair glinting in the firelight. A familiar pang plucked at her heart when she looked into his hazel eyes, glimpsing her own regret reflected in them. She took a breath and returned his welcoming smile. Halfdan reached his chubby arms out and tried to squirm out of the sleigh.

Brenna passed Halfdan to her and she set the boy on the ground. He ran to Olaf and wrapped his arms around the tall man's legs.

Åsa climbed down from the sleigh, handing the reins to the waiting stable boy. He cowered at the sight of the wolf. "He's friendly," Åsa assured him. To prove it, she put out her hand and Fylgja sniffed, then licked it.

"Isn't that Hrafn's wolf?" said Olaf.

Åsa nodded. "He was. Hrafn's dead," she said shortly. "The wolf has bonded with Halfdan."

Olaf stared at her for a moment. "Well, I'm glad to hear that evil wizard's finally dead." To her relief, Olaf didn't pursue the matter. Perhaps he realized she didn't want to relive the incident. "We have a new winter guest," Olaf continued, picking up his son. "I can't wait for you to meet him. He's a Svea trader, and he's come from the Eastern lands."

Åsa smiled uncertainly, not sure why Olaf's tone held such enthusiasm.

"He has a cargo of wootz," said Olaf.

Åsa caught her breath. Wootz steel yielded the finest swords in the world, swords that held an edge and never broke, but its manufacture was a closely guarded secret and it could only be obtained in the distant Serkland. Their previous supplier of the rare metal, a trader named Bjorn, had retired from long-distance travel. He said he was rich enough and now wanted to settle down and raise a family, far from the dangers and excitement of foreign travel. Tromøy's blacksmith, Ulf, had forged the last of his wootz ingots and waited eagerly for more.

Olaf put the squirming Halfdan down and let him run ahead of them, the wolf on his heels. "Sonja's waiting for you in the bower. She's eager to see you and Halfdan."

Åsa hurried after her son. She still wore her trews and tunic under her furs—her gown for the evening was packed in her chest, along with her sword and helmet. The men would lug it up to the bower.

Sonja was waiting at the bower door. She gave a happy cry and scooped Halfdan into her arms. "So good to see you. Come, sit, and tell me all your news. Rognvald has grown even more since you were last here."

Åsa felt a rush of warmth for her. Sonja was always so happy to see her and Halfdan.

The wolf curled up outside the door while Sonja pulled her guests inside. Soon Åsa was seated by the fire with a cup of ale in her hand, and she launched into the tale of Toki's murder and Halfdan's abduction.

"You're so brave," Sonja exclaimed.

"You'd do the same to save Rognvald."

Sonja gazed down fiercely on her sleeping son. "Yes, I would."

Åsa had no doubt.

~

THAT EVENING, Åsa dressed in her fine red wool gown trimmed with tablet weaving at the cuffs, neckline, and hem. None of the handiwork was hers—Tromøy had far more skilled weavers than she—though she presided over the weaving ceremonies where the fine work was created. This gown had been woven, sewn, and trimmed by Heid's apprentices. The tablet weaving was infused with silver threads and galdr chants to give Åsa power and victory, peace and plenty. Though Åsa led those chants along with the sorceress Heid, she did not participate in the weaving itself. She focused on running the kingdom, seeing to the livestock and crops, the defense, and trading the wealth of Agder for such things as they could not get for themselves. Furs and walrus ivory from the far north, wheat from Daneland, amber from the Eastern Sea, the all-important combs fashioned from antler, spoons carved from horn.

Sonja escorted Åsa to the guest seat, then turned back to meet the newcomer at the door. A handsome man. He was not as tall as Olaf, but broad-shouldered and slim-hipped, and he walked with a confident grace. Åsa thought he was perhaps in his late twenties. His hair and beard were glossy brown, freshly washed, and his beard trimmed neatly. His eyes glowed the vivid blue of glacier ice in a face tanned from days in the sun. Squint-lines at the corners of his eyes made him look like he was perpetually laughing.

The Svea trader wore a soft blue tunic that accentuated his eyes. The tunic was trimmed in silk weaving far finer than anything seen in Vestfold. Silver rings glinted on his neck and arms. A man of wealth.

His gaze flicked over to Åsa and lingered. She returned his look with a smile. He nodded to her as Sonja led him to the guest seat beside her.

"Åsa Haraldsdottir, Queen of Tromøy," said Sonja, "please meet Eyvind Arneson. He's the son of Jarl Arne of Alsike, in Svealand."

"Second son," added Eyvind. He bowed to Åsa before he took his seat. "Honored to meet you, Åsa, Queen. I'm but a landless trader, and my ship is my kingdom."

"A sea-king," said Åsa.

"If you will," Eyvind replied.

She was eager to find out about the wootz steel. "I am told you have traded in the East," she began.

"Yes, I have traveled to Bolghar and beyond, as far south as Serkland."

"Olaf tells me that you trade in wootz steel," said Åsa, unable to hide the eagerness in her voice. So much for clever negotiation. The truth was, she'd pay almost any price to get more of the ingots.

"Yes, I picked some up in Serkland and have been hauling it around for months with no takers. Everyone's afraid of trying to forge it. It's tricky to work. I've heard that you have a blacksmith who knows how to handle it."

Åsa was surprised that he was so forthcoming about not finding a buyer. Not the cagey trader she expected. She relaxed and decided to respond in kind. "I am so glad you have brought it so far. You are correct, my blacksmith on Tromøy is skilled in forging wootz."

Eyvind leaned forward in his seat. "Where did he learn the technique?"

"In Serkland," Åsa said shortly. She wasn't sure how much she wanted this man to know about Ulf. "He'd be overjoyed if I brought home some wootz ingots for him."

"Perhaps we can arrange a trade—if your smith could forge me a sword in exchange for the cargo of wootz."

"That may be acceptable," said Åsa, realizing this would entail

Eyvind's visit to Tromøy. And she realized that she wouldn't mind that. "You would be welcome in my hall."

"Very well. Perhaps when we finish our business here, we could travel to your home in company?"

"Yes, that would be fine."

Eyvind turned to Olaf. "May I impose on you to lend me a sleigh for the trip?"

Åsa glanced at Olaf and was surprised to see his face contorted in a scowl like thunder. Could he be jealous? He had no right to be. She frowned, and watched him marshal his countenance. In an instant, the storm cleared and he smiled. "Yes, of course."

Åsa listened while Eyvind and Olaf traded tales of their travels in the Eastern lands. She had been raised on her father's and Ulf's stories of Serkland, and she never tired of hearing about the far-off place. She tried to imagine a land where it was always warm and snow was unknown, where silk was as common as wool, and flowers bloomed all year round. She'd always longed to visit the Eastern lands, but it seemed that her life had no room for such a journey.

Eyvind's gaze strayed to her often, and lingered while Olaf told his tales. His attention suffused Åsa with a warmth of anticipation. She was looking forward to spending more time with him.

That night she settled into Sonja's bed in the women's bower with Halfdan. Sonja tucked her infant son into the cradle that hung from the rafters, then climbed into the great bed beside her guests.

"Eyvind seems to be attracted to you," she said.

"He's interested in trading his wootz," Åsa replied complacently. But as she snuggled next to her son beneath the eiderdown, a tiny thrill of anticipation bubbled inside.

Two days passed while Åsa traded her soapstone, bog iron,

woven cloth, and tools for new combs of reindeer antler and furs from the North. Eyvind seemed to find reasons to linger near her, and his presence sent little tingles through her.

Åsa was ready to depart before dawn on the third day, her sledges loaded with furs and antler. Eyvind followed in the sleigh Olaf had supplied. The dull gray ingots of wootz steel were stacked and lashed securely beneath a hide. The snow made the trip smooth and the sleighs seemed to fly as the horses raced along the trail, the blind wolf keeping pace. They reached the ferry landing just before dark.

Once on the island, they navigated the woodland track by torchlight. Upon pulling into the yard, Åsa dropped Halfdan and the wolf with Brenna at the hall and guided Eyvind straight to the smithy. "I can't wait to see Ulf's expression."

They found him working in the glow of the forge, his hammer sending sparks flying. He laid down his hammer as the sleighs pulled up.

Åsa could barely contain her excitement as she hopped down from her sleigh. "Ulf, this is Eyvind, a Svea trader. He has a surprise for you."

The old blacksmith's eyes lit up when Eyvind lifted the hide and revealed the gray metal cakes.

"I understand you learned to forge the wootz while you were in the East," said Eyvind.

"I was enslaved to the greatest swordmaker in Damascus," said Ulf. "He must be dead by now."

"But in the East, a swordmaker's slaves are never freed—they work them until they die, taking their secrets to the grave," said Eyvind.

"You have the right of it," said Ulf. "My master didn't intend for me to survive. He crippled my legs so I couldn't escape."

"Like Völund," said Eyvind, naming the smith-magician of legend. Ulf looked pleased by the comparison.

Eyvind leaned forward in his seat. "How did you escape such a fate?"

"Åsa's father," said Ulf, "King Harald—he was not king then, but the leader of our expedition. He wouldn't leave without me. He rescued me and nearly lost his life in doing so."

Eyvind looked to Åsa with admiration. "Your father must have been a great man."

"He was." She bit back the grief that rose up in her throat. Fortunately, the conversation veered to metallurgy, giving her time to recover. When she had mastered her emotions, she said, "Ulf, I must see to the cooks. Will you show Eyvind to the guest-house so that he may refresh himself?"

The blacksmith nodded absently. Åsa left the two men deep in conversation about metals and smithing techniques. She hurried to the hall where preparations were already in motion for the evening meal. She ensured that it included the finest of their smoked meat, porridge, and skyr as well as some of their precious stored root vegetables, then retired to her bower room to change. Brenna had already laid out one of her best dresses.

While the fóstra arranged Åsa's hair, she said, "He's a handsome man."

"An interesting one," Åsa replied. "He's traveled all over the Eastern lands. His stories are fascinating."

Brenna grinned. "I think you are fascinated by more than his stories."

Åsa fussed with her jewelry to hide her blush. As soon as Brenna turned her loose, she hurried to the great hall and took her place on the high seat. She forced herself to sit serenely while Vigdis ushered Eyvind to the guest seat.

Once Vigdis had served the welcome ale and they had drunk toasts all around, the Svea merchant rose and presented a linen-wrapped package to Åsa. "Lady, please accept this small token from distant Serkland."

She opened the wrapping and caught her breath at the length of vivid blue silk that lay folded within.

"It's one of the rarest colors," he said with pride. "And it matches your eyes."

Åsa hoped her blush didn't show in the dim firelight. "You are most generous, Lord Eyvind. I will be the envy of all women." She folded the silk and set it beside her. "Please, I am sure you have many more tales to tell us about your travels."

Eyvind shot a glance at Murchad. "I understand that you have an Irishman in your household. I haven't traveled to Ireland, but I'm very interested in it."

"I'll bet you are," Murchad said under his breath. Åsa stiffened, hoping her guest hadn't heard. Aloud, Murchad said, "It's a long journey from here, and the route is infested with pirates. We fought off an attack in the Orkney Isles."

"I'm glad you were the victors." Eyvind shrugged. "Pirates are an occupational hazard in my business. It seems that a trip to Ireland might be worthwhile. Tell me, do you have a need for silver or gold? I know that Irish workmanship is some of the finest in the world, but I've heard you lack for precious metal."

"That's true," Murchad allowed. "We have become expert at gilding base metals."

"Perhaps your countrymen would welcome some silver dirhams."

"Yes, they may," said Murchad cautiously.

"Perhaps we could discuss the sea route while I'm here."

Murchad said, "I'm not eager to send strangers to my homeland. Traders so often become raiders, and the Irish always seem to fall prey. Hundreds of my countrymen have been killed or enslaved."

Åsa frowned. Murchad had a right to be cautious, but these were bordering on fighting words. She quickly changed the subject. "Eyvind has brought us wootz steel. Ulf is thrilled."

From the benches, the blacksmith grinned and raised his horn in a toast.

"Our guest has sailed all over the East, as far away as Serkland. Eyvind, you must tell us of these foreign lands."

Placated, the Svea settled back with his drinking horn. "The people in Serkland are dark of hair and eye. Their homes are very different from our dark halls. It is summer all year round, and they build their dwelling rooms around an open-air garden, filled with trees and flowers."

Eyvind continued. "The Serklanders are very learned. They are master falconers, and, as Ulf can attest, master weapons makers. Their techniques are kept with the upmost secrecy. Ulf here may be the only man alive outside of Serkland who knows their methods. Even the steel itself is manufactured in a secret location, using a closely guarded process known only to a few specialists. The Serklanders have silk in abundance and foods we have never tasted. Though it is summer year round in their lands, they prize our northern furs as symbols of their wealth and rank, and they'll trade almost anything they have for black fox pelts. That is how I got the wootz. I traded a load of black fox furs for it."

"What kind of fighters are they?" asked Einar.

"They are smaller in stature than we are, but fierce warriors, expert at fighting from horseback."

"The Irish, too, fight from horseback," said Murchad. "It would be fascinating to learn their techniques."

"They use a curved sword. The blades are the strongest, and sharpest, the best at holding an edge."

With a shudder, Åsa recalled the wicked, curved Serkland sword with which Gudrød had killed her father. Ulf had spent months forging her sword, Gudrød's Bane, which proved to be the equal of the Serkland sword when she killed Gudrød in a duel.

Though the evening ended on a friendly note, Murchad

avoided the Svea after that. Åsa didn't blame the Irishman. His country had long been beset by raiders in the guise of traders. Eyvind was amiable, but she sensed a thread of steel running through him. To have traveled so far, the man must have seen much danger and fought many battles.

As she said goodnight to her guest, she decided to invite him on an outing. "Tomorrow promises to be fair," she stammered. "Perhaps you would like to hunt?"

"I would like that very much," Eyvind replied.

"Good. Good. I will see you then." She hurried off, pleased but flustered.

The morning dawned sunny as Åsa had promised. Eyvind met her outside the hall and they donned skis. She settled Stormrider on her shoulder and they set out, Halfdan following on his tiny skis, the wolf lolloping along beside him.

"That's an interesting pet your son has," remarked Eyvind.

"Yes," Åsa replied.

"It's unusual for a wolf to be so tame."

Åsa nodded. "The wolf's blindness makes him tame. I think he's grateful to us for food and shelter. He's devoted to Halfdan— a very good protector." She hoped Eyvind wouldn't probe too deeply into that subject. She didn't know him well enough to tell him the story of Hrafn, to reveal her shapeshifting abilities.

"I can see that," he said. To Åsa's relief, Eyvind let the matter drop.

A hare broke cover and she set Stormrider on it. Watching the falcon stoop, Halfdan was beside himself with excitement. When they set out once again, however, the boy began to wobble on his skis and started to whine. "He's tired," said Åsa. "We should turn back."

Eyvind knelt down and said to Halfdan, "Would you like a ride home?"

Halfdan nodded vigorously.

"Let's take off your skis, then." Eyvind unlaced the little boy's skis and handed them to Åsa. He hoisted Halfdan onto his back and started out at a brisk pace, Åsa and the wolf scrambling to keep up. Tiredness forgotten, Halfdan shrieked with excitement all the way home.

The Svea stayed for a week while Ulf forged his sword. He spent quite a bit of time in the smithy, and Åsa found herself drawn to look in on the progress of the work.

Eyvind looked up as she entered the warm workshop. His gaze met hers and held across the blazing forge, his eyes as intense as the fire. She settled in beside him contentedly and watched. As a child, the smithy had been her favorite place. She loved the warmth of the forge, the smell of hot iron, the sparks that flew when Ulf hammered the steel. Eyvind's presence added to the excitement of the atmosphere. During Ulf's rest breaks, the two men traded stories of their travels to the East. Though Åsa had heard Ulf's tales before, she never tired of them, and Eyvind's stories gave her a new view into a great civilization. He told about their advanced navigation techniques and mapmaking, their libraries full of written knowledge, their wealth and skill.

All too soon, Ulf finished the blade. Once the pommel was fitted, Eyvind picked it up and swung it hurtling through the air. "It compares favorably to the Serkland swords," he said. "Light yet durable, flexible yet hard." He turned to Ulf. "You are a great master."

Ulf nodded, accepting the homage.

Eyvind turned to Åsa, regret evident in his eyes. "Now I fear I must depart. Spring is only a few weeks away, and I must hurry if I want to reach Serkland this year. It has been a great pleasure, Lady."

"The pleasure has been all mine," said Åsa truthfully. She was sad to see the Svea depart, yet also relieved. Eyvind made her feel unsettled in a way she hadn't felt in a long time. "I hope you will bring me more wootz in the fall."

"Indeed I shall, and I will deliver the ingots to you directly here, if I may."

"You're always welcome, as is your wootz steel."

Once Eyvind departed, Åsa threw herself back into training the troops. The winter was drawing to a close and before they knew it, it would be time for Ragnhild and Murchad to set sail for Gausel.

CHAPTER 18

Tromøy
April, AD 823

The full moon of April heralded the beginning of summer, just before the barley was planted. The inhabitants of Tromøy set to work getting Ragnhild's little fleet ready to sail to Gausel, *Raider Bride* and the two refurbished Danish ships. Ragnhild had named the Danish ships *Raven's Loot* and *Eagle's Treasure*, appropriate, considering how they'd been won.

Each of the three vessels would carry thirty rowers and five qualified helmsmen. From the veteran warriors and trainees, enough had volunteered to sail with Ragnhild to fully crew her ships.

Over the winter, they had repaired the sails and woven new ropes of walrus hide to replace halyards and shrouds. The recruits had sewed their padded battle jackets and coated them with varnish hard enough to deflect an arrow. They'd spent days in the smithy, helping Ulf forge their helmets and new spear tips for their practice shafts, refurbished their wooden shields, fletched arrows and notched bows.

Now that the snow had melted, they dragged the boats out of the boathouses and onto the beach where they set the pitch pots to boil. The smoke-filled air rang with the sound of hammers as they drove new wool roving between the planks and replaced rivets, then sealed the seams with pine tar.

"I thank you, Lady, for the Danish ships," Ragnhild told Åsa. "They will serve me well. The finest ships in the world are built near Gausel. After I take power, I will send you new ones. But I fear I'm taking too many of Tromøy's warriors."

"I managed to recruit a few more farmers over the winter," Åsa reassured her. "They will arrive as soon as planting is done on their family's farms. I should be able to pick up some experienced warriors at the Midsummer assembly, but as it is, I have enough trained fighters to deal with any raiders that might be foolish enough to attack us. The Danes are preoccupied with the Franks, and their own internal strife."

Åsa gathered a council to discuss Ragnhild's plans.

"Harald is expecting us, Ivar made sure of that," said Ragnhild. "If we take the sea route, his spies will see us coming. But we've come up with a strategy." Ragnhild nodded at her three húskarlar. "My brother will expect me to bring a fleet to take Gausel. Rather than sailing together under the eyes of Harald's spies, we will travel separately and make landfall on the western coast, at Solavika. It's far enough south of the entrance to the inland fjords that we should escape Harald's notice. We'll portage the ships overland to the Hrafrsfjord, then row across the fjord. All the ships will rendezvous on the eastern shore. From there we can easily reach Gausel on foot, leaving the fleet under guard."

"It's a good plan," said Einar. "We have a fair chance of getting past his spies undetected, and it gives us at least some element of surprise. But even with that advantage, three ships' crews will hardly stand up to Harald. He's bound to outnumber us."

Murchad said, "We won't fight him only on foot. If one of you will guide me, I'll bring a dozen trained horses and horsemen overland to meet the ships in Gausel."

"I'll guide you," said Svein. "I know the overland route well."

"I'll ride with you," said Ursa. The shield-maiden had become a master horsewoman, and she was eager to make a name for herself.

"With your horsemen coming over the mountains, he will underestimate us all the more," said Ragnhild.

"That will give us a solid advantage," Murchad agreed. "But how will the inhabitants of Gausel receive us? Are you sure they'll be glad to see us?"

Ragnhild shrugged off his caution. "They know I am my mother's rightful heir."

Einar would command *Raven's Loot*, and Thorgeir *Eagle's Treasure*. They chose their crews carefully, mixing the experienced sailors with the newcomers.

Preparations continued, until there was nothing left to do but to load their sea chests on the ships. That morning, the inhabitants of Tromøy gathered on the beach while Åsa presented Ragnhild with the battle-flag. She took it with a proud smile and hoisted the pennant up the mast. When the wind caught the fabric, the Valkyrie appeared to be riding. Ragnhild stared at it without words.

"May your enemies be taken, and victory be yours," said Åsa. She and Heid sacrificed a goat and blessed the ships and crews. Hogni and his crew set the meat to cook all afternoon while the sailors brought their gear aboard.

That evening they feasted around a bonfire.

"I will miss you, shield-maiden," Åsa said. "And you, Irishman."

For the first time, it hit Ragnhild that she was leaving Tromøy —possibly forever. If she defeated her brother, she would rule her own kingdom, far from Tromøy. Would she ever see Åsa again? She sipped her ale to calm the troubled feeling that rose in her stomach.

That night in bed, Murchad took her in his arms and stroked her hair. For a moment it seemed the barrier between them had dissolved.

"Having second thoughts?" he murmured.

Ragnhild set her jaw. "No."

"That's my warrior queen," said Murchad, kissing her. She let go of her misgivings and melted into the warmth of his body, relishing his strong arms around her. She clung to him as they made love.

Afterward, lying beside Murchad, she couldn't get comfortable. This was their last night together for a week or more, perhaps forever. She'd come so close to losing him to the haugbui. She hated to be separated from him again, especially with all that had come between them. But it was the best course of action.

The feather mattress bunched in hard fists and her thoughts swirled endlessly. *Harald denies me my right to Gausel. What about Orlyg?* Their younger brother was caught between the two of them. So far he'd remained neutral. Would he take sides in the coming conflict? Ragnhild's gut roiled.

I'm the rightful heir to Gausel, but will the people there accept me? What if everyone turns against me?

What if I'm wrong?

I've had it so good here on Tromøy, as Åsa's right hand. What makes me think I can become a queen in my own right?

Will I regret leaving Tromøy? It's too late now to stop what I've set in motion. I've already forfeited my place at Åsa's side. And I've promised Murchad to help him protect Ireland.

Right or wrong, I have no choice but to move forward with my plans.

She slept fitfully, and woke bleary-eyed and filled with doubts.

In the morning, Murchad woke and took her into his arms

again. They made love with the knowledge that it could be the last time. Afterward, they lay entwined, reluctant to separate.

"I will miss you," he whispered into her hair.

Ragnhild didn't want to let go of him, but she gave him one last embrace and tore herself from his arms. "And I will miss you. But we will meet again soon." She slid from the bed and picked up her tunic.

Together, they strode to the beach where her crew gathered, surrounded by a throng of people. All of Tromøy had turned out to see them off.

The skies were cloudy, with a light drizzle and no wind at all. Ragnhild made her way through the crowd to *Raider Bride*. She gripped the gunnel and vaulted aboard, then turned to wave at Murchad and Svein, standing among the folk of Tromøy on the shore.

Those staying behind cheered as the crews shoved off. Ragnhild took the tiller while the rowers clambered aboard and fitted their oars. She looked back to see Åsa at the head of the crowd, waving. Ragnhild raised her hand in reply. Confidence filled her, chasing the doubts of the night away. This was her destiny, for good or ill.

The three ships cleared Tromøy's harbor to a light northerly, strong enough to fill the sails and allow the rowers to save their strength.

"Raise sail," Ragnhild shouted. Half the crew shipped their oars, threw off the ties, and hauled the yard up the mast, the blue-and-white striped sail spilling free. The wind caught the heavy fabric and the sail bellied out. *Raider Bride* surged to life, a cheery trickle of water sounding beneath the keel.

The sun broke through the clouds and the wind strengthened. The little fleet rode the sparkling waves, sailing in company for the familiar voyage to the southern cape. As evening fell, Ragnhild led them into a sheltered cove where they built a fire and ate a quick meal of dried meat and flatbread.

The sunshine and brisk wind had done their work. Shortly after they'd finished eating, yawns began to make the rounds of the crew and one by one they found their way to their hudfat.

Ragnhild crawled gratefully into her sheepskin and stretched out on her back, letting the tension flow out of her body. She looked up at the stars, wondering how Murchad and his party fared as they made their way over the passes. She whispered a prayer to Ullr, the mountain god, to look after them. Sleep took her in mid-prayer.

In the morning, dark clouds threatened to make the passage less friendly than the day before, as the sea swell rolled in. The ships ducked into the skjaergarden, the rocky archipelago that stretched the length of the southern cape, providing shelter from the open sea. Ragnhild took the lead, mounting an experienced lookout on the bow with a white signal flag to point out hazards. The oarsmen fought tide rips and capricious currents, maneuvering in the narrow, skerry-littered passage, dodging rocks and playing the currents.

At noon, they pulled into a cove so that Einar's ship could take the lead and give Ragnhild's crew a rest.

The day's rowing brought them near Lindesnes, the most southern point of land. Einar led them into a protected bay to spend the night, resting up before rounding the treacherous headland in daylight. Summer was the only time of year to brave the seas off the southern cape. There was a portage across the peninsula for safe passage when the winds and currents were fierce, but portaging was hard work, taking the crews a full day to haul each ship across the narrow neck of land. The weather promised to be fair the next day, so they would sail around.

The hard work of rowing had exhausted them, and once again after a quick meal they all sought their sheepskins.

It wasn't until Ragnhild crawled alone into her hudfat that she had time to think of Murchad. He would be high on the mountain plateau by now. He was in good hands with Svein. Only a few more days and they would be together, she thought as she fell asleep.

In the morning, they rowed out of the archipelago and skirted the rocky headland. As they came out from the shelter of the last islet, the wind hit them, kicking up choppy seas.

"Ship oars," Ragnhild cried. "Make sail!"

The crew raced to unlash their sail and haul the yard up the mast. The fabric bellied out as the crew sheeted the big sail in. The ship heeled as *Raider Bride* took the wind's force across her beam. The sailors clung to the shrouds, exulting in the sea and wind.

They rounded the cape and put the wind behind them. Ragnhild felt a quiver run through the steering oar. She was tempted to let *Raider Bride* have her head, but she saw Einar was taking a reef, so she reluctantly ordered the crew to shorten sail. Ten sailors manned the halyard, lowering the yard, while another half dozen gathered the foot of the sail, tying off the reef points.

Once they were safely past the headland, Ragnhild led them back into the shelter of the skjaergarden and the wild ride was over. She guided her little fleet through the archipelago, plying their oars through the rocky channels.

When the skerries ended, Ragnhild raised sail and took a tack well offshore, avoiding the familiar reefs she'd known since childhood. They sighted whales and fishing boats in the distance, but no warships. The gods must have appreciated Åsa's sacrifice, for the weather held fair. The following seas lifted the hulls and gently set them down again with a shushing sound in a vast, calming rhythm.

Halfway up the coast, they put into a sandy cove for the night so they would arrive at Solavika in daylight.

They built a fire and broached a keg of ale, and ate their last meal together. Now that they had weathered the southern cape and entered home waters, the ships would split up.

The day's sail had been exhilarating and the sailors were in the mood to celebrate. While the crew roistered around the campfire, Ragnhild stared pensively at the waves lapping on the beach. She was coming home for the first time in a year. So much had changed in that time. Her father and mother dead, her brother estranged. A longing swept over her.

She shook off the emotion and joined the conversation.

"Remember when we raided my father's hoard?" she said.

Einar smiled. "And Harald chased us. You jumped overboard to lead him away from us."

"He brought me back to Father, who sent me to Ireland to marry Murchad. *Raider Bride* was built to be my bridal ship. But Åsa rescued me."

"And then a year later, you became his wife."

Ragnhild nodded ruefully. "There was no escaping it." *All the bloodshed could have been avoided.* Ragnhild fell silent again, staring into the fire, doubts flooding into her inexorably as the tide.

CHAPTER 19

Mountains of Southern Norway

M urchad rode Svartfaxi, following Svein up the well-worn trail into the breathtaking southern highlands. Behind them came the rest of the cavalry, including Ursa, nine more horsemen, and two pack animals. They traveled light, carrying only food, ale, their armor and weapons, and their hudfat, sleeping in the open. This time of year the weather could be wet, but the tanned outer hides of their sheepskin hudfat kept them dry. So far the early summer weather was warm and mild.

Murchad had a creeping feeling that the mountain spirits were watching him, and that they were not altogether pleased to see an Irishman in their territory.

The highlands were densely forested, dotted with granite boulders, plunging to mountain valley lakes and bogland. Sheep and cattle grazed in the high meadows, tended by cowherds and dairy maids who lived all summer in the lonely saeters, dairy huts scattered through the mountains. The milkmaids and cowherds were hospitable, sharing their skyr and cheese with the travelers in exchange for news. Some of them expressed the desire to join Åsa's army, and Murchad was tempted to recruit a few of them for Ragnhild.

"Let them finish their summer's work first," advised Svein. "Their families depend on the dairy products to survive the winter." He invited them to come to Gausel or Tromøy in the fall. "If you want to train as a warrior, that's what we'll do all winter."

Murchad did not really feel he was in command of the company. Svein was their natural leader. The big Norseman knew the way through the mountains, but he was more than a guide. The others trusted him and were accustomed to looking to him for leadership.

For all he'd gotten to know the Norse during their training sessions, Murchad could not really say they had warmed to each other. The Norse showed respect for his skills, but there was a begrudging quality to it.

They all shared a passion for horses and a unique understanding of the animals that enabled them to train quickly. Svein rode Ragnhild's horse, Hofvarpnir. Ragnhild had a strong bond with her horse, though Murchad knew she still missed Brunaidh, the Irish horse he'd given her. It had been hard for her to leave Brunaidh behind when they sailed from Ireland.

Svein spoke little as they rode the trail. He was a man of much experience in battle and many other things, and he was devoted to Ragnhild. In the evenings when they drank ale around the campfire, Murchad tried to capitalize on that shared devotion to draw the húskarl out. His efforts were rewarded as Svein became more garrulous and revealed much about Ragnhild. He'd known her and her brothers since they'd been born. Their mother died when Ragnhild was very young, leaving them to be raised by their father and an ancient nurse. Solvi was too busy to spare much notice for his children, and as the siblings grew older, their upbringing fell to the three húskarlar.

"All Solvi's children ran wild," said Svein. "Ragnhild every bit as much as her brothers. There was always competition among them. Harald dominated the two younger ones, and Ragnhild and Orlyg formed a bond from a young age. They often stood together against Harald."

"What do you think Orlyg will do when Ragnhild makes her claim?" Murchad asked, topping off Svein's ale.

The húskarl shook his head. "That's a tough one. If he sides against Ragnhild, it will break her heart. That boy means the world to her. But he's in a difficult position. Harald holds his inheritance, and all the power."

Murchad nodded. Ragnhild found herself in a fraught situation. "I know of betrayal first hand. My cousin and I were raised like brothers. Yet he deposed me—in part because of my marriage to Ragnhild, when I refused to put her aside and marry a Christian wife."

"That must have been a very hard decision for you," said Svein, a note of approval in his tone.

"It was." Murchad was pleased at the húskarl's show of sympathy. A delicate bond seemed to be forming between them. He decided to quit while he was winning. "I think I'll get some sleep."

Svein nodded.

Murchad burrowed into his hudfat and lay looking up at the stars, just beginning to peep out. He sighed. No matter how well he got to know the Norse, they were not his people. He prayed for the skill to guide his hot-tempered young wife. If they succeeded in taking her kingdom, she had promised him they'd guard the seaways and send out spies to thwart raids on Ireland. Then he would return the necklace to Ireland, no matter what Åsa and Ragnhild said. He would keep his vow to his people.

Murchad rolled over and pulled his hudfat tighter. He missed Ragnhild.

CHAPTER 20

The Jaeren Coast, Western Norway

Ragnhild launched *Raider Bride* at dawn, ready for the treacherous tides and currents of the Jaeren coast. Einar would sail at midday, while Thorgeir was scheduled to leave the next morning.

Ragnhild watched the familiar stretches of dunes and sandy beaches go by, all territory subject to Gausel, part of her birthright.

When the lookout sighted Solavika's broad, sandy beach, Ragnhild hove to offshore, waiting for the tide to change before putting into the bay. When the tide flooded, the longship rode in on the mild surf. The hull slid onto the sand and the waves retreated, setting them gently on the beach.

The sailors jumped off and dragged the ship out of the tide's reach. Though the bay was open to the western swells and therefore not a practical anchorage, it was a portage used often by traders to avoid the dangerous waters off the entrance to the

Boknafjord. By dragging their ships a few miles overland, they had access to a vast network of protected fjords and waterways reaching far inland.

Most important, they were far from Solbakk and Harald's watchful eye. Her brother would not expect her to make the arduous portage. He knew she wasn't a strategist, and he'd expect her to make a bold move. His spies would be watching for her to sail into the Hrafrsfjord, or into the Boknafjord itself. She chuckled as she imagined Harald's chagrin at underestimating her.

The crew made camp on the beach that night, resting up for the heavy trek ahead. Ragnhild stared east across the land toward Gausel. She was so close to her goal—yet so many things stood in her way.

They unloaded the ballast stones and stacked them on a pile of rocks left by other ships. To save time, Ragnhild decided to keep the mast up and their sea chests on board, and focus the entire crew to portaging.

The next morning, the crew felled a dozen small pine trees from a grove a short way inland. They spent the rest of the morning cutting the limbs and peeling off the bark to create smooth logs, still slippery with pine sap.

At noon, the lookout sighted Einar's ship. Relief washed over Ragnhild. That was one group she no longer had to worry about. She hurried over to help them pull the ship high up onto the beach.

"Welcome. You must be exhausted," she said to Einar as he climbed down off the ship.

"That I am," he said, seating himself gratefully and accepting the cup of ale she handed him. His crew joined him, while *Raider Bride's* sailors passed out the ale cups.

"How was your passage?" said Ragnhild.

Einar took a drink of ale. "Uneventful. We made good time, but we are glad to be here."

"I'm glad too," said Ragnhild, topping off his ale. "Get some rest, we have work to do."

The following day, they laid the logs out to form a short boardwalk. They attached a heavy mooring line to a small hole in the fore section of the keel. It took both crews to heave *Raider Bride* onto the logs. Once the ship was positioned, the sap of the freshly cut trees enabled the hull to slide easily across the logs. Ragnhild left ten sailors to guard Einar's ship while the rest turned to. Half of them were stationed along the hull to lift and steady it, while the rest hauled on the hawser. Those in the rear were assigned to fetch the logs from behind and lay them in front of the ship.

Ragnhild called out a rhythmic hauling shanty to keep the crew working together, heaving *Raider Bride* over the short distance to the Hrafrsfjord. A man could walk across in less than an hour, but hauling the heavy oaken ship was an agonizingly slow process.

It was late afternoon when they finally made it across. Portaging was hot, backbreaking work, and they were grateful to see water again. After a short rest, they turned back for Einar's ship, leaving a lucky few behind to guard *Raider Bride*.

It was fully dark by the time both ships lay on the western shore of the Hrafrsfjord. The crews were too tired and sore to do more than eat some dried cod and burrow into their hudfat.

In the morning, they launched the ships into the Hrafrsfjord and rowed across the fjord. Before noon they beached on the eastern shore. Ragnhild could see the hills of Gausel in the distance. Her goal was so close. She looked to the south, hoping to see Murchad's party riding up, but she knew it was too soon.

"We'll make camp here," she said. "We don't know what kind of reception to expect from the locals."

"Looks like we're about to find out," said Unn, nodding toward a contingent coming over the fields.

Ragnhild scanned their oncoming ranks. There were perhaps

one hundred of them. For a moment she regretted arriving ahead of Thorgeir. In the front ranks, about twenty men carried spears and shields. Behind them came a crowd of farmers, armed with scythes and hooks. Despite their numbers, Ragnhild realized her trained warriors could easily take them on.

"Arm yourselves and get ready to form a shield wall," she commanded quietly. "Easy. No need to appear hostile." The boat crews picked their shields off the rails and hefted their spears, forming a line along the shore.

At the head of the contingent walked a mature woman dressed in finely woven garments, her red cloak fastened with an intricate silver brooch. Ragnhild recognized her and strode forward to meet her.

"Greetings, Jofrid."

The woman bowed her head, and the others followed her lead. "Welcome, Lady Ragnhild. You have grown up. You look just like your mother."

Ragnhild stared at her. Did she really look like her mother? She didn't know—she had only memories of a sweet smile and soft voice.

Jofrid nodded. "We welcome you all to Gausel. Please, accompany us to the hall, where we can receive you properly."

Could this be a trap? Ragnhild had known Jofrid and the people of Gausel all her life. She decided to trust them. "Thank you." She assigned a dozen crewmembers to stay behind with the ships, promising to send a relief crew the next morning.

The crowd escorted them the two and a half miles overland to the settlement, where the great hall stood on the hill. Ragnhild remembered it from visits with her parents when they came to collect their taxes in wool, cheese, and barley. They had made the trip in a big, beamy ship, sailing down the Gandesfjord from Solbakk to Gausel. That was the route Harald would take to attack them.

To Ragnhild's relief, no one asked them to surrender their

weapons at the door. It was a good sign. She fingered her sword-hilt for reassurance while Jofrid ushered them inside. Their hostess conducted Ragnhild to the high seat, while the boat crews were welcomed on the benches.

Jofrid brought a horn brimming with ale. "Lady Ragnhild, I offer you the hospitality of this hall."

Ragnhild accepted it and raised it in a toast. She decided to make her position clear right away. "To my people of Gausel." To her relief, her statement raised a cheer.

When Ragnhild had drunk, Jofrid carried the horn around the room, naming each person as she served them. Ragnhild remembered many of them from her childhood visits. She began to relax a little. She looked at Einar, seated on the bench at the head of her crews. He seemed perfectly at ease among these people he'd known all his life.

As soon as everyone had drunk, stewards carried in platters of roasted goat and pots of barley porridge. Ragnhild was impressed with the impromptu meal these people were able to muster, especially so early in the spring when stores were usually low. The plentiful repast told her this remained a very prosperous area. The fact that the meal was ready meant spies watching the coast had given Jofrid ample warning of their arrival. Ragnhild wondered if that information had reached her brother yet.

When they had eaten, Ragnhild rose and raised her horn. "You all know me. I am Ragnhild, daughter of Ingfrid, your former queen. I am my mother's rightful heir. My brother, Harald Gold-beard, would withhold Gausel from me.

"I have come to reclaim my inheritance. I ask you all to accept me as your ruler, as my mother before me. I promise we will defend you from my brother, and all other invaders, and bring peace and prosperity to this land. If you accept me, you will pay no more tribute to Harald. All the wealth of this land will remain here, and we will establish friendly trade with Ireland."

There was silence in the hall. Ragnhild's bravado began to sag.

Jofrid rose. "Lady Ragnhild, we acknowledge you as your mother's heir, and we have no wish to anger you. But we are simple farmers. We have lived for many years in peace and prosperity with your father, and that peace continues under your brother. We want no fight with Harald."

Ragnhild stared around the hall at the fearful faces. "I wish to live among you in peace, as is my right."

"I fear your brother will not allow that," said Jofrid. "Your claim will bring us war, destruction to our lands, and death to our people."

"Are you refusing to accept my leadership?" Ragnhild bit back her disappointment and kept her tone moderate.

"Lady, we fear the consequences. Your brother will descend on us, and we will be caught between you. Please, bide here tonight. In the morning we will talk more."

Ragnhild raised her voice. "Good people of Gausel, I thank you for your hospitality. I will not endanger my people by remaining under your roof. My crews and I will return to our ships and camp there while we find another way to deal with Harald."

As they filed out of the hall, Einar said, "I'm sure your brother's spies will report our presence."

She nodded. "He'll come soon. With any luck, our ruse has succeeded, and Harald thinks I only have two ships." She wished Murchad was there to advise her. She was glad he'd arrive in a few days.

~

THE NEXT MORNING, Jofrid arrived at the ship camp on horseback. Behind her came men driving a wagon. A pair of horses were hitched to the wagon, and three milk cows and six goats were tied on behind.

"We thank you, Lady, for your consideration for our safety.

Please, accept these supplies and livestock." She gestured to the wagon, laden with barrels of ale, sacks of grain, and a half a dozen hens in willow cages.

"I thank you for the bounty, Lady Jofrid." This tribute was an encouraging sign. Perhaps Ragnhild would be able to win her people over.

When Jofrid had departed, Ragnhild said to Einar, "I don't want to endanger these people. There must be a better way."

"Nor do I. We need them on our side," said Einar. "Perhaps we can keep the battle away from Gausel."

Ragnhild thought about it. "That might work. We'll post lookouts to the north to watch the seaways. If Harald brings a war, we will go to meet it. We can have it out with him far from Gausel."

"I suggest we scout the beaches and choose a battleground to our advantage," said Einar. "I know a good place."

"We'll go look at it today," said Ragnhild. "I doubt if Harald will come himself. He'll send Orlyg. Harald knows I won't kill our little brother on sight."

Einar nodded grimly. "He knows you well."

CHAPTER 21

Mountains of Southern Norway

Murchad's party had reached the highest point of their climb and made camp in a wooded copse in the shelter of a granite cliff. They picketed the horses in a nearby meadow where the grazing was good.

The stars sparkled in their millions and Svein pointed out the constellations. Murchad had learned their Latin names during his formal education in Ireland, but the Norse had their own: Ursa Major was Odin's wagon, containing the North Star so vital to navigation. Orion was Frigg's distaff, and Gemini contained the eyes of Thjazi, where Thor had tossed them when he'd killed the giant.

They set watches and bedded down. Murchad crawled into his hudfat and lay watching the dying embers of the campfire, thinking of Ragnhild. Soon he would see her, hold her in his arms. As he drifted off to sleep, that uneasy feeling of being watched made his neck hairs prickle. He turned on his side, determined to ignore it and get a good night's sleep. They had many more miles to put behind them before he saw his wife again.

Unrest among the horses brought him awake. They were snorting and milling. It was a slight sound but Murchad was used to rousing whenever things changed.

Svein was already up and heading toward the pickets. Murchad wriggled out of his sleeping-skin, picked up his spear and shield, and followed.

The horses neighed in distress, crashing in the brush. Missiles flew from the forest. Murchad flung his shield up to fend off rocks and arrows as he dashed toward the horses.

A hard-slung stone struck Svein in the head. The big húskarl crashed to the earth.

By this time the entire camp was armed and moving. Ursa ran up beside him. "Look to Svein," said Murchad, dashing toward the horses.

Metal flashed in the firelight and he deflected a spear flung from the trees. In the darkness, the attackers were all but invisible. "Shield wall!" he cried as the others caught up with him. They got their shields locked overhead as a volley of spears and arrows hailed down on them. "Get out of the firelight," he warned. Locked together, the shield wall maneuvered into the safety of the shadows.

The assailants charged out of the darkness, wielding spears and axes. Murchad's shield wall bristled with spears and short swords, holding them at bay. The attackers circled, trying to flank them, but the defenders bent their line around to cover all sides, forming a fortress of shields.

The raiders circled the shield fort, trying to find a weakness. The defenders showed no opening, jabbing their blades at the attackers when they came within range.

Even in the bad light, Murchad could see the assailants were well-armed, with helmets, shields, and good weapons. Too well-armed for mountain brigands.

One of the raiders barked an order and the attackers backed away, shields up.

"Steady," said Murchad. The shield fort held firm while the assailants were swallowed up by the darkness.

Men shouted and horses whinnied. Murchad cursed. "They're taking the horses!" The shield fort broke and he ran, spear cocked, in time to glimpse the raiders riding into the forest—with his horses.

He drew up, panting, realizing it was useless to chase after mounted men in the dark. He nearly stumbled over the body of the sentry, a farm boy named Bo who had a special gift with horses. His throat had been neatly cut from behind so he didn't have a chance to cry out.

The others gathered around their fallen comrade. "Carry him back to camp," said Murchad. They picked up the boy's corpse and bore him back to the fire.

Ursa and several others had already brought Svein to camp. The big húskarl lay as if dead, his face pale as Bo's.

"He breathes," said Ursa. "But I have not the healing skill of my sister."

"Do what you can for him," said Murchad. He took stock of their situation. They had lost one of their most promising horsemen, and all of their horses. They had their provisions and weapons, but their only guide lay unconscious, perhaps dying.

"We need to tend to Svein and pray to whatever gods you like that he wakes," Murchad told his horse soldiers. "He's the only one who knows the way through these mountains. We can't leave him, and we can't carry him on foot, so for now we stay here."

Nobody could sleep after what happened. They gathered around the dead campfire, weapons close to hand.

"Keep a sharp lookout for another attack," Murchad said

grimly. "We can't escape without our horses. As soon as there's a little light, I'm going to track them."

"I'll go with you," said Ursa.

He regarded the shield-maiden. She was nearly his height and strongly built, possibly outweighing him. The scar on her face made her look as if she were scowling, but Murchad had grown used to it and learned to read her eyes and her voice. Now they conveyed determination.

"Very well," he said, then chose three of the most experienced warriors. "We're going to get our horses back. Ursa and you three will come with me. I want the rest of you to stay here and tend Svein. Keep him safe. He's our best chance of making it out of here alive."

They dug a shallow depression and laid Bo in it, his dagger and shield by his side. Each of them found stones to lay over him. Murchad stood by silently as they commended him to their pagan gods.

At first light Murchad and his party filled their skins with water, packed two days' worth of food, several lengths of rope, all the horses' bridles, and their weapons, and set out on foot.

Fourteen horses were easy to track, though the raiders had put a great distance between them. They followed the trail for hours, and in the late afternoon a fine mist began to fall. Fresh horse droppings told Murchad they were getting close to the horse thieves.

In the early evening, they smelled woodsmoke. "Spread out and creep silently through the trees. When you sight the horses, stop and take cover until dark. Keep your eye out for the sentries, and wait for my signal. When you hear it, we'll go in for the horses." He demonstrated an owl's hoot.

He hid in the trees, watching the camp. He counted at least twenty of them, too many for the five of them to dispatch. He hoped their superior numbers would make them lax.

They were very well equipped for a band of outlaws. They

had hudfat, horses, and good weaponry. And there were a lot of them. It made him wonder again if they really were just a band of thieves preying on travelers.

He waited, chewing on flatbread to ease the growling of his stomach while the breeze carried the scent of roasting meat and men's laughter. Eventually the voices trailed off as the raiders bedded down.

He was glad to see only three men took up sentry posts on the outskirts of camp, one of them guarding the horses.

When all was quiet, Murchad gave his owl's hoot. The sound blended into the forest noises, and only those who awaited it knew it for what it was.

The slightest rustling of branches told him his crew was on the move. They crept up behind the guards and halted, waiting. When silence told him they were all in position, Murchad gave another hoot. In a flurry of movement, his crew fell on the sentries and cut their throats before they could cry out.

The horses nickered softly in greeting and stood quietly as their familiar riders bridled them. Each of the party led two horses away from camp, one on a lead-rope, while Murchad took three. Murchad listened for the sound of pursuit, but the enemy was silent.

As soon as they were out of earshot, they swung onto horse-back and rode away, leading the other horses.

When they got back to camp at dawn, Svein was still unconscious. Murchad began to lose hope that the big húskarl would wake again.

"They'll come after the horses," said Murchad. He didn't share his suspicions that these raiders were after more than their horses.

Ursa said, "We can't risk moving Svein. It could kill him."

Murchad nodded. "Trying to flee with Svein slowing us down would be suicide. The enemy would catch us easily and we're outnumbered. We're better off strengthening our position to fight them here."

He posted two sentries high above on the rocks where they could spot anyone coming from a long way off. Murchad placed four archers in the trees surrounding the horses and the camp.

All they could do now was wait.

~

Gausel

DARKNESS WAS FALLING and Ragnhild's crew were letting the campfire burn down when the Hrafrsfjord lookout shouted, "A ship!" Ragnhild tensed as everyone jumped up and went for their weapons. Could Harald be staging a sneak attack from an unexpected quarter? Then, moments later, the lookout called, "It's Thorgeir!" Ragnhild's shoulders slumped in relief.

They put down their spears and axes, broached a keg of ale, and built up the fire. The longship hove into sight, the rowers pulling wearily. Ragnhild and her sailors sloshed into the water to take hold of the gunnels. They ran the ship into the beach and helped the exhausted crew tumble over the sides.

Thorgeir's bearded face split into a wide grin when he saw Ragnhild. She threw her arms around the big húskarl, inhaling his familiar scent of sweat and wet wool. "I'm so glad to see you!"

"Sorry it took us so long. We ran out of wind shortly after departure, and had to row the whole way," he explained. "That pretty much wore us out, and we had to rest overnight before we had enough strength to portage." He peered at the crowd. "Where's Svein? And the Irishman?"

"They're overdue," said Ragnhild. Heid's prophecy echoed in her mind. *Be careful, for in gaining what you desire, you may lose what you hold dear.* "They should have been here by now, but we haven't seen or heard from them."

Thorgeir shrugged. "You know Svein. He likes to take his time. I'm ready for food and ale!" In spite of the big man's nonchalance, worry niggled at Ragnhild's gut.

At dawn one of the lookouts on the Gandesfjord side came running. "Three ships are sailing down from the north."

Harald.

Ragnhild was relieved to hear he'd sent only three ships. It seemed their scheme had worked. Her brother must believe she only had two ships, and by sending three, he'd have her outnumbered. Perhaps Thorgeir's tardiness was an advantage.

"We must prepare a welcome for my brother," she said. "Even without Murchad and Svein, I reckon we match his numbers." Leaving a small guard with the ships, they set out for Gausel with one hundred warriors, armed with spears and axes. Ragnhild, Thorgeir, and Einar rode ahead on the horses Jofrid had provided.

When they reached Gausel, the headwoman was waiting with furrowed brows and a worried look.

"Keep your people inside," Ragnhild said to her. "My warriors are on their way. I will fight my brother, but I have decided to keep the fighting away from Gausel. We'll intercept Harald's forces north of here, and do battle there."

Jofrid's face relaxed. "For that we are grateful, Lady."

Ragnhild's forces arrived and she led them north to the beach Einar had proposed. Once they had mustered, she faced her troops. "Line up three deep. Don't look excited, but be ready to form a shield wall."

They quickly got into position, and her standard-bearer raised her battle-flag for the first time.

As the ships neared, she saw that she'd guessed right. Orlyg's ship, *Wave Rider,* was in the lead, and Harald's *Battle Swan* was not among them.

Ragnhild rode forward as the vessels reached shore. A hasty count confirmed that her forces did indeed match his.

Orlyg scowled as his bow touched the beach and he leaped over the side, a dozen warriors splashing into the shallows beside him. Ragnhild nodded to her warriors and they locked shields behind her.

"Greetings, brother."

"Sister, I see you've brought your farmhands."

Orlyg's remark was met with a rattle of spears as Ragnhild's troops straightened their lines.

"Well-trained farmhands," she said, keeping her voice mild. "And they number the same as your crew. So nice of you to bring a welcoming party."

"I have a message from Harald," Orlyg said stiffly.

His tone cast a shadow on Ragnhild's spirits. "I'm sure you do. Well, let's have it, brother."

"Harald bids you leave Gausel and report to him at Solbakk."

Ragnhild's mood darkened even more. Orlyg had always been her ally. Where was the brother she'd done mischief with? It seemed he'd chosen Harald's side. "I have no intention of leaving my property. I will remain here."

Orlyg frowned. "Sister, please, do not resist Harald. You won't win."

"You know I'm in the right, Orlyg," Ragnhild cried. "Harald is being unfair."

"That may be, but neither you nor I can stand against him."

"Maybe you're afraid to stand up to Harald, but I'm not."

"Sister, I beg you not to fight him. He's too powerful."

"We'll see about that!" Ragnhild retorted.

"He knows about your horsemen coming over the mountains," Orlyg said. "He's sent men to stop them."

Ragnhild's mind reeled in panic. Murchad was in danger. She had to get rid of Orlyg and go to his aid. "And now you've delivered your message," she said brightly, hiding her fear. "I wish I could invite you to eat with us, brother, but we didn't know you were coming. Next time, send a messenger ahead and I will prepare a feast for you and your men. And bring Harald and Signy, of course. I long to see them. I believe they have a child now?"

Orlyg's face purpled. "A girl," he stammered.

"Please send my congratulations. I am very happy for them. So sorry you must be going so soon, but bring my love to them all."

Orlyg stared at her triple row of stalwart warriors. Apparently they looked better trained than he'd anticipated, for he turned to his crew and said, "Shove off."

His warriors wore startled expressions, but did as he ordered.

"So much for my favorite brother," Ragnhild said softly to Einar as they watched the ships row away.

"Orlyg risked much, telling you that Harald sent men against Murchad," said Einar.

Ragnhild nodded. "When I catch the spy who betrayed us, I'll make him wish he was dead." She started toward her horse. "I'm going to find Murchad. He's in danger."

Einar grabbed her shoulder. "What if Harald comes while you're gone?"

"I'll go," said Thorgeir. "You'll need Einar here if Harald comes."

Ragnhild breathed a sigh of relief. Thorgeir was a perfect choice. He'd grown up here and knew the country as well as the sea. Ragnhild trusted his judgment, more than her own. And he was Svein's best friend. Ragnhild longed to accompany them, but she knew she must stay here in case Harald came. Murchad would expect nothing less. "Choose your party and take what you need."

Thorgeir picked out two seasoned warriors and they armed with spears, axes, and shields. Along with their weapons, they carried only their hudfat, food, and water.

Unn rode with them, armed and carrying a saddlebag loaded with her medical supplies. "If there are injured, we'll most likely build a shelter and treat them where we find them. A cart would slow us down, and jolting across the rough mountains is not an ideal way to transport wounded. It could do more harm than good."

Ragnhild didn't argue. Unn had come so close to losing her sister once, and now Ursa was in danger again. "May the gods go with you."

She watched them ride off, fearing what they would find, but even more afraid they would find nothing. Svein knew the country better than any of them, but if Harald's men had attacked their party, they could be lying dead at the bottom of a ravine and never be found.

Ragnhild forced her mind away from these thoughts. They were useless, only sapping her energy. It was time to get ready for her brothers' next visit.

She turned to Einar. "Orlyg's seen our forces, and he'll report to Harald."

"He won't underestimate us next time," said Einar. "He'll come as soon as he can muster a superior army, and when he does, he'll attack without mercy."

"If he attacks before Thorgeir gets back with the others, we'll be hard put to defend against him," said Ragnhild.

They had faced Harald twice, once in Ireland, where he fled before a superior force. When he attacked Tromøy the year before, they'd sent him packing. But now, without three of her war leaders, Ragnhild quailed at the thought of facing down her older brother. He'd always been bigger, stronger, tougher than her. Turning that around would take enormous effort.

But he was coming, whether she was ready or not.

CHAPTER 22

Tromøy

The barley and flax fields were sprouting, the dairy maids and farmhands had long since herded the cows to the summer pastures. The spring shearing was completed, the sheep's rich winter coats collected, washed, and combed. Every female over the age of three carried a distaff tucked in her belt wherever she went, dropping a spindle and winding up the thread while talking, cooking, minding children.

Halfdan and Fylgja were everywhere. The blind wolf never left the boy's side and Åsa gladly let him sleep in the bower on a sheepskin. After the kidnapping, she was grateful for the added protection. Most mornings she found the boy curled up with the wolf on the floor. For his part, she doubted the old wolf had ever been fed so well or had so warm a place to sleep. All trace of bond to his former master seemed to have gone. Åsa wondered if Halfdan would one day be able to enter the wolf as Hrafn had—

as she did with Stormrider. It was said the ability ran in families. When he was older, she would see.

The spring weather brought a visit from Eyvind. Åsa was surprised at how pleased she was to see the Svea trader. Her gaze lingered on his broad shoulders and glossy brown hair while he supervised the mooring of his ship. When he turned to look at her, his glacier-blue eyes captured hers. For a long moment, neither of them could look away.

"Welcome, Eyvind," she said formally. "I thought you would be on your way to the Eastern lands."

"I am, Lady. Since it's only a short sail from Skiringssal, I thought I would stop to take on a load of soapstone vessels and whetstones, and more of Ulf's fine metalwork to trade."

Åsa warmed to the idea. This would greatly cut the transport time for herself and the producers. "I am so glad you did. We'll sail down the coast and I will take you to the quarry in Fjaere, where you can pick up the soapstone and whetstones directly, as well as smelted bog iron. You and your men are welcome to refresh yourselves in my guesthouse, and after we shall feast to celebrate your arrival."

Eyvind gave her a slow smile that sent a quiver down her spine. "Thank you, Lady."

While the visitors found their way to the guesthouse, Åsa hurried off to the hall to arrange the meal. She set the stewards to work, then retired to her bower to get ready. While Brenna helped her dress, Åsa was annoyed to find her heart beating hard in anticipation. *There's no reason to get so excited. It's only business.* But her heart told her it was more than that.

Åsa took her place on the high seat, her nerves still jangling. While she waited for Eyvind, her hand strayed to her belt pouch where her fingers found the Irish necklace. The power shimmered up her arm and her jitters calmed.

Eyvind entered the hall and approached the high seat. He offered her a tiny wooden box. "A gift, Lady."

She opened the box and broke into a delighted smile. Inside gleamed a string of faceted carnelian beads alternating with rock crystal.

"I brought them back from Serkland last season, and I intended to trade them in Haithabu, but I knew they must belong to you."

"They're lovely. Thank you, Eyvind." She took the beads from the box and bowed her head forward. "Will you fasten them for me?"

He stepped forward and brought the strand over her head. As he clasped them behind her, his breath warm against the back of her neck sent a tingle down her spine.

He stood back to admire them. "I was right. They were made for you."

Åsa's face warmed under his scrutiny. *Don't be such a fool. It's not like a man has never given you a gift.* Yet the truth was, such gifts had been rare in her life. For the traditional morning gift, her husband, Gudrød, had presented her with her own mother's jewels, which he had looted when he killed her father and brother and forced her into marriage. She had reason to be touched by Eyvind's straightforward gifts.

During the meal, they had little attention to spare for anyone but each other. "Tell me more about your coming voyages," she asked Eyvind.

His eyes took on a faraway look. "First, I will sail to Haithabu and trade there, then to the Eastern Sea where I can get the best amber. From there I'll work my way north to Gotland and Birka, before crossing to the land of Finns, and Aldeigja. I will follow the rivers as far east and south as I can get, I hope all the way to Bolghar and beyond."

Åsa listened avidly. She had been raised on tales of the exotic East, told by her father and Ulf. Olaf had made that trip as well. She wondered if she would ever see those far-off lands. Looking around her at the hall, she shrugged. This was what she'd fought for, her home, her son, her people. Here she must stay to keep them safe.

At the end of the evening, Åsa was tempted to invite Eyvind to her bed. She opened her mouth to speak and thoughts clamored in her mind. *What if he says no? What if I've misread him? Even worse, what if he says yes?*

She cleared her throat. "Ulf is working on some knives and axes I had planned to take to market. If you can wait a few days while he finishes them, you can take them with you."

"That sounds most agreeable," Eyvind said.

"Will you hawk with me tomorrow?" she asked.

"I would like that."

"Well, I'll let you get your rest. We'll leave at dawn." She thought there was disappointment in his eyes, but perhaps he was just tired.

In the morning they rode out, Stormrider perched on her leather-clad shoulder, a goshawk on his. The spring weather had taken a turn toward summer, and the sun gleamed gently on their heads.

When they came upon a flock of quail, she let him fly his hawk first, while Stormrider waited patiently for her turn.

"You have fine control of your bird," he said admiringly.

Åsa smiled. "We have a...special rapport."

Eyvind seemed to take her reply at face value. For the rest of the day, they hunted easily together, without the need for conversation.

That evening, she bade Brenna light the brazier in the chamber off the main hall. The fóstra smiled but said nothing.

Heid gave her a smirk. "Clever choice. A sea-king. He'll be good for trade."

Åsa chuckled. Of course the völva would see the practical side of things. But she was right. Eyvind was the ideal choice. As Heid said, his trading connections could enhance Åsa's own status and wealth. In the past she'd always brought her trade goods to Vestfold, but Eyvind changed all that. Now she didn't have to transport all her goods there.

After the meal, as the fire burned low and the others found their beds, she turned to Eyvind and said, "I am happy that you came."

His blue eyes held hers as he reached for her hand. He squeezed her hand gently and she caught her breath. "The truth is, I had to see you again." He leaned toward her until his breath warmed her cheek. His eyes closed and his face came nearer.

He's a sea-king. Second son of a king. It's only natural for him to want a kingdom of his own—and here is mine for the taking, if I let him get too close. She drew her head back. His eyes flew open. "I'd best let you go off to the guest house. We must depart early tomorrow." She turned away from the disappointment in his eyes. "Good night." She rose.

"Of course." Eyvind rose and bowed. "Until tomorrow." He stepped down from the guest seat and made his way to the door.

Åsa set out for the bower, but instead she went to the chamber door and opened it. Within, the brazier cast its glow on the big bed with its down pillows and quilt, the walls hung with vivid tapestries embroidered with scenes from legend. In the flickering firelight the gods seemed to come to life. Memories of her nights here with Olaf sprang to life. His scent of new-mown grass seemed to hang in the air with a pall of regret.

She shook off the feelings and banished Olaf's ghost, then turned and headed to the bower.

Heid sat up in bed and shook her head as Åsa entered their chamber. "Coward."

"How can I trust him?"

Heid gave her a knowing smile. "How indeed." The old sorceress turned her face to the wall and snuggled into her down comforter.

Åsa undressed and slid into bed next to Halfdan and Brenna.

The little boy was sound asleep, but Brenna whispered, "It's not as easy as the völva makes it sound."

Åsa heaved a sigh. "No, it's not. So many depend on my actions and decisions. What if he is really after Tromøy? What if he wants to wheedle his way into my affections only to become king?"

"You should wait until you're sure. He's not the only man you'll meet."

But he's the only man I've wanted since Olaf.

Every man in her life had betrayed her in one way or another—her husband, Gudrød, had murdered her father and her brother and taken her by force. Olaf had betrayed her to his father, then married another woman. Even her father and brother had left her alone, dying when she needed them so much. How could she ever put her trust in a man again?

Worn out from the day's activities, Åsa fell asleep and dreamed of glacier-blue eyes.

In the morning, she wondered how Eyvind would behave after the previous night's rejection. Would he be angry? She might as well find out what kind of man he was once and for all. She dressed and hurried to the hall.

"Good morning, Lady," Eyvind greeted her.

His smile was as warm as before. *No hard feelings*, she thought, relieved. "Good morning. I hope you slept well."

"Your guest quarters are most comfortable," he said with a mischievous grin, "though my mind was elsewhere."

A blush rose in her cheeks, and Åsa turned to instruct the cook. The remark pleased her more than she wanted it to. She was glad he hadn't given up.

After breakfast, they readied Eyvind's ship for the passage down the coast. Halfdan, not to be denied a sailing trip, bounded aboard, his wolf on his heels as always.

The spring weather was brisk, sending gusty winds that splattered them with chill rain, but between the cloudbursts the sun shone. Fylgja huddled in the stern behind Åsa while Halfdan romped the decks, secured by a long lifeline. Åsa turned her face into the wind, relishing the refreshing breeze, the motion of the ship.

Eyvind watched her with a smile. "You love being at sea," he said to her.

"I do," she admitted. "If I didn't have Tromøy, I'd spend all my time on a ship."

"We share the same passion," he said. "I love the freedom. I could never give it up. I'm sorry that you had to."

"It's worth it," she said. "I love my home and my people. But sometimes I wish I could just sail away."

"I made that choice years ago."

"I thought your brother inherited?"

"My father wanted to divide his kingdom between me and my older brother."

"Didn't your brother object?" She thought of Ragnhild and her brother, squabbling over their inheritance.

Eyvind shook his head. "My father's holdings are vast and my brother was happy to have me take some of the responsibility. But I said no, and set sail as fast as I could."

"Clever of you," she said. He only smiled and turned to watch the sail.

Eyvind was an expert sailor, as she'd expected, handling his ship with the skill of a long-distance trader accustomed to navigating unfamiliar waters. He knew how to read the riptides and unsettled currents that belied hidden rocks and shoals. She didn't really have to advise him until midday, when they neared the Hesnes Isles, where they had to thread their way through the skerries and islets into Fjaere's harbor of Vikkilen.

The boat landing lay at the base of a ridge that supported several steadings. Merchant's tents lined the beach, surrounded by piles of raw soapstone and schist, stacks of pots and querns. Eyvind's eyebrows rose at the sight.

"The stone comes from inland quarries," she explained. "It's transported by boat on the River Nidelva to the nearby Lake Rore, then hauled on sledges overland to the coast."

"An impressive operation," he said.

Åsa and Eyvind bartered for loads of soapstone, both raw stone and finished pots, as well as whetstones and quern stones. When they both bid on the same stack of finished pots in progressive sizes that nested together, Eyvind bowed and said, "They are yours, Lady."

"Oh no, Lord," said Åsa. "You are my guest. Take them, I insist. I can get a set later."

Much to the vendor's chagrin, it became a reverse bidding war. Fortunately, Eyvind gave him a fair price in the end.

Eyvind's crew loaded the heavy stone beneath the floorboards, where they would serve as ballast until he traded them. They departed in midafternoon and a favorable wind brought them back to Tromøy before sundown.

That night after the meal, Asa summoned her courage. *This is what I want. What I need.*

She swallowed and reached for his hand. "I would like you to spend the night with me in my chamber."

His pale blue eyes stared into hers as he squeezed her hand. "That I desire above all else."

She leaned over and kissed him. His lips were soft, but she felt the power of his underlying desire. She rose and led him to the chamber off the main hall.

Åsa smiled to see that Brenna had lit the brazier. The fire warmed the room and cast a mellow glow. They embraced again, unpinning cloaks and letting them fall onto the rush-strewn floor, pulling off tunic, hose, and gown, taking time to relish each expanse of skin revealed. She ran her hands over his shoulders, muscled from work, scarred from battle. He brushed his fingers across her back, causing her skin to quiver beneath his touch.

But something stopped her. She drew back, arms crossed over her chest.

His hand stilled. "Lady, you have nothing to fear from me."

Her gaze met his, searching his eyes for the truth.

"I want nothing from you but the pleasure of your company. To know the joy of touching you."

He spoke with such sincerity that she believed him. The tension flooded out of her shoulders and she pressed her body to his.

They made love while the gods carved in the bedposts looked on. He was not like Olaf. There was nothing tentative about his lovemaking. He touched her with sure but considerate hands, and her body turned to molten liquid. She was able to let herself go in a way she never had before, trusting him as she had trusted no man.

After a slow lovemaking, she fell asleep in his arms.

In the morning she woke to find his arms still around her and smiled into his sparkling eyes. They made love again, and finally rose.

After breakfast, she rode down to the shore to see him off. As he supervised the final distribution of the iron goods from Ulf, Åsa found herself wondering if Eyvind had a lover in every port he sailed into. Oddly, she felt no twinge of jealousy. He didn't belong to her, and she surely did not belong to him.

He looked up at her and his gaze captured hers. "I don't want to leave you, but I must."

"I wish I could go with you," she said. "I would love to see those distant lands."

"You would be welcome on my ship."

Åsa sighed. "I must stay and defend my kingdom. But a part of me sails with you."

"And part of my heart remains here, with you. I'll see you in the fall with a load of wootz ingots."

She watched his ship depart from the dock, still wishing she could go with him. The temptation was strong. She rode back up to the hall and retired to her bower, where she slipped into Stormrider and set off after Eyvind's ship. From aloft, she watched it sail out into the Skagerrak, toward the land of Danes, to the port of Haithabu.

He would be back in the fall.

~

WITH MOST OF the spring work done, Åsa loaded her ships and took her little fleet north to Skiringssal where she would trade the stone and iron for what the folk in the hinterland needed. She also brought more of Ulf's wares and extra wool from the spring shearing.

Halfdan and the wolf came along as always. Halfdan seemed to be born for the sea, though Åsa still made him wear his lifeline. As usual, Fylgja vomited once and then got his sea legs.

When they arrived in Skiringssal, Sonja met them at the shore, her son beside her. At just over a year, Rognvald had learned to walk since their last visit. He recognized Halfdan with a crow of delight and tottered toward him. He fell on the wolf, petting him vigorously. Sonja sucked in her breath in alarm, but Fylgja rolled over on his back and lay splay-legged, obviously enjoying the rough handling. Åsa wondered if the wolf had ever been shown affection before he became Halfdan's.

Olaf arrived and stood watching his two sons, his face aglow with pride. A tender warmth spread in Åsa's chest at the sight. She was glad that he'd found someone like Sonja.

"Come up to the hall," said Sonja. "I have a fresh batch of ale ready. I've tried new herbs and I'd value your opinion." They all trooped up the path. They took seats on the outdoor benches where Sonja served the ale while they watched the boys rough-house. Soon Rognvald was astride Fylgja, riding him around the yard, Halfdan trotting at their side, guiding the wolf and making sure the younger boy didn't fall.

Åsa took a sip of ale. "I approve. Do I detect meadowsweet?"

"Yes," said Sonja. "Refreshing, don't you think?"

Åsa nodded and sipped some more.

"Eyvind should be in Haithabu by now," said Olaf.

"Yes, he stopped at Tromøy to pick up a load of soapstone and schist to trade in the East," said Åsa, commanding herself not to blush.

"Did he?" A worried frown passed over Olaf's face. "Eyvind seems to spend a lot of time on Tromøy."

Åsa shrugged. "It's just good business." She turned to Sonja. "How was your spring wool this year? Ours was the best we've seen in a long time."

"It was a cold winter," Sonja observed. "That will always bring on a good coat."

When Åsa's gaze returned to Olaf, his face had regained its placid expression.

CHAPTER 23

Gausel

Three days passed with no word from the search party. Ragnhild fretted, itching to go after them, but she knew she couldn't, not with Harald's imminent attack looming over them. She had to be in command when he arrived.

Jofrid and the folk of Gausel remained friendly. Ragnhild visited them often, getting to know their ways. She walked the fields with the headwoman. The mild coastal climate produced farmland rich with barley, rye, flax, and even wheat. Horses, sheep, and cattle abounded in the rich pastureland. Frey, the god of peace and plenty, had truly blessed the region. The people themselves were friendly, hospitable, hardworking. No wonder they didn't want war. They had much to lose.

Who was she to bring battle to these fertile fields, death to these people? She was determined to ensure their safety while establishing her claim. She had to face Harald, but she would keep the battles away from Gausel.

"Your land is well tended, your crops do well," Ragnhild said.

"You have brought many mouths to feed," said Jofrid.

What the headwoman said was true. Another way in which Ragnhild imposed hardship on these people. "Many of my crew are farmers as well as warriors. It's early enough for them to break ground and plant an extra field of barley, and other crops to offset our consumption."

Jofrid nodded. "That would help."

"I'll assign a crew to fish in the Gandesfjord as well."

Jofrid smiled.

Ragnhild's crew worked side by side with the local farmers, clearing and ploughing the new field with an ard. It was heavy work, driving an ox hitched up to the plough. It took four people to accomplish this—one to go ahead of the ox to clear big rocks out of the way, one guiding the ard's single iron blade as it scratched a furrow in the sod, another to lead the ox and keep the beast moving. They ploughed a furrow in the sod one direction, then drove the ard across the field again, perpendicular to the furrow they had just made. Behind them came another farmer sowing seed. Children ran about the fields, scaring the birds away.

Ragnhild's crew shared varying methods of planting and fertilizing from east of the mountains with their hosts. A rapport grew up among the two groups born of work and shared knowledge. The days passed quickly, full of hard work and comradery.

No word from Murchad or Thorgeir. Ragnhild barely slept, and she could see the concern etched on Einar's face too.

~

THE WAR HORN sounded early in the morning. Ragnhild tumbled from her hudfat and joined the others to dress and arm themselves.

"Harald?" said Ragnhild, heart beating fast. She stared up at the lookout on his lathered mount. He'd ridden in from the coast of the Gandesfjord and obviously not spared his horse.

"I only saw one ship," gasped the lookout. "I didn't recognize it, but they looked like raiders. It's too late to intercept it. They're heading for Gausel."

Ragnhild's warriors donned their padded battle-jackets and iron helmets and armed themselves with spears and axes. The archers shouldered their bows and picked up quivers of arrows. Ragnhild led her hird to Gausel, covering the two and a half miles quickly.

They arrived just as the enemy ship landed on the beach. The farmers were grouped outside the longhouse, armed with their scythes and wood-axes, desperation in their eyes. They raised a cheer as Ragnhild led her warriors in front of them.

"Stay behind us. We'll defend you."

Jofrid stepped forward. "Thank you, Lady! Thor bless you!"

Ragnhild led her army down to the beach to meet the ship—packed with men and bristling with spears. Ragnhild estimated there were forty of them. They were raiders, all right, ill-armed, without armor or even helmets. But still more than a group of farmers could fend off.

"Fire at will," Ragnhild cried. Her archers sent a volley into the attackers' midst before they could get their shields up. Shrieks filled the air as several raiders fell. But those who survived vaulted ashore and regrouped quickly, forming a ragged shield wall on the beach.

"Swine horn," Ragnhild shouted. Her warriors gathered in the familiar wedge-shaped formation, Ragnhild at the apex. "For-ward!" she cried, and they charged into the enemy ranks.

She hurled herself at the opposing line, thrusting her spear between the enemy shields, raising a shriek when her spearhead pierced flesh. The raiders were ill prepared for any real resistance and their ragged formation dissolved before Ragnhild's charge. Her warriors fell on the enemy, impaling them with javelins, hacking them with swords and axes. The raiders fled to their ship and struggled to launch it, but Ragnhild's warriors chased them into the water and cut them down. By the end of the battle, the shore was littered with enemy bodies, the water red with their blood. Ravens and gulls wheeled above, fighting to be the first to feed.

"We've won a new ship," said Ragnhild, pausing to catch her breath.

"Sorry ship it is," said Einar.

"It just needs some maintenance," Ragnhild replied. "We'll soon set it right. The best part is that we now have a ship on the Gandesfjord as well as the Hrafrsfjord, without the need to portage."

The raiders' ship was laden with spoils from other farmsteads —sacks of grain, a live pig trussed in the stern, some woven cloth.

"Shame on them, stealing from poor farmers," said Jofrid.

Ragnhild smiled. "I would hardly call farmers such as yourself poor. Is there any way we can find out who owns these things and return them?"

"Perhaps at the next assembly," said Jofrid.

Ragnhild stiffened. Jofrid did not need to say that the assemblies were usually presided over by Harald Goldbeard. "Where is my brother? Does he not defend you?"

"Nay, Lady, he is too far away to keep watch on our shores, nor to spare warriors to protect us."

Ragnhild scanned the citizens of Gausel. They looked strong and healthy. "Perhaps you should learn to defend yourselves."

"We fight when we must, but we're farmers," protested Jofrid.

"As were half my warriors, until we trained them." Ragnhild remembered what Jarl Borg always said. "Farmers are tough and strong. They already know how to handle a blade, they need only learn to reap men instead of barley."

Jofrid nodded. "I'm sure everyone would appreciate the training."

"Tomorrow, then. Send all your able-bodied men and women to my camp."

The next morning a crowd of two dozen sturdy men and women appeared at the ship camp. Ragnhild assigned those of her warriors who had been farmers to lead the citizens of Gausel in their training. The farmers armed themselves with sticks and shields and lined up in two shield walls on either side of a fallow field. While Ragnhild and Einar called out orders from the sidelines, Ragnhild's warriors followed the well-known drills that Jarl Borg had taught them, taking turns to form a swine horn and attack the opposing ranks, then fighting hand-to-hand when the formations dissolved. From the sound of wood rending and cries, everyone was getting a good thrashing.

It kept Ragnhild's mind off of Murchad.

CHAPTER 24

Mountains of Southern Norway

In the afternoon, the lookouts stationed on the cliffs gave their birdcalls and soon hoofbeats sounded. With their arrows, the sentries picked two of the riders off from above, before the raiders reached the camp. The archers in the trees managed to kill one more as they attacked.

Murchad formed his five warriors into a shield wall around Svein to face the dozen surviving attackers. The sentries on the cliffs and archers in the trees rushed to their horses and rode in, spears cocked.

The raiders' horses had not been trained for battle and in the face of armed horsemen hurtling down on them, they bolted. Two attackers were thrown while the rest managed to hang on as their mounts fled.

Murchad's shield wall took the two fallen men prisoner while his crew caught their mounts.

When the captives were bound, Murchad questioned them. "You're too well equipped to be bandits. Who sent you?"

They both set their jaws and said nothing. Murchad drew his knife and tickled one under his chin, drawing a thin line of blood. The raider winced, and Murchad pressed the point of his knife deeper, grinding it into the skin.

The raider grimaced. "We were sent by Harald Goldbeard," he blurted. His companion scowled.

Harald must have had a spy on Tromøy. He probably knew all their plans.

"This is but a respite," Murchad said to his crew. "The rest will be back. There are at least ten of them left, plus however many stayed behind guarding the camp. They'll come after dark and attack tonight. They'll try to pick us off with arrows. It's difficult to guard against such an attack. We'll have to use subterfuge."

They moved Svein away from the fire and hid him nearby in the undergrowth. The pain of moving roused the húskarl and he groaned. "I'm glad to see you're awake, brother," Murchad said. He assigned Ursa and one other to guard him. "You're going to have to keep him quiet."

The shield-maiden nodded grimly. "I'll try."

"Remember, we need him to lead us out of here." Murchad didn't say, *If we survive.*

As darkness fell, he had his men gag the two captives and shove them into empty hudfat. Their dead companions were put into sleeping skins as well. Murchad's crew built up the campfire and laid the bandits around it. When the scene was set, Murchad and his warriors climbed into the trees and waited.

The attackers took the bait. Late that night, dark figures stole into camp and cut the throats of their own men, living and dead. In the firelight the raiders made excellent targets for arrows shot from the trees. The first volley eliminated three of them. Then Murchad's warriors stormed the camp and the rest of the attackers fled.

Murchad counted bodies. "Harald won't welcome back failures. We can expect another attack."

Nobody slept that night. Not knowing when the surviving raiders would come, Murchad set them in the trees to keep a silent vigil over their horses and the corpse-strewn campsite.

Morning came without further attack. Murchad set two sentries to watch from the trees while they took turns sleeping that day. In the evening they all took to the trees again, watching their campfire to see if it lured in any more attackers.

The attack came after dark.

Murchad heard them creeping through the brush and gave his owl's hoot. The raiders were wary this time, knowing their quarry lurked in the trees.

As the attackers crept through the forest, Murchad gave another signal and his warriors dropped onto the raiders as they passed beneath their hiding places. But the enemy was prepared for them. Knife drawn, Murchad landed on a raider who had his own blade ready. Murchad twisted away from the knife and stabbed his blade into the raider's stomach. The man's chain mail stopped the knife and he thrust his blade. Murchad knocked the knife from his hand, but this man was quick and strong. He lunged again and brought Murchad to the ground, straddling him and pinning his arms with his legs. He grabbed Murchad by the throat and throttled him. Murchad writhed, struggling to breathe as he tried to heave the man off his knife arm.

All around him he heard sounds of struggle as his warriors fought the attackers. Sparks flew before his eyes as his air was cut off.

Hoofbeats sounded in the distance. More raiders. Despair overwhelmed Murchad as his vision went dark. He heard the horsemen crash through the brush with a war-cry.

He recognized the war horn voice as Thorgeir's. Murchad felt his assailant's grip falter. He took a huge gulp of air and convulsed, throwing the man off. He rolled onto his attacker and drove his knife up under the man's chin.

The horsemen rode into the melee, driving their spears down on the enemy while Murchad's party dispatched the rest.

When the work was done, Thorgeir reined up beside Murchad.

"I am glad to see you, brother!" gasped Murchad.

Thorgeir grinned down at him. "Your wife is getting cross and sent us to hurry you home."

"That I'll be glad to do, but Svein cannot be moved yet. I am glad to see you have brought Unn."

Unn had dismounted and consulted with her sister over the fallen húskarl, who was awake and groaning. "He's conscious, that's a good sign. You've done well. We need to feed him up but not move him until he can sit a horse. A litter over this rough terrain would kill him for sure."

They stayed at the camp three more days. At last Unn decreed Svein well enough to sit a horse if they went slowly, and they set out for Gausel.

~

Gausel

THE SENTRY CAME RUNNING. Ragnhild looked up and saw the little group of horsemen behind him. For a moment she simply stared. The harness she was mending fell from her hand as the first rider resolved into Murchad's wiry form, his raven hair streaming out behind him like a flag.

She stared a moment longer, then ran. Murchad kicked Svart-faxi into a gallop. As they came together he leaped off his horse and scooped her into an embrace, his lips whispering over her hair. "*A mhuirin*," he murmured. "*A chroi.*"

Tears coursed down her cheeks. She let them fall. "We must never be separated again, husband," she whispered. "We must stay always together after this."

"I never want to be without you again," Murchad replied.

Someone had taken Svartfaxi's bridle and led him off. Ragnhild embraced the others as they tumbled from their saddles. Svein grinned weakly as they helped him off his horse, and let the women herd him off to a tent.

When the newcomers had seen to their horses and settled themselves for a cup of ale, Murchad told their tale. "If Thorgeir hadn't arrived when he did, I'd be dead."

"Bah!" said Thorgeir. "You would have bested those worthless sots, even if they'd outnumbered you ten to one."

"You certainly outsmarted them," said Ragnhild.

"Now, wife, tell me how things stand here," Murchad said. "Why are you camped here, rather than in Gausel's hall?"

Ragnhild explained the situation with the people of Gausel to him. "I promised not to put them in danger. We expect Harald's attack any day, and we will meet him on the shore, away from the steading. What is your counsel, husband?"

Murchad gave it thought. "You have a rightful claim, but in claiming it you endanger these people. In Ireland, that would make no difference to any king. They would press their claim regardless of the destruction that followed. And so we have a land in continual turmoil. I think for now, you should continue as you are. We'll wait for Harald. I don't know if any of the men he sent after us survived. He may or may not know that we got through."

CHAPTER 25

Tromøy
June, AD 823

Åsa set out for the Midsummer Ting. She brought a wagon load of trade goods and a small oak chest filled with silver arm rings and cloak pins to entice warriors to join her. Olvir took charge of Tromøy in her absence, commanding the majority of her forces. Halfdan and the wolf stayed behind with Brenna. The boy was too young to participate, and the wolf was liable to create a stir.

After a chaotic morning they set out on the track to the ferry landing. Åsa rode Gullfaxi beside Jarl Borg, Stormrider perched on her leather-clad shoulder. Heid drove her cart, her apprentices following on foot. A week of dry weather left the ground firm, and the little party made good time on the three-day trek to the assembly grounds in the highlands.

They were among the first to arrive. While they set up camp in Åsa's ancestral spot, she sensed the presence of her father and her mother, and the ancestors that came before them—except perhaps for one, the queen in the mound, who lay on Tromøy, neglected and forgotten.

More warlords rode in and soon the site thronged with their encampments, banners streaming over a sea of tents. The cacophony of trading and greeting filled the air late into the night.

In the morning, Åsa joined the other council members outside the law circle, waiting patiently while Heid and two other völur made a sacrifice and sanctified the enclosure. Jarl Borg entered first, bearing a large gold arm ring which he placed on a rune-carved altar stone in the center of the circle. Åsa stepped over the hallowed bounds and took her place among the other lords. She settled Stormrider on the back of the chair, and looked around at the other council members— grizzled warlords, muscular jarls, petty kings resplendent in embroidered tunics and silver arm rings. As before, she was the only woman in the council circle. Fighting back anxiety, she slipped her hand into the leather pouch and found the necklace. The power flowed up her arm and flamed in her heart, giving her courage.

The council members each nodded to her, some grudging, others friendly. She was their equal, and she'd proven it in battle. Her gaze found Olaf, smiling at her from his place across the circle. Seeing him still made her heart beat harder.

Jarl Orm leaned forward, eyes gleaming with malice. "I hear your shield-maiden has gone against Harald Goldbeard." The other men watched them with interest.

"The Lady Ragnhild only seeks to claim what is hers by right," Åsa answered tautly.

"I hear she's got an Irishman in tow," Orm jeered.

"Lord Murchad is her husband," Åsa replied.

"Well, it will take more than a girl and an Irishman to bring Harald Goldbeard down."

Åsa bristled. "Ragnhild has no intention of bringing her

brother down. She only seeks to rule her lands in peace as is her right."

The men sat back, murmuring amongst themselves.

Jarl Borg cleared his throat. "Perhaps we should hear our first case." As he was the eldest among them, the rest of the assembly followed his advice.

Two húskarlar escorted the first plaintiff to the boundary. The man stepped inside the ropes.

"Come forward, name yourself, and state your business," said Jarl Borg.

The plaintiff approached the altar and laid his hand upon the golden ring. "I am Sorli, son of Gorm, and I swear to tell the truth to this council. Last winter I killed my neighbor, Stein Thorsson. We disagreed over a land boundary. We came to blows, and I struck him dead, by accident."

The council members looked at each other. Their first job was to decide whether the killing was truly accidental, and whether it was properly handled.

Jarl Borg said, "Were there any witnesses to the killing?"

"No, there were not, but as soon as I had killed Stein, I went to my neighbor and declared my deed." Secret killings were always considered murder.

The neighbor came forward, and affirmed that Sorli had reported the killing to him and showed him the body.

"Do you have any more witnesses on your behalf?"

"I do." Sorli called three witnesses to attest to his good character.

"Who speaks for the dead man?" said Borg.

A woman stepped from the crowd. "I do. I am Liv, wife of Stein." After Liv had sworn on the ring, she said, "I was not witness to the killing, but Sorli has ever been after that piece of land. I believe he killed my husband deliberately."

A murmur arose from the crowd. Sorli's face reddened, but he held his tongue. He was not allowed to speak while Liv held the floor.

"Have you any proof of this?" Borg demanded.

Liv hung her head. "No, I do not."

"Very well. If you have no more to say, the council will deliberate."

The crowd dispersed to browse the market while the council discussed its verdict.

"So, is it murder?" said Jarl Borg. If they decided it was, the killer could be outlawed or executed, depending on whether the criminal posed a threat to others.

"There were no witnesses to the killing, so we only have the killer's word as to his motives, and the wife's suspicions," said Olaf.

"True, but he reported the killing properly," said Jarl Orm.

Åsa remembered the case of Onar and Jokul. She wondered if Sorli planned to force Liv into marriage, thereby gaining her land. If that were the case, perhaps it was murder after all. "But his wife believes he killed Sorli to take his land."

"She has no proof," said Jarl Orm.

"And he has good character witnesses," said another.

"I wonder how much he paid them?" Olaf said. This remark was met with cynical laughter.

"His defense seems to be in order," Orm said.

Jarl Borg cleared his throat and stood. "Based on the evidence, I think we have to call it an accidental killing."

Åsa found that by the evidence presented, she had to agree, though in her heart she believed the wife. "What wergild should be paid to the widow?"

"Stein was an able man in his prime, so his wergild is three marks," Jarl Borg decreed.

This did not sit well with Åsa. "His widow has three children, all of them too young to be much help to her, and she has no other kin. She'll have to hire a man to do the heavy work. Her husband's wergild won't cover that expense. She's not a wealthy woman."

"Well, she can always marry," said Orm.

"And I can tell you who will be the first man to propose," Åsa snapped.

Most of the council nodded in agreement.

"Suspicion is not evidence," said Jarl Orm. "It falls beyond the purview of this council to act on it."

Though Orm was correct, Åsa could not bring herself to sentence the widow to marry her husband's murderer. She knew how that felt. "I have a solution." The men all turned to look at her. "As well as the wergild, the killer should be made to perform some of the labor of the man he's killed."

"Have him work for her like a slave? Sorli's a free man," Jarl Orm objected.

"Well, make Sorli supply her with a slave, then." Åsa hated the idea but it might be the only way to keep Liv independent.

"That's beyond the prescribed penalty."

Åsa thought of the other widows who struggled to survive. "A woman should not be left destitute by the loss of her husband. The law should serve all people. It needs to change."

"The law was set down by our forefathers. If it was good enough for them, it's good enough for us. I say, let her marry," said Orm again.

The others voiced their agreement, all but Åsa, Olaf, and Jarl Borg.

After the council ended for the day, Olaf walked back to her camp with her.

"I'm so angry about Liv," she said. "The law is wrong."

"It makes me angry, too, but we can't change it if the others don't agree," said Olaf.

"I'll think of something," she muttered.

Olaf smiled. "I'm sure you will." He cleared his throat. "I want to talk to you about Eyvind."

She stared at him. "Eyvind? What concern is he of yours?"

He shook his head. "It's just that none of us know him that well. I'm not sure he can be trusted."

"You introduced him to me," she said.

"I know. I know. I just didn't think…"

"Didn't think what?" She felt her face heating up.

"Look, the man's a sea-king. And Tromøy is just there for the plucking."

"Olaf, I think I've proven I'm not helpless. I've fought off the Danish navy."

"I know you're a great warrior," he said. "I'm just not sure you're as good when it comes to guarding your heart."

Hands on hips, she glared at him. He lowered his head and hurried off.

As she watched him depart, worry niggled in her gut. Olaf had known Eyvind longer than she had. If he was worried enough to say something, perhaps she should heed his warning.

~

THAT EVENING, Åsa searched the encampment for Liv. She found her at her tent, three young children clinging to her skirts.

"I know what it is to be forced to marry a murderer," Åsa said. "You need not fear Sorli. You are welcome to join my entourage and I will see you home."

"Thank you, Lady," Liv said, "for believing me, even though I couldn't prove it, and for protecting me from Sorli."

Liv moved her children and their belongings to Åsa's camp. Though the widow did not complain, Åsa worried how she'd manage to keep the farm afloat without kin or husband.

People approached, hovering in the darkness.

"Show yourselves," Åsa commanded. "Name yourselves."

One by one, six young men and four women came forward and stated their names, and their wish to join Åsa's hird. Some of them carried their own weapons, whether a wood-axe or a homemade spear. Two even wore swords on their belts, obviously family heirlooms, much honed.

"Come forward, and tell me your names and your families." Åsa hauled up Gudrød's Bane and laid the sword across her knees.

She questioned them, turning away some who were too young. "Come back in a few years," she told them.

By the evening's end she'd accepted seven recruits of varying experience—three men and four women, all young but not the raw trainees she'd taken on in the past.

That night, Åsa lay awake in her tent, worrying about Liv and her children. The widow deserved more support than the council offered. Yet Åsa could only provide temporary assistance. This was Sorli's responsibility, but she had no power to make him pay. She thought of other widows she knew, who ran their farms with the help of grown children or hired hands.

In the morning Åsa rose, bleary-eyed. They heard several cases: another killing, this time accidental, divorces, property disputes. She brought up Liv's plight once more, but Orm and his cohorts made it clear the matter was closed.

That evening, two men approached her fire.

"Come forward," she said.

The men stepped into the firelight. Brothers, by the looks of them. They were in their mid-to-late twenties, lean but filled out with muscle. They each bore swords and shields, with axes tucked in their belts.

"Name yourselves," she ordered. "State your business."

"Lady, I am Sune Leifson, and this is my brother, Hjorleif. We come from the mountains. We wish to serve you in your hird."

"Why have you left your home?"

"We have two elder brothers who will inherit the family farm. There is not enough land for all of us."

This was a common tale. A farmer would have many children

to work the fields, but not enough land to divide among them all when the time came for them to marry and have children of their own. The younger sons must find their own way, most often the way of the sword. At least Sune and Hjorleif's father had supplied them with weaponry.

"And why would you serve me and not some other lord?" Åsa remembered Behrt's reply to that question the year before—that no other lord would have him. She stiffened, waiting for Sune's answer.

"We have heard that you are brave," said Sune, "and that a man may make a name for himself serving under you."

His words filled Åsa with pride. "Tell me, Sune and Hjorleif, are you willing to perform a service for me?"

"Anything, Lady."

"I've taken a widow and her children under my protection. Are you willing to escort her home, protect her, and help her set her farm to rights?"

The brothers exchanged a proud glance. "We are honored that you would entrust us with such a mission, Lady."

Åsa beamed. She drew her sword and laid it across her knees.

Sune leaned forward and laid his hand on the blade. "I am Sune, son of Leif, a free man. I swear to serve you faithfully with my life."

When he looked up, his eyes were glowing.

Hjorleif came forward and did the same.

"Find a place among my hird, Sune and Hjorleif, sons of Leif," said Åsa. She reached into her oak chest and drew out two silver arm rings, one of twisted silver terminating in a serpent's head, the other etched with runes. The two men donned their rings and bowed to Åsa. "Bring your hudfat to my camp," she said. The brothers dashed off to retrieve their gear.

Åsa assigned two girls to help Liv as well. She knew it was only a temporary solution. She didn't have the manpower to provide permanent assistance to every widow in her district, but perhaps a few of her people could make the rounds of the farm-steads, lending help where needed. It was a start. Åsa went to sleep happy that night.

When she packed up to return home, Åsa had gained nine new recruits. Not enough to fill the ranks Ragnhild had taken with her, but it was a good start. The summer was young and she hoped more would find their way to Tromøy before winter.

When Åsa told Liv that four strong young people would accompany her home, the widow burst into tears. "I'll never be able to thank you enough, Lady," she said. "I will find a way to repay you, somehow."

"I am sure you will," Åsa said.

CHAPTER 26

Gausel
July, AD 823

The war horns sounded before dawn. Ragnhild scrambled out of her hudfat, Murchad right behind her.

Warriors were already building up the fire. The lookout was sitting on a log, drinking ale and catching his breath. "A fleet is on its way down the Gandesfjord. I can't tell how many."

Murchad took his riders to ready the horses. They grabbed their weapons and shields and hurried out into the yard, strapping on swords, hefting spears, while the rest pulled on their helms and padded battle jackets by firelight. Murchad's party returned within minutes leading the saddled, bridled mounts. Ragnhild, wearing her chain mail brynja and helm, heaved herself into the saddle and accepted a piece of flatbread from the cook. Flanked by Murchad and Einar, she led the warband out of camp just as the sky began to lighten.

They rode the few miles to the beach, foot soldiers bringing up the rear. Ragnhild and Einar dismounted while Murchad led his mounted warriors, armed with javelins and axes, behind the hills where they stayed hidden in reserve.

As the sun rose, Ragnhild made out five sails. Her heart plummeted. At least one hundred and fifty warriors. As they drew closer, she recognized the lead ship. *Battle Swan.*

Harald, come at last. Her eyes flicked over the fleet, and she was relieved that Orlyg's ship was not among them.

As the vessels neared the shore, she saw that they were loaded with men. She quickly revised their numbers upward to two hundred. Dread sent a chill through her body. Ragnhild faced her brother with one hundred and sixteen warriors. Worse, Harald knew about Murchad's cavalry. She only hoped he didn't know the full extent of their capabilities.

She swallowed hard and turned to her troops.

"We're outnumbered," she cried, "but each of us is worth five of them. Today we must call upon all of our skill, all of our training. We can take them!"

Their cheers thundered as Harald's fleet neared the shore.

Harald would be forced to do battle on her chosen ground. Her archers and spearmen could wreak devastating damage on them while they beached their boats. She lined them up three rows deep, shields locked, spears ready. Behind the front lines she had placed fifty archers, then took her place at the head of the shield wall, next to her Valkyrie battle-flag.

Harald's fleet turned toward her shield wall arrayed on the beach. The enemy ships rode in on the surf, loosing a hail of arrows. There was little wind, but the ships' motion hampered their aim. "Shields up!" Ragnhild barked. Most of the missiles fell short, but a few arrows smacked into wood as her shield men caught the volley.

"Archers! Loose!" she cried, and they sent up a deadly cloud toward the ships. The sailors got their shields up but from their screams she knew some arrows had found their marks.

"Spears ready!" They waited as the fleet drew near. She spotted Harald, glaring beneath his helm.

She locked eyes with her older brother as his ship ground into the beach. His men vaulted over the side and formed a loose shield wall.

Harald leaped into the shallows, sword drawn. Ragnhild drew Lady's Servant and stepped forward to meet him.

"I see you have a battle standard, little sister," Harald sneered. He stood beside his own flag of a swan in flight. The breeze lifted the swan's wings as if the bird were flying at them.

"Yes, brother, I've come to claim what's mine." The wind rippled through her standard, and the Valkyrie's horse appeared to canter toward the enemy.

"I've had enough of your girlish fantasies," Harald said. "Yield, sister, or it will be the worse for you."

"Make me," said Ragnhild, hefting Lady's Servant.

"I will." Harald turned to his men and cried, "Charge!"

Ragnhild stepped back into the shield wall, locking her shield to her neighbors'. The warriors beside her held their spears ready between their shields as Harald's men attacked, spears leveled, axes swinging. The two forces collided with a deafening clash of metal on wood. Axes hacked into shields, spears penetrated leather armor. Men fell, screaming.

Ragnhild's shield wall crumbled quickly in the face of Harald's onslaught, and the formations disintegrated into skirmishes. Time for horsemen. Ragnhild blew her battle horn.

An eerie shriek split the air and Murchad galloped in at the head of the cavalry. The horsemen swooped down on Harald's forces, casting their light spears into the startled enemy. Judging by the screams, their missiles reaped a goodly toll, but Harald's men regrouped quickly and charged the cavalry.

At a horn's blast from Murchad, the horsemen wheeled their mounts and pretended to flee. Harald's men pursued them, hurling their javelins at their backs. But the horsemen wore their shields slung across their backs, and the spears clattered off harmlessly.

Murchad blew his horn again. The horsemen wheeled their horses and turned back on their pursuers. Harald's men were caught off guard with no time to regroup. The cavalry rode into their midst, slashing swords and axes into the disorganized throng. The enemy turned to flee, only to meet Ragnhild's warriors.

Murchad cast his spear straight at Harald, who sent his own missile soaring at the Irishman. The two spears passed midflight and glanced off the other's shield. Murchad drew his sword and charged the Norse king, hacking his blade down on Harald's helmet. The steel rang and Harald stumbled. Murchad pivoted Svartfaxi and swung again, connecting with the helmet once more and knocking the Norseman off his feet. Harald lay gasping on the ground, staring at the Irishman riding down on him. He managed to roll aside as Murchad's sword slashed down.

Murchad wheeled his mount and spurred back to Harald, who scrambled to his feet and blew his horn to rally his men. In an instant they had formed a shield wall around their king.

Murchad reined up. Svartfaxi snorted, still game, but it was time for Ragnhild to take the lead.

Her foot soldiers rallied to her call. They formed a wedge-shaped swine array, with Ragnhild at the apex, and charged Harald's shield fortress.

They hit the shield wall with all their force, but Harald's men held firm against the battering.

More of Harald's men surrounded Ragnhild and her foot soldiers while Murchad's horsemen charged the perimeter, hurling javelins at the enemy. In spite of the hail of spears from the cavalry and the sword blows from Ragnhild's infantry, Harald's men held firm. They fended off missiles and slashes with their shields, closing in on Ragnhild and her warriors.

Above the sea of helmets and shields, she glimpsed a warrior get hold of Murchad's leg and try to drag him from Svartfaxi's back. Murchad hacked at him with his sword while Svartfaxi lashed out with his hooves. The assailant let go of Murchad and rammed his spear into the horse's chest before he was trampled under the hooves.

Svartfaxi lurched to his knees. Murchad leaped off his back, swinging his sword in a broad arc to keep the enemy at bay. Ragnhild screamed and hacked into the shields before her, trying to fight her way to him. As the enemy swallowed her into a chaotic melee, she met her husband's gaze.

"I'm sorry, *a chroi*," she cried.

"No regrets," he shouted, slashing his sword into the throng of men.

He disappeared in a sea of shields and helmets. Was he down? She strained to catch sight of him, but he'd vanished into the crowd.

"Murchad!" she cried, ramming her sword into the man before her. He folded over her blade, then fell as she jerked it out of his gut. "Murchad!"

Her gaze searched frantically, sighting Murchad slumped over Svartfaxi.

Horse and rider lay still, covered in blood.

Ragnhild rushed to him, but enemies barred her way, crushing in on her with shields and blades. A warrior lunged at Ragnhild, all but impaling himself on her blade. She yanked her sword free of his corpse and let him fall while she kept hacking through the enemy. Rage turned her vision red and she thrust viciously into their ranks, drawing screams. But for each man that fell, two more filled in the gap. She killed and killed, until they all lay bleeding at her feet, and still they came.

The last shield fell and her way to Murchad was clear. She stumbled over the dead and dying, shoved the corpses away and knelt over his body, sheltering him beneath her shield. He lay still and pale in a pool of blood.

"No!" she screamed. Harald's men descended on her and she sprang to her feet, hacking and slashing. She stood over Murchad's body, cutting down all who came near. She chopped a spear shaft in half and rammed her blade into the spearman's gut. She ripped it out as he fell and drove it into the next man's throat, then turned to meet a new attacker.

A horn sounded in the distance and she glanced up. A crowd of people marched toward them, bristling with spears and axes. Her heart sank. They couldn't take on more.

Then she recognized the farmers of Gausel. Jofrid strode at their head, bearing spear and shield.

The farmers fell on the diminished outer ring of Harald's warriors with spear and axe, hacking their way with workman-like strokes toward Ragnhild and Murchad.

Attacked from both sides, Harald's men were overwhelmed at last and they fled. The cavalry chased them down to the beach. Many were cut down in the water, but enough managed to reach their ships to launch them and row away.

Chest heaving, Ragnhild dropped to her knees beside Murchad.

Jofrid approached. The headwoman gazed sorrowfully down on the fallen Irishman. "He was brave, and skilled."

Warriors clustered around them, heads bowed. Ursa and Unn rushed in and fell to their knees beside Murchad. "No!" cried Ursa.

"Shh!" Unn hissed. She eased his helmet off and put her cheek near his mouth. After a moment, she peeled back his tunic and held her ear against his chest.

She sat back on her haunches and looked at Ragnhild. "He lives, Lady."

Ragnhild's arm began to tremble. Her sword fell from nerveless fingers. For a moment, she couldn't catch her breath.

He lives.

～

BLINKING BACK TEARS, Ragnhild stroked Svartfaxi's face. The horse lifted his head, looking up at her with eyes that begged for release. "Good horse, brave horse. Ride with the Valkyries today." The horse gazed up at her with trusting eyes as she drew her knife and ended his suffering.

Some of those who were uninjured carried the wounded to the steading, while others collected the dead. Harald's men and their own were all laid together on a huge pyre.

Ragnhild walked beside the stretcher bearers who carried Murchad to the hall. Jofrid fell in with her. "Thank you, Lady," said Ragnhild. "You saved us."

"We owed you that, and more," said Jofrid, "I will send my healer to help tend to your wounded. Then come to the hall to rest yourselves."

They brought Murchad and the other wounded into the guest house, where Unn joined Gausel's healer, Thyra.

"Murchad was knocked unconscious," Thyra reported briskly. "The blood was not his."

"We lost twelve," said Unn, tearfully.

"A great loss." Grief filled Ragnhild. Was it worth it?

She stayed by Murchad's side until he opened his eyes.

"Hello, Oison," she whispered in Irish. "Did you have a nice visit to the other world?"

He smiled. "I had to come back for you."

～

THAT NIGHT they burned the dead. Svartfaxi and two other fallen horses were laid on their own pyre. For the first time, Ragnhild recited the rites. As the fires burned down, Jofrid welcomed everyone to the hall. Ragnhild helped Murchad in from the guesthouse.

Jofrid ushered Ragnhild and Murchad to the high seat and served them mead. They drank to the fallen, naming each one.

When all the dead had been toasted, Jofrid turned to Ragnhild. "We have reached a decision," she announced. "You've done more for us than Harald ever has. You helped us with our work when you could have just taken what you wanted. You kept the battle away from us. You've shown us how to fight. Now we can defend ourselves and make our own decisions."

"And when Harald comes back?" said Ragnhild.

"We'll fight him again. We've already proven we can stand up to him." Jofrid turned to the benches and raised her horn. "I propose that we accept Ragnhild and her husband as rightful leaders of Gausel, as her mother wished." The populace of Gausel beat their weapons on their shields in approval.

Ragnhild turned to Murchad, her eyes gleaming. "Husband, we've won our kingdom."

Murchad raised his horn and smiled. "Now we must keep it."

⁓

Solbakk

Signy held her infant daughter and watched her brother-in-law with concern. Now that Harald was openly at war with Ragnhild, Orlyg was beside himself. He and Ragnhild had always been close. The young warrior paced the shore like a caged beast, staring off to sea as if searching for his sister, the worry and frustration coming off him in waves. When Orlyg refused to join his elder brother in his attack on Gausel, Harald had cut him off. He acted as if his younger brother didn't exist. Worse, he could withhold Orlyg's inheritance as he had Ragnhild's.

Harald was tearing the family apart. She had to find a way to reason with him.

Signy handed her daughter off to the fóstra and hurried down to the shore to intercept Orlyg.

"We have to stop this feud," he muttered.

"I know. But how?"

"Ragnhild is just as stubborn as he is. I tried to reason with her, but she won't hear anything I say."

Signy sighed. "I tried to convince Harald to let her be, but he's determined to run her off."

"Ragnhild is within her rights," said Orlyg. "I'll never join Harald against her."

"He's not making things easy on you," Signy observed. "I can talk to him again. I can't promise he'll listen to me, but I'll do my best."

"You're the only hope this family has," said Orlyg.

Signy squared her shoulders and set off up the hill.

She found Harald in the cow-byre where one of the cows was birthing a late calf. Birth was the purview of women, but here was Harald hunched among the dairymaids at the cow's hindquarters, his arm up to the elbow inside the cow.

"Easy, easy," he murmured as the cow lowed in distress. He probed a little further. "The calf is breach."

Signy hurried over. "Why did no one call me?" she said, laying a reassuring hand on the cow's flank. She felt the contraction and the cow bellowed in pain.

"We weren't sure where you were," said one of the dairymaids. "None of us had arms long enough to reach the calf so we had to call the king."

"I've got a hoof," said Harald in triumph.

"As soon as the contraction eases, pull," said Signy. She raised a birthing chant and the four maids joined in. The sound calmed the distressed cow.

"I'm pulling," said Harald. "It's coming. Just a little farther..." The cow's sides heaved in another contraction and Harald stopped. The women continued their chant as the contraction subsided.

"Now find the other hoof and pull it into line with the other," said Signy.

Between contractions, Harald pushed his arm far up inside the cow. "Got it. It's aligned with the other."

"One more good pull," said Signy.

When the next contraction eased, Harald grunted and pulled hard. The cow gave a bellow and the calf shot out so fast that Harald stumbled, landing on his back, the slippery calf gripped in his arms.

"There, little one," he whispered.

Signy stared at her husband, sitting in the straw crooning to a newborn calf.

She hurried over to clean its muzzle off with a handful of straw. Together, they helped the calf to stand up and nurse, while the cow licked her baby contentedly.

"How can you treat your livestock better than your own sister?" Signy said.

"My livestock doesn't rebel against me." Harald's eyes were defiant.

"Your sister is only claiming what is hers. You have no right under the law to withhold her property and you know it. Will you withhold Orlyg's inheritance as well?"

"No one will stand against me."

"She does. And from what I hear, so do the people of Gausel. Even your brother takes her side." She rose and brushed off her skirt. "And me. Will you trade your whole family?"

She walked out of the byre, Harald staring after her.

CHAPTER 27

Tromøy
Autumn, AD 823

The lookout scurried up the trail to announce a ship's arrival. Åsa rose from the bench outside the hall where she was playing with Halfdan. Shading her eyes against the late afternoon glare with a hand, her heart quickened as she recognized the red-and-white striped sail.

Eyvind.

Brenna looked down at the harbor and nodded wisely. The old fóstra took Halfdan by the hand and led him off. Åsa smiled gratefully and hurried to the stable where she saddled Gullfaxi and rode down the trail to the harbor, anticipation bubbling in her chest.

Eyvind's ship surged onto the beach. On deck was a familiar looking pile covered by a hide. Following her gaze, the Svea grinned and twitched the hide back to reveal a stack of gray ingots.

"Greetings, Far Traveler," she called. "I see you've brought a welcome cargo."

He gave her a sultry smile. "I hope I'm welcome for more than my cargo."

Åsa felt the color rise in her face as it always seemed to do when Eyvind was near. She was pleased to see him—more pleased than she wanted to be. She tried to slow the quickening of her heart as she greeted him. "Come to the hall, you and your crew. I've got some ale freshly brewed."

"Gladly, Lady." His blue eyes twinkled at her. She rode ahead as he led his crew up the hill to the hall. Ulf waited impatiently outside the smithy and Eyvind stopped off to tell the smith he'd brought him wootz ingots.

Åsa rode on, arriving at the hall well ahead of her guests. She dismounted and handed Gullfaxi's reins to the stable boy, and set the kitchen staff scurrying. "Brenna!" she cried, bursting into the bower. "I need you!" The fóstra got up from the floor where she'd been playing with Halfdan and threw open Åsa's garment chest. She pulled out a dress of fine blue wool and shook it, scenting the air with packing herbs. Brenna helped Åsa dress, then sat her on the stool and unbraided her red-gold hair, combing the shining torrent smooth, then twisting it into a knot at the back of her head.

"Your eyes have a sparkle I've not seen in a long time," Brenna said fondly.

Åsa hurried to the hall, arriving a bit out of breath. She greeted Eyvind at the door and led him to the high seat while his crew found places amongst Tromøy's hird. She accepted the ale horn from Hogni and offered it to Eyvind. "Drink, Eyvind, and be welcome," she said formally.

"I thank you, Lady." Eyvind accepted the cup and drank. Åsa took her own seat beside him while Vigdis carried the ale horn around the room.

"I have brought you a small gift." From his belt pouch, Eyvind withdrew a leather bag and opened it. Inside lay a ring of silver, set with a huge chunk of amber.

"You shower me with gifts," Åsa said, beaming.

Eyvind took the ring from the bag and slid it on her finger. He sat back and gazed at her, a look in his eyes that made her heart quicken.

As she sat through the welcome feast, Åsa couldn't stop her toe from tapping impatiently. Eyvind's proximity on the guest seat kept her unsettled. She was keenly aware each time his blue gaze returned to her throughout the evening.

As soon as the others began to find their sleeping places, she took Eyvind by the hand and led him to her chamber.

He kicked the door shut and took her in his arms. She cupped his face in her hands and kissed him. The desire born of long separation welled up between them and she let herself drift in a warm sea of passion. Still entwined, they edged toward the bed and fell onto the eiderdown.

After their lovemaking, he pulled her close and murmured into her hair, "I don't want to leave you again. I want to stay here for the winter."

Åsa stiffened. A chill passed over her as she remembered Olaf's warning. She pulled away. "You take much for granted."

He frowned. "Am I not welcome?"

Åsa took a deep breath. "I will never make you a king."

Eyvind glared at her, a storm brewing in his eyes. "That's the last thing I want."

"Are you sure of that?" Åsa's blood rose. She stood. "You're a landless sea-king. How convenient it would be to gain a kingdom by marriage."

"I can't believe you think that's why I'm here. If I threaten you that much, I'll leave." He rose, snatched his tunic from the floor and jerked it over his head. He yanked his breeks on and grabbed his swordbelt and boots.

Though she longed to reach out and stop him, to take back

her words, she couldn't. *He'll say whatever he thinks will win me. And then he'll take my power. I will be no better off than I was with Gudrød.*

From the corner of her eye she watched him stalk out, slamming the chamber door behind him.

She sat for a long time in stunned silence. *It's happening again. I lost Olaf this way, and now Eyvind. Where will it stop? Will I be alone forever—like the queen in the mound? Perhaps she's right, that's my destiny. I'll protect my people, my son. That's all that matters.*

And when I'm old, I'll turn Tromøy over to Halfdan, and go into the mound to be forgotten too.

Now in the chamber's dim shadows the tears fell, the tears she'd held back so long. She picked up her leather pouch from the floor and reached in. Her fingers found the golden necklace, taking comfort from its strength.

It seemed all men were the same. They wanted power. Eyvind was no different. To keep her power, she must remain alone.

She would accept her fate, and make the best of it. Holding the necklace, she lay back on the bed and cried herself to sleep.

～

EYVIND STORMED DOWN THE BEACH, his chest tight with rage. "I'm a fool," he muttered. "She'll never trust me. She thinks all I want is her kingdom. She doesn't know me at all. She judges me by the same measure she has every man she's known."

He was so angry he'd come away with no food or water. Well, there was no going back tonight. Time to shelter. He veered inland from the beach, toward the forest. The trees seemed to part before him, as if inviting him in. As he stepped into the woodland, the moonlight picked out a faint pathway before him. A game trail, no doubt.

The early autumn canopy shed the worst of the rain and the forest litter crackled, dry beneath his boots. He caught the welcome music of trickling water in the distance. He followed the sound until it brought him to a spring bubbling from a rock, where he drank his fill. It was full dark now, and he leaned against a sheltering hillock. The earthy scent of the leaves mixed with the astringent smell of pine, and the forest stilled save the hoot of an owl.

At some point he must have fallen asleep, for he dreamed that a tall, fair-faced woman came to him. There was a glow about her and he realized she was no mortal. Eyvind's scalp prickled.

"Greetings, Lord," she said in a silvery voice. "You are far from home."

CHAPTER 28

At dawn, fingers of light filtered in through the gable end and touched Åsa's face. Memories of the night came flooding back. *What have I done?* Regret swept over her in waves.

She rose and dressed, hastily wrapped her cloak around her shoulders, and hurried into the hall.

Perhaps he's still here. At least we could part friends.

The hall loomed empty. She hurried through the cavernous depths and burst out of the door into the morning light and ran down the trail to the shore. With a sigh of relief, she saw his ship on the beach, the crew moving about. Eyvind must have spent the night there, and still be aboard. Her heart quickened. She had to see him before he left, even if only to say farewell.

She reached the ship and scanned the men for him. But he wasn't among his crew. "Where is Eyvind?" she asked.

A sailor shrugged. "We haven't seen him." His look said, *We thought he was with you.*

Dread welled up in her. Suddenly, nothing mattered but that she find him. He could be anywhere on the island. She hurried to the bower room where Stormrider drowsed on her perch. Åsa lay on the bed and slid into the falcon's body, then lofted out of the gable end and soared over the steading.

She followed his trail along the beach until it entered the forest. As she glided through the trees, her keen falcon's vision discerned the delicate traces he left on the foliage and woodland floor. His trail took her deep into the forest, to a lonely place that she knew well. A jolt of fear pierced her.

The trail ended at the queen's mound.

She soared up above the trees and winged back to the bower where Heid had taken up vigil beside her still form. Concern creasing the völva's ravaged face.

Åsa flew into her body. "The queen has taken Eyvind into her mound." She stumbled out of bed. "I must go to him."

"I'm coming with you," said Heid, rising from her stool.

Åsa didn't wait for the sorceress. She grabbed her sword off the wall and ran out the door to the horse-byre, where she saddled Gullfaxi. She threw herself into the saddle and rode off down the trail, into the forest.

The grave mound hulked, dark among the trees. She dismounted and took a deep breath, striving to quell her fear. The memory of the haugbui's power shook her.

The Irish necklace inside her belt pouch called to her, its power emanating through the leather.

She reached in and touched the gold. Power surged into her fingers and flowed up her arm, tingling in her chest. She took a deep breath.

"Grandmother, awake! I am Åsa, daughter of Harald Redbeard, queen of your lineage. I demand entry."

The mound sulked among the trees, inert.

"Open to me, ancient one. You cannot deny me."

Silence.

If such power flowed into her when she merely touched the necklace, what would happen if she wore it? Heid had warned her that it was hostile to her, but she'd suffered no harm from it. And now she was desperate.

Åsa drew the necklace from the pouch. Hot to touch, the metal sent vibrations up her arms. Hands trembling, she brought the links over her head and settled it around her neck. The golden disks touched her chest and a great welling of power seared her heart. It pulsed there, spilling over until her whole body vibrated. Her head blazed, her limbs seemed alight with flame, her heart beat hard and fast.

She took a deep breath and summoned her galdr training, charging her voice with power. "Obey me, Lady, or my curse will fall upon you. Worms will gnaw your bones, wild animals will scatter them in the forest. I swear this will come to pass. I am mighty, and you cannot withstand my will."

From deep within the mound, a rumbling growled. The earth trembled.

"Open to your daughter, Grandmother," Åsa commanded.

The mound shook and a rift gaped in its side, emitting an unearthly glow.

"Enter, child," came the silky voice.

Suppressing a shudder, Åsa stepped into the mound.

The eerie light revealed Eyvind's still form on the bed, his face white as a swan's wing. His eyes were open, but he didn't register her presence. Åsa's throat tightened.

The draugr's form emerged from the gloom. "Daughter, you've neglected me." Her eyes flicked to the necklace, and Åsa pulled her cloak over it protectively.

The queen frowned. "You gave your word that you would honor me on the sacred days."

"Yet when I came, you tried to lure me into the mound."

"I was lonely," sulked the ghoul.

"You know I cannot leave my people without a leader. You would never have done so." When the haugbui did not reply, Åsa turned to Eyvind's still form. "You have taken this one of mine. You must return him to me."

The queen pouted. "You rejected him. What makes you think he wants to come back to you, after the way you've treated him?"

Her words stung.

"Oh yes, I know all about it. You fear that if you give him your heart, he'll take your kingdom too. And you're right. That's all he wanted you for."

Åsa's hand trembled.

"Leave him with me, daughter. Keep your kingdom safe from men like him."

Åsa raised her chin. "I've fought off raiders and warlords, I've fought off entire fleets to keep my kingdom safe. I don't need your help."

"Oh, but you do, daughter. You are mighty with the sword, but your heart is your weakness."

Åsa flinched at the ring of truth in her words. She stared down at Eyvind, whose glassy eyes stared back. *This is my fault. I drove him here to become the victim of the haugbui, my ancestor. I can't leave him here.*

She drew Gudrød's Bane. "This man is not for you. He belongs to the living. Release him, or I'll cure your loneliness permanently."

The queen cackled and drew her own sword, and held it to Eyvind's throat. "Daughter, I'll never wake him. If you send me onward, he will sleep forever, and I will take your hamingja with me. Nature will turn against you, the seasons will be ill, sickness will come where you expected joy."

Åsa fought the dread that rose in her stomach. The only way to save Eyvind was to dispatch the queen, hamingja be damned.

Somehow, she had to lure the haugbui away from Eyvind, within striking distance.

Then she knew what she had to do.

She hesitated only an instant before opening her cloak to reveal the golden necklace.

It seemed to burn with its own light, flaring in the dim mound. The draugr's metallic eyes riveted on it and her mouth hung open. She reached for the glinting gold.

"Just let me touch it," the draugr rasped.

Åsa pulled the necklace over her head.

Before the haugbui could read her intent, Åsa hung the necklace on her sword point and held it out toward the ghoul. The draugr hissed and reached for the gold.

Just as the haugbui's fingers closed around the golden chain, Åsa swung Gudrød's Bane. "I make my own luck." She sliced her blade into the ghoul's neck, severing it in one stroke.

The haugbui's head flew across the chamber and smashed into the timber wall. The draugr's body collapsed, the golden necklace clutched in a skeletal hand.

A staggering sense of loss gut-punched Åsa. She lowered her sword, hands shaking. The haugbui was gone. But Eyvind still lay like the dead.

The sound of the vardlokkur drifted into the mound. Outside, Heid and her apprentices chanted.

Åsa sheathed her sword. She bent over the queen's corpse and grabbed the necklace, tugging. The bony fingers held it fast. She jerked hard, but the draugr's hand clutched the golden chain.

A shadow fell over her. Glancing up, she saw the gap in the mound narrow. She dropped the necklace and took hold of Eyvind, pulling him. His body was limp and unresponsive as a corpse. He was heavier than a man should be, already taking on the density of a draugr.

The vardlokkur sounded louder, taking on an urgent tone. The air rang with the chants, swelling into the trees.

Eyvind's body moved. Not much, but he moved.

Åsa hauled with all her strength and managed to drag him to

the opening. She heaved him upright and propped his inert body against the side of the mound.

"Help me!" she cried.

Heid's eyes snapped open and she left off chanting. "Lend her a hand, you fools," she barked.

The apprentices reached in and took hold of Eyvind. Åsa pushed from behind as the women hauled him through the narrowing entrance. She wriggled through and tumbled after him, landing on the ground with a thud just as the mound closed. She lay in the dirt, panting.

"Get him into the wagon," Heid ordered. "We must bring him back to the bower quickly." She looked at Åsa. "Where's the necklace?"

"She's got it." Åsa nodded toward the mound.

"Good riddance," said the völva.

"Murchad won't be happy." Åsa got up from the ground and brushed the grave-dirt from her clothes and hair. Her legs felt loose and flimsy.

It took all the apprentices to manhandle Eyvind's body into the back of the cart. Then they helped the völva into the driver's seat and Åsa mounted Gullfaxi. Heid took up the reins and set off through the forest, her apprentices trotting alongside.

They brought Eyvind into the bower, where they lay him on the bench by the fire. Heid gathered the apprentices around the unconscious man, and resumed the vardlokkur. Åsa joined in with fervor.

They sang until their voices began to falter, but there was no change in Eyvind. "Rest, ladies," said Heid. "He lives. That will do for now."

The apprentices departed to eat and rest. Heid sat down beside Åsa and fixed her with a stern gaze.

"Who rules here?" she demanded.

Åsa looked at her, startled. "I am queen here."

"And how did you become such?"

"I was elected by my people."

"How have you kept your kingdom?"

"I have fought battles to keep it."

"Whom have you fought?"

"The Danes. King Solvi. Raiders. And Gudrød."

"And you have won every time. Who were these that you have overcome?"

"Kings—land kings, sea-kings, warlords…"

"What do they all have in common?"

Åsa pondered a moment. "They were men."

Heid nodded. "And so you have defeated all these mighty men to keep your power and defend your kingdom."

"Yes."

"Then why do you fear one landless man so much?" The völva nodded at Eyvind's still form. "Is he so dangerous? What has he got that all those vanquished men did't have?"

Åsa swallowed. "He has my heart."

The sorceress frowned. "And is your heart so weak that this man can take your power?"

Åsa stared at the völva, her mind at a standstill.

"He'll wake when you will it so." Heid rose. "I need some food," she said, and stalked out of the bower.

Åsa looked down at Eyvind, lying helpless on the bed. It wasn't him she feared. She feared her own heart.

After her treatment at the hands of men, how could she bring herself to trust one again? When she'd refused Gudrød's suit, he'd rained hellfire on her family, murdering her father and her brother and burning Tromøy. She had borne a heavy guilt over that. If she'd given in to him, married him, her father and brother would still be alive. And Ragnhild. Åsa had fought a war to preserve the shield-maiden's freedom from marriage to the Irish king—yet she'd returned, married to him after all, and happier for it. If Ragnhild had given in to her father…how many lives would have been spared?

But the truth was they'd both fought for their right to make their own choices. And she'd do so again. If she was wrong, so be it.

She didn't have to trust Eyvind. He was only a man. If he posed a danger, she would deal with him just as she had all the other men who'd threatened her.

But Eyvind had threatened nothing. He'd only said he wished he didn't have to leave her. She wished the same thing.

She took his hand and whispered, "Eyvind, I want you. I accept you. I believe you. Come back to me."

As her tears fell on his face, Eyvind's eye twitched. His milk-pale face began to gain color. His breathing intensified, the rise and fall of his chest strengthened.

Eyvind's eyes fluttered open. She found herself staring into their blue depths and smiled.

~

Gausel
August, AD 823

THE LOOKOUT CAME RUNNING. "Ships are coming down the Gandesfjord. More than one, though I couldn't tell how many, with the fog."

Ragnhild's heart contracted.

Harald.

She sounded her battle horn. Her people came running, pulling on their battle jackets and helms, snatching up shields and weapons. Murchad's cavalry formed the rear ranks. They set out for the same beach where they had fought Harald before. This time, the people of Gausel marched with them, their ranks bristling with spears and axes.

Ragnhild stood on the shore at the head of her army, watching the ships emerge from the mist. She only counted three so far. Her heart sank as she noted Orlyg's among them. So he, too, had sided with Harald in the end.

Battle Swan materialized, Harald standing in the prow as it bit into the sand.

"Shield wall!" Ragnhild cried. They formed up with a rattle and waited.

Harald's crew jumped into the shallows and dragged their ship up the beach, then stood aside. No weapons were drawn, no shields raised.

Harald stepped down from the bow. With a shock, Ragnhild saw that behind him stood a woman, holding a baby. It was Signy. The child must be her new daughter.

Harald helped his wife and daughter from the ship. He turned to Ragnhild and inclined his head. "Greetings, Ragnhild, queen of Gausel."

Ragnhild's throat caught and she could not speak.

"Greetings, sister," said Signy, holding out the baby. "We thought it was time you met your niece. Her name is Ragnhild."

AUTHOR'S NOTE

Like all the Norsewomen novels, this book includes a mixture of real and fictitious characters. Olaf and his son, Rognvald, were real historic figures, though I could find no reference to Rognvald's mother. Ragnhild is a fictional character, but Harald Goldbeard is mentioned in the sources, and he had a daughter named Ragnhild.

Murchad mac Maele Duin was a real Irish king. He was truly deposed by his cousin, Njal, and then vanishes from the Irish Annals for a decade. There is some speculation that he had a Norse wife and a son by that marriage.

Åsa's concerns about marriage were based in fact. The laws cited in this novel are based on Norse law codes written shortly after the time period. The law gave unmarried adult women the right to inherit property and serve as head of households, including the duties of vengeance and paying wergild. When a woman married, these rights ceded to her husband.

Fosterage was commonly practiced throughout Europe through the high medieval era. It was the practice of sending children out to be raised and schooled in another household for several years. The practice built alliances between families since the bond of foster-child with their foster-parent was nearly as strong as that of birth families. The child usually returned to their birth family after a few years. Sometimes the foster children were sent to a lower-ranking subject and the cost of the child's upkeep was paid to the foster parents, and for the lower ranking family it was considered an honor. In the case of Asa and Sonja, the families were of equal rank so it was more an alliance-building.

Gausel is a settlement near Stavanger, Norway. During the Viking Age it appears to have had a high population of wealthy women landowners who inherited their land. High status female burials here are twice as common as male burials. These graves contain the highest concentration of Irish metal objects in the world, indicating a strong relationship with Ireland, whether through raiding or trading.

Grave #1883, known as the Gausel Queen's, is one of the richest graves in Norway, approaching the splendor of the Oseberg ship burial. It is dated to about AD 850-860 and the occupant was buried in a wooden coffin with female grave goods, many in the Irish style, including fine brooches of gilded bronze and silver, silver arm rings, drinking horns with Irish mounts, an Irish hanging bowl, and a horse's head wearing a harness with gilded bronze-mounts in the Irish style.

Nearby, three boat graves have been discovered that also contain horse's heads with bridles. Since no human bones survived, these burials are designated male because they contained full sets of weapons. The largest of them contained a full set of blacksmith tools in a boat estimated (by rivet placement) at 30 feet long and dated about the same time as the Gausel Queen (AD 850).

Gausel is an intriguing area and I look forward to setting more novels there, as well as Ireland and, of course, Tromøy.

- **Ard**—a primitive form of plow
- **Álf**—elf, male, often considered ancestors (plural álfir)
- **Berserker**—warriors said to have superhuman powers. Translates either as "bear shirt" or "bare shirt" (also berserk)
- **Bindrune**—three or more runes drawn one over the other
- **Blót**—sacrifice. i.e., Álfablót is sacrifice in honor of the elves, Dísablót is in honor of the dís
- **Bower**—women's quarters, usually a separate building
- **Breeks**—breeches
- **Brisingamen**—Golden necklace belonging to the goddess Freyja
- **Brynja**—chain-mail shirt
- **Dís**—spirits of female ancestors (plural: dísir)
- **Distaff**—a staff for holding unspun wool or linen fibers during the spinning process. About a meter long, usually made of wood or iron, with a bail to hold the wool. Historically associated with witchcraft.
- **Draugr**—animated corpse

- **Fylgja**—a guardian spirit, animal or female
- **Fóstra**—a child's nurse (foster mother)
- **Flyting**—a contest of insults
- **Galdr**—spells spoken and sung
- **Gammelost**—literally "old cheese"
- **Gungnir**—Odin's spear
- **Hamr**—"skin"; the body
- **Hamingja**—a person's luck or destiny, passed down in the family
- **Haugbui**—mound-dwelling ghost
- **Haugr**—mound
- **Hird**—the warrior retinue of a noble person
- **Hnefatafl**—also Tafl, a chess-like board game found in Viking graves
- **Holmgang**—"isle-going"; a duel within boundaries, sometimes fought on small islets
- **Hudfat**—sleeping bags made of sheepskin
- **Hugr**—the soul, the mind
- **Húskarl**—the elite household warriors of a nobleman (plural: húskarlar)
- **Jarl**—earl, one step below a king
- **Jotun**—giants, enemies of the gods. Plural: Jotnar
- **Jól**—Yule midwinter feast honoring all the gods, but especially Odin
- **Karl**—a free man, also "bonder"
- **Karvi**—a small Viking ship
- **Kenning**—a metaphorical expression in Old Norse poetry
- **Knarr**—a merchant ship
- **Lawspeaker**—a learned man who knew the laws of the district by heart
- **Longfire**—a long, narrow firepit that ran down the center of a hall
- **Mjölnir**—Thor's hammer, a symbol of fertility

- **Norn**—the supernatural sisters who weave fate named Skuld, Verdandi, and Urd
- **Odal land**—inherited land
- **Ørlög**—personal fate
- **Primstave**—a flat piece of wood used as a calendar. The days of summer are carved on one side, winter on the reverse.
- **Ragnarök**—the final battle of the gods—the end of the world
- **Runes**—the Viking alphabet, said to have magical powers, also used in divination
- **Seidr**—a trance to work magic
- **Shield-maiden**—female warrior
- **Shield wall**—a battle formation
- **Skáld**—poet
- **Skagerrak Sea**—a body of water between Southeast Norway, Southwest Sweden, and Northern Denmark
- **Skerry**—a small rocky islet
- **Skjaergarden**—a rocky archipelago on the southern cape of Norway
- **Skutching**—scraping the flax stalk from the inner fibers
- **Skyr**—a dairy product similar to yogurt
- **Small beer**—a beer with a low alcohol content, a common drink
- **Stook**—a group of sheaves stood on end in a field
- **Sverige, Svea**—Sweden and Swedes
- **Swine horn**—a v-shaped battle formation
- **Thrall**—slave
- **Tiercel**—a male falcon, usually smaller than the female
- **Ting, Allting**—assembly at which legal matters are settled
- **Ulfhed**—"wolf head"; another warrior like a berserker (plural ulfhednar)

- **Urdr**—(Anglo-Saxon *wyrd*) the web of fate, the name of one of the Norns
- **Valhöll**—"corpse hall," Odin's hall
- **Valknut**—"corpse knot," a symbol of Odin
- **Valkyrie**—"choosers of the slain." Magical women who take warriors from the battlefield to Valhöll, or Freyja's hall Sessrumnir
- **Vardlokkur**—a song to draw the spirits
- **Völva**—a sorceress. Literally, "wand-bearer"
- **Wergild**—the value of a person's life, to be paid in wrongful death
- **Wights**—spirits of land and water
- **Wootz**—crucible steel manufactured in ancient India

IRISH TERMS

- **A chroi**—my heart
- **A ghra**—my love
- **A mhuirin**—my darling
- **Currach**—an Irish boat
- **Ban na Sidhe**—"banshee," a faery woman
- **Fae**—the Sidhe or faeries
- **Finn Gaill**—"white foreigner"--Norse

CHARACTERS

CREW OF *RAIDER BRIDE*

- Ragnhild Solvisdottir, age 17, leader of Tromøy's shield-maidens, daughter of the deceased King Solvi of Solbakk
- Murchad mac Maele Duin, age 30, Ragnhild's husband, deposed king of Aileach of the Northern Ui Neill— Cenel nEoghan
- Einar, Thorgeir, Svein—warriors formerly of Solbakk, now sworn to Ragnhild
- Unn, age 17, shield-maiden and healer
- Ursa, age 16, Unn's younger sister, also a shield-maiden
- Tova, age 15, their younger sister
- Ylva, age 14, their younger sister

ORKNEY

- Ivar, the chieftain
- Gudrun, Ivar's wife

- Kol, a ship captain

TROMØY—AN ISLAND OFF THE EAST COAST OF AGDER, NORWAY

- Åsa, age 19, queen of Tromøy, daughter of the murdered King Harald Redbeard
- Halfdan the Black, Åsa's three-year-old son
- Brenna, Halfdan's nurse (fóstra)
- Toki, Brenna's husband, steward of Tromøy
- Hogni, Toki's assistant
- Olvir, head of Åsa's household guards
- Jarl Borg of Iveland, Åsa's military advisor
- Ulf, blacksmith of Tromøy
- Heid, a famous völva (sorceress), Åsa's mentor
- Vigdis, one of Heid's nine apprentices
- Knut, a famous traveling skáld (poet and historian)
- Helga, (deceased) eldest of five sisters from a farm in Agder's hinterlands
- Stormrider, Åsa's peregrine falcon
- Flekk, Åsa's dog
- Gullfaxi, "Golden Mane," Åsa's horse
- Svartfaxi, "Black Mane," a horse Åsa awarded Murchad
- Harald Redbeard, King of East Agder, Norway, Åsa and Gyrd's father (deceased)
- Gunnhild, his queen, Åsa and Gyrd's mother, a noblewoman of Lista (deceased)
- Gyrd, their son, Åsa's brother (deceased)

VESTFOLD

- Skiringssal, the Shining Hall of Vestfold, Norway

- Borre, another stronghold of Vestfold, north of Skiringssal
- Olaf, age 20, king of Vestfold, son of King Gudrød
- Sonja Eisteinsdottir, age 18, Olaf's wife
- Rognvald, their infant son
- Kalv, captain of Olaf's guard
- Gudrød, deceased king of Vestfold, Olaf's father, formerly Åsa's husband
- Alfhild, Gudrød's first wife, Olaf's mother (deceased)
- Halfdan the Mild, Gudrød's deceased father—Olaf's grandfather
- Hrolf (deceased) Gudrød's natural son

SOLBAKK, ROGALAND

- Solvi, deceased king of Solbakk, father of Ragnhild and her brothers
- Ingfrid, his deceased wife, mother of Ragnhild and her brothers
- Harald Goldbeard, king of Solbakk, brother of Ragnhild and Orlyg, Solvi's eldest son, age 20
- Signy, daughter of the king of Sogn, Harald's wife, age 17
- Orlyg, Solvi's younger son, brother of Harald and Ragnhild, age 18
- Katla, Ragnhild's foster mother

GAUSEL—A FARMING SETTLEMENT IN SOUTHWEST NORWAY

- Jofrid—headwoman of Gausel
- Thyra—Gausel's healer

OTHERS

- Hrafn, an outlawed berserker and sorcerer
- Eyvind, a Svea trader
- Jokul, a farmer
- Onar, a farmer
- Helga, Jokul's sister, Onar's ex-wife
- Jarl Orm, member of the high council

NORSE GODS AND HEROES

- Hervör –legendary shield-maiden, daughter of the berserker Angantýr, demands his sword Tyrfing
- Angantýr—one of twelve berserker brothers, owner of Tyrfing
- Tyrfing—a legendary sword, cursed by the dwarves who made it. Though it would always bring victory, it would kill a man each time it was unsheathed, and it would be the death of the owner's bloodline.
- Odin—lord of the Aesir gods, of many names
- Valhöll—Odin's hall—literally, "corpse hall"
- Einherjar—heroes slain in battle who come to Valhöll and Sessrumnir
- Gungnir—Odin's spear that marks an army as his
- Sleipnir—Odin's horse
- Thor—Odin's son, god of thunder, preserver of mankind
- Mjölnir—Thor's hammer
- Freyja—originally of the Vanir gods. Goddess of love and magic. She gets first pick of the slain heroes for her hall her Sessrumnir.
- Frey—Freyja's twin brother, fertility god of peace and plenty

- Loki— a jotun trickster
- Hel—Loki's daughter, mistress of the dead not killed in battle
- Nifleheim—cold and misty land of the dead, ruled by Hel
- Ran—goddess of the sea
- Yggdrasil—literally "Odin's steed," the world tree, that holds the nine worlds. Odin travels between the worlds on the tree.
- Norns—three sisters who spin the lives of men and gods

IRISH GODS AND HEROES

- Finn Mac Caimhill—Irish hero
- Oisin—Finn's son
- Niamh of the Golden Hair—a fae princess, daughter of the sea god
- Manannan mac Lir, god of the sea
- Tir na nOg—land of youth
- Tuatha de Danaan—children of the goddess Danu, the Sidhe, or Fae
- Cu Chuilain—an Irish hero, son of the god Lugh
- Lugh—the sun god, father of Cu Chuilain
- Mebdh—ancient queen of Connacht
- Ailill—ancient king of Connacht, Mebdh's husband
- Scathach—a woman warrior who trained Cu Chuilain

ACKNOWLEDGMENTS

I have so many people to thank in bringing this novel into being: My beloved mother who first introduced me to Åsa and the Viking world; my wonderful fellow writers at Kitsap Writers, each of whom contributed so very much and kept me going; and to critique partners DV Berkom, Chris Karlsen, and Jennifer Conner. Thanks to my dear husband Brian who is always on my side and eager to read more, and beta readers Colleen Hogan-Taylor and Linda S., each of whom gave me priceless insights. I owe many thanks to editors Ruth Ross Saucier, Kahina Necaise, and Laurie Boris. Any errors that exist in this book are entirely my own.

ABOUT THE AUTHOR

Johanna Wittenberg is the author of The Norsewomen Series. Like her Viking forebears, Johanna has sailed to the far reaches of the world. She lives on a fjord in the Pacific Northwest with her husband, whom she met on a ship bound for Antarctica.

For a free short story, join the mailing list: https://johannawittenberg.com/free-short-story/

Website: https://JohannaWittenberg.com

facebook.com/TheNorseQueen

twitter.com/JoWit5

amazon.com/Johanna-Wittenberg/e/B084H88R6J

bookbub.com/authors/johanna-wittenberg